FORTUNE'S TRAIL: A NEVADA STORY

KAARAN THOMAS
AND
A. J. HICKS

Jeff –
Hope you enjoy
this story!

(Happy trails to you –

Bud

Other works by Kaaran Thomas:

Trip in the Dark: It Began With the Kennedy Assassination (2012)

Published by Tradeworks Publishing, St. Louis, Missouri

IBSN 978-0-9914408-0-1

Fortune's Trail: A Nevada Story is a work of fiction. Apart from the well-known actual people, events and locales that figure in the narrative, all names, characters, places and incidents are the products of the authors' imaginations or are used fictitiously. Any resemblance to current events or locale or to living persons, companies, or institutions is entirely coincidental.

Cover Photo: *The Silver Slipper on the Scenic Highway*
by Justin Bowen/LAS VEGAS SUN

Typesetting and cover design by Gorham Printing
Author photo by Marissa Tolotti

To our spouses and best friends,
Suzette Hicks and Andy Nielsen

CONTENTS

PREFACE

For millennia, the meadows clung to life along the banks of an artesian spring gurgling through the rocks in a hidden valley in the brutal Mojave Desert. They were unknown to the white man until 1829, when a Mexican trader traveling along the Spanish Trail decided to explore the surrounding territory and found the small oasis.

In 1855, Mormon settlers built a 150-foot square fort of sun-dried bricks in its midst to protect the mail route from Pueblo de Los Angeles to the new towns springing up along the edge of the Great Salt Lake. But hostile Indians frequently raided the fort and the Mormons deserted it.

By 1890 the meadows had become a water stop for the railroad. The workers started a small town around the tracks. Later, the town—the last western city to outlaw gambling—became the first metropolis to change its mind. The artesian spring dried up—consumed by a hundred spectacular fountains. In its place flowed a mighty green river of cash.

The meadows that had once given sustenance to Indians and pioneers attracted gangsters and grifters, outcasts and misfits. They came from all over America, dreaming big dreams, running from the law, looking to make a fast buck on a street whose name conjured images of glamour and vice all over the world. Some made it big, some were buried in the desert, some lost their souls, some gained redemption. Some bet their last dollar on red and watched as the roulette wheel spun and the little ball bounced along, finally settling in place.

They transformed the little oasis in the desert into the emerald city of their dreams. Its streets were given monikers like Glitter Gulch and The Strip. And they baptized their city with the Spanish translation of the meadows that had given it life: Las Vegas.

This is their story.

Chapter 1: When Harriet Met Sam

Selma, Mississippi, 1939

Harriet turned her face from side to side in the morning sun, studying her reflection in the looking glass. She had seen herself this way only once before, on her twelfth birthday when the glass emerged from her ma's hope chest.

"Hold it gentle now, Harriet. It's genuine silver-backed glass all the way from New Orleans," Ma said, lifting it tenderly from its cradle in her hope chest. Ma had brought the looking glass to her new home on the day she became a bride. There it stayed, under her marital bed, until the day Harriet, her eldest daughter, became a woman.

On that day five years ago, Harriet had her first monthly. She was terrified. Her family did not discuss bodily functions. Nobody told her women were supposed to bleed. She ran through the early morning mist to the stream, sobbing quietly from the cramps, trying to scrub the blood from her nightdress. She heard her mother's footsteps crunching through the fall leaves behind her and realized she had been caught out. There was nowhere to hide the disaster–her only nightdress now ruined by some event she could not understand.

"Ain't nothing to be ashamed about Hat." Ma crouched down beside her and showed her how to rub the stained fabric against the mossy rocks till it turned white again. They stood together arm in arm watching the red-tinted water wash away the last evidence of her first period. "It means you're a woman now's all."

Then Ma showed her how to line her undies with rags; how chamomile tea helped ease cramps. Finally, when her pain and tears subsided, Ma led her by the hand into the sleeping room where she pulled out the hope chest from under her bed and opened it for the very first time. Harriet's breath had caught at the wonders inside. A white dress: "My dress when I married your Pa," Ma had said. "It's made from Brussels lace". Harriet had no idea what that meant but from the way Ma said it she could tell that Brussels lace was the most special thing in the world.

"I saved it for you, for when you get married," Ma said, pulling out a veil, long and fine as a spider's web for Harriet to feel. Underneath the veil lay a prayer book with a bouquet of dried flowers pressed inside and a pair of silver slippers. "The shoes'll fit you perfect, Hat." Her ma wiped away a tear. "You'll be a beautiful bride."

And at last the wondrous looking glass. It was better than looking at yourself in the clearest lake on the stillest day. Harriet glanced quickly into the surface. Maybe it was a sin of pride, to think about how other people saw you. But Ma said it was fitting for a girl just become a woman to see her real image: "The way you look in the eyes of God."

Ma put the looking glass away without peeking at herself, Harriet noticed. Harriet wondered what the eyes of God saw the last time Ma looked at herself in the glass? Before her hair went grey? Before her back got stooped from totin' the water from the well day after day?

Harriet was no longer interested in the eyes of God. She had already decided she would never end up like Ma, old and tired and poor. If that meant she never got to wear the wondrous dress and veil and slippers, so be it. Ma's wedding was the highlight of her life. After that it was all having to take in washing for a living.

Harriet couldn't see anything her parents had done to deserve their fate. Her pa worked their cotton farm hard to give them a good life. But everything seemed to go wrong for them. Ma kept having babies, "More mouths to feed," she would say when her belly started to swell. "But it'll be a blessing," she added when she saw the look on Harriet's face.

The boll weevils came. Their pastor said it was punishment for their sins, but Harriet couldn't see how her family had sinned more than any of the other parishioners. They stood by the fields each day and watched their cotton turn to rot. Finally, when all that was left of the beautiful white blossoms was grey moldy wads on bent brown stems, Pa and Old Tom the mule plowed it under. After the plowing was done, the family stood and looked at the grave holding all their hopes.

"Land, it's everything, Hat," Pa said, looking out across the ruined fields. And Harriet thought, well that's all we have.

Then the bankers foreclosed on chunks of their farm and sold them off piece by piece, till there was nothing but the cabin and a plot for vegetables, a hen house and a little barn for the cow and Old Tom.

"We shouldn't complain," Pa, said, "They did us a favor. They could've taken everything. What's left is not much but it's ours free and clear." Harriet didn't understand free or clear. It seemed to her they had paid for their little wooden house, their rickety barn, and their split rail fence with all they had left in the world. They had no money for new clothes or shoes. They lived off what they could raise and what they could get selling eggs and potatoes in town. Ma saved the wash money in a jar. "For Christmas," she said, holding it to her chest with her chapped hands.

The first winter after the bankers left there was no Christmas. The wash money went to buy meat and salt and flour to keep them alive. Ma lost another baby and Pa said he didn't know whether to curse the Lord or bless him. That night he took his rifle off the hook and headed for the hills.

"He'll be back," Harriet told her Ma. She tried to sound confident, but she wasn't sure what he had to come back to. She tried to dig a grave for her little sister but the ground was frozen solid. She carried the sad little bundle to the barn, promising to bury her as soon as the ground thawed.

When Pa did come back he was a moonshiner.

"I won't see us starve," he told Ma. "If the gov'ment doesn't want us making whiskey they need to find some other way for me to feed my family."

Ma was too weak to make a fuss. She stumbled back to her bed and stayed there.

"I lost my baby and my farm and now the Lord's taken everything else," she mumbled to herself, lying stiff and straight under her quilt like she was already dead.

Harriet made the meals as best she could. She carried bowls of porridge to Ma's bedroom in the morning and bowls of stew in the evening. In between she tried to shut out the sound of crying.

A few weeks later Pa came home with sacks of flour and sugar, a small glass bottle of vanilla and even raisins and an apple for each of them.

"It's time we had something sweet around here, Lavinia," he had said to Ma. The last thing he pulled out, in a package from the dry goods store wrapped in brown paper, was a bolt of gingham. It was so fine you could hold it up to the window and see the light coming through. Ma started crying again, but this time it was a happy sound. She gave Pa a big hug. Then they went into the bedroom and didn't come out for a long time and things were good at home after that.

The trouble was, their home was surrounded by other people's land; people who whispered behind their back after the Sunday service at their church and giggled to each other at school about whiskey and drunks and the gov'ment.

Harriet loved her classes. Her teacher told her she was a good learner. That didn't make up for the teasing she got from the students. She came straight home from school each afternoon, gathering her brothers and sisters protectively and walking through the fields to avoid the places where they used to join the local children at play. The family kept to themselves. Ma read to the children—stories from the books she had brought with her as a bride—old books with leather covers cracking from use. Harriet's favorite was The Wonderful Wizard of Oz about a girl caught up in a tornado and carried away to an Emerald City. Harriet wished a tornado would come and carry her off, far away from Selma, Mississippi. But she was a smart girl. Before her seventeenth birthday she had figured out that if she wanted to get away she had to do it all by herself.

Which was why Harriet was holding the looking glass. In a way it was due to Pa's moonshining. The week before, he said he had to go to Natchez on business. She begged him to take her along. It was a long rough ride over pitted roads behind Old Tom's switching tail, but she was unfazed. She waited patiently for her first sight of the Mighty Mississippi as the two of them finally made it to the top of the last hill and the city spread itself out below. They ambled down the main street to the county courthouse. Harriet had never been to the courthouse. It was pretty on the outside with lots of decorations around the big double front doors. On the inside, though, it was dim and dusty. Harriet sneezed. People were running around in the gloom holding bunches of paper and looking serious. Pa stopped in front of a room that had "Sheriff" printed in gold on a frosted glass door. He told her to sit in a waiting room while he talked to the man in charge. He disappeared behind another door that separated the waiting room from the sheriff's office.

Pa wasn't inside but a few minutes when she heard shouting

coming through the door. She hadn't meant to eavesdrop, but they were talking so loud she couldn't help herself. They were arguing about money. How much should Pa pay the sheriff to look the other way? She had no idea someone in the government got paid for looking one way or another. She stood with her ear pressed against the door and listened, fascinated. She hardly noticed when a man came into the waiting room.

"Hi there, young lady," he said, and she jumped back, blushing from embarrassment.

"Sorry." He tipped his hat. "Didn't mean to startle you." But he didn't look sorry. He was tall, with big brown eyes, dark wavy hair and a pert little mustache that twitched as he smiled at her. He was older than Harriet, but not by too much, she guessed. Maybe five years or so. She had no idea what to say. She didn't want to appear flirty like the girls at her school. She had to think of something grown up–something a smart girl would say.

"Are you here to see the man about looking the other way," she said, finally. She was sorry right away. The man burst out laughing.

"Why would you ask such a question?"

"That's what my pa is doing."

"Oh, I see. Well, maybe your pa and I should have a talk."

Just then the door opened and Pa walked out. He was smiling. She was relieved. The stranger stood up and shook his hand.

"I'm Sam Wilson. I understand you had some business with the sheriff."

Her pa looked at her, then back at Mr. Wilson.

"My daughter here has big ears, and a bigger mouth. Why would you be interested in my business?"

"I plan to set up a tent at the end of Confederate Street, down where the carny show is. For cards, you know, poker and such. I was curious if you were planning something similar. Maybe we could join up."

"I see. Well, that's not my business. Sorry. I'm in the...uh...liquor business."

"Liquor...who do you sell to?"

"Depends."

"We could use some quality liquor, assuming we can get the sheriff there to, uh, look the other way." Mister Wilson nodded towards Harriet and smiled back at Pa like he had just cracked a joke. Harriet felt another blush creep up her neck.

"I'm Ray Lane," her Pa said. "I'm gonna take Harriet here for a walk. We'll be back in twenty minutes. Go see the sheriff. If you're still interested, let's talk." Pa opened the door, then turned back towards Mr. Wilson and smiled.

"By the way, the sheriff's cut's ten per cent. For liquor at least."

"Thanks," Wilson smiled back.

That was how she met Sam Wilson. She saw him again when he drove up to their farmhouse in a truck. Pa said the road to their farm wasn't fit for a motorcar, but Sam Wilson had made it. His truck was a wonder, with a huge tire in a special compartment behind the doors and running boards she could stand on and sneak a peek inside while Mr. Wilson and Pa walked off into the woods with Old Tom and their wagon. The interior was soft brown with shiny metal handles and knobs.

She jumped off the running board when the men returned with the wagon loaded with barrels. Mr. Wilson and Pa loaded the barrels into the truck. She stood in the yard and watched.

"Do you like it?" Mr. Wilson asked.

"It's mighty fine," she replied.

"Would you like a ride?"

"Oh...more than anything!"

"Let me go talk to your folks. Then maybe we can take a spin."

He and Pa finished loading and went into the kitchen. It seemed like they came right out again. Sam hurried towards his truck.

"Harriet Lillith Lane, you git yourself into the house this minute!" That was Ma.

"I'm afraid I've made your ma angry," Mr. Wilson said sadly as he started the engine. It roared like an angry cougar. "I asked her if you could come to work for me."

She stood in the yard till the truck disappeared from sight. Then she marched into the kitchen. Ma was kneading dough. Harriet thought she was punching the ball with more vigor than usual.

"What'd he want with me," she asked.

The dough received another thump.

"He wanted you to come work in his poker tent."

"What's that?"

"It's where men play cards and drink and God knows what all."

"What'd he want me for?"

"He said you could be a dealer."

Ma spit out the words. The flour was flying off her hands, powdering her face.

Pa was standing by the door looking down.

"Pa, what's a dealer?"

He looked at her mother. She gave the dough ball another righteous punch.

"It's somebody who passes out cards in card games. Why would you ask such a question?"

"I heard what Mr. Wilson asked. About me working as a dealer in his poker tent. Can I do it? Please?"

Another look passed between her parents.

"Well, let your ma and me discuss it some more."

"Ain't gonna be no discussin'." Another whack at the dough.

"She's seventeen, Lavinia," he said. "It's time she took out on her own. And it would mean one less mouth to feed, at least for a few weeks while he's in town."

"This family's deep enough in sin. I'll not have my oldest work in a gamblin' tent." The dough ball slammed onto the kneading board, ending the discussion in an explosion of flour.

Harriet was determined to get the job.

Which was why she was holding the looking glass this bright Sunday morning while the rest of the family was at church in Selma. She had told Ma and Pa she had a tummy ache. The wagon was no sooner over the hill then she dove under the bed and retrieved the treasure. She was bound and determined to find Mr. Wilson and his tent and she wanted to know exactly what he would see when she turned up.

Now she inspected herself carefully. She had nice teeth. They were straight and none were missing. Her eyes weren't blue like Sallie's, but they were greenish brown and looked friendly, at least to her. Her nose had a little bump on the end. That was a minus. She had piled her long brown hair on top of her head and fixed it with hairpins, also taken from Ma. She admired the overall effect. She looked good, all things considered.

She stuffed her belongings into an empty feedbag. She found an old piece of wrapping paper and a pencil and wrote out a note for Ma so she wouldn't worry. It was the only time she had ever written a note to her parents. She kissed it softly, smoothed the paper out carefully and left it under a rock on the kitchen table. She told Ma she could take care of herself. She hoped they would understand. She put her Sunday shoes in the bag and tugged on her work boots. She could change shoes when she got to Natchez. She would throw the boots away, she decided. It would seal her promise to herself. She would never spend another day in the dirty, heavy things.

She was lucky, the day was sunny and the roads were dry. When the spring rains came the dirt got churned up into a mud pie. She walked fast the first few miles before she got to the cutoff for Selma. She had to pass the cutoff before the family came back from church. After the cutoff she slowed to her usual steady gait, singing to herself to pass the time. For the first few hours she looked behind her whenever she heard a noise, afraid she would see Old Tom and Pa coming after her, but the road behind was as empty as the road ahead. She thought about that. Did it mean they didn't care? Or that they had changed their mind? Finally she decided, whatever the reason, she was on her own. She squared her shoulders and walked on.

It was almost dark when she came up over the last hill. There was Natchez, with the sun setting behind it and the Mississippi turned all red and gold. Somehow it was even more special because she had got there under her own power.

"The Emerald City," she whispered to herself, even though Natchez was brown and grey against the evening sky. Maybe Sam Wilson could be her Wizard of Oz.

She realized suddenly that getting to Natchez was only half her challenge. She had to find Mr. Wilson. She remembered he said something about Confederate Street and a carny. She stopped a policeman and he pointed her in the right direction. It was dark by the time she reached the carny show and she was tired and hungry. But as anxious as she was to find Mr. Wilson and maybe get him to buy her somethin' to eat, she just had to stand still admiring the colorful lights strung up around the tents. Her mouth watered from the smell of roasted peanuts. Somewhere somebody was playing a lively fiddle tune that made her tap her feet.

People were wandering along the sawdust paths between the tents, laughing and talking. She asked two or three men where Mr. Wilson's tent was before a big man asked if she meant the poker tent. She nodded shyly.

"And what would you be wantin' the poker tent for, little lady?"

"I'm going to work for Mr. Wilson," she replied nervously, trying to look her most grown up.

"Really? I see." The man looked down at her boots, caked with dust from her journey. "Well, he's at the end of that row on the left."

She found a stump to sit on and tugged off the offending footwear. She left the boots and socks by the stump in case somebody else might want them. Then she pulled out her Sunday shoes and put them on. They were much prettier than the boots, but they were not beautiful like the silver slippers in Ma's hope chest. She had thought about taking the slippers but she decided she would leave them for Nellie, her next younger sister. She would have to earn her own silver slippers.

◆❉◆✦◆❉◆

Sam surveyed the action from his corner seat in the poker tent. Thirty men sat at tables looking at their cards. Tonight was blackjack night and the house was making serious money. And people were having fun. Every so often someone yelled "blackjack" and the whole place broke into cheers.

Ray Lane's liquor had been a great addition. What a lucky break to run into Ray at the sheriff's office. His instincts told him Lane was an honest man. His visit to the farm confirmed the opinion. The place was neat and well kept. And the wife was obviously from good people. A God-fearin' woman. He smiled at the memory. Ray had led him to the small hut in the woods, stacked high with barrels, where he pulled a cork from one of the barrels and let Sam sniff the golden liquid. Sam could tell from the smell it was made with good corn mash and barley, not the Jamaican ginger and other chemicals some moonshiners used. He was relieved. His circuit took him through Arkansas, where he saw too many men's legs twitching uncontrollably from drinking "jakeleg 'shine". Sooner or later, rumors of bad liquor could ruin a business.

And the Lane's corn mash 'shine was strong enough to loosen pocketbooks and cloud judgment. That was good, because he only had thirty days in Natchez. He had tried to convince the Sheriff to give him two months so he could leave with the carny show but the SOB flat refused. Not at any price. Not if he wanted a chance to come back the next year. He was sorry to have to part company with the carny show. He had joined up with them at Fort Adams and quickly become friends with the owner, Big Mike and his energetic, jovial wife Lucy. They traveled together to Natchez.

People like Mike were rare in Sam's life. He had been a loner since the day he ran away from the Memphis orphanage where he had been unenthusiastically housed and fed and taught readin' writin' and 'rithmatic, but otherwise left to his own devices until he was old enough to make money pitching pennies and tossing dice in the back alley. He left without saying goodbye. He didn't know his parents or his age. He measured his life by his ability to earn his keep.

At first the craps games produced just enough profit to scrounge a meal from a local restaurant. Then he was able to pick up the fundamentals of poker by working in a local bar, bringing rounds of fresh whiskey to the poker players. He had an excuse to hang around and listen to their bets while sneaking peeks at their hands. When he could finally sit at the card tables and play, he won enough to buy himself a good suit of clothes and a nice pair of boots.

Sam's next revelation came when he grew his first set of whiskers. He was good-looking. The hookers who worked the bars took a liking to the dark slender young man with the soft brown eyes. Before long he augmented his poker winnings with a percentage of the revenue from his own flock of working girls. They were happy to pay him in exchange for his protection. He earned enough to buy his truck, which almost killed him before he learned how to drive the damned thing.

He pressed the clutch for the first time and released a flood of wanderlust. He heard stories in the bars about the river men who traveled from town to town setting up card games. They worked for different bosses, "kingpins" who split up the gambling circuits among themselves by a process known only to them. He dreamed of the places his truck could take him if he could work for such men and maybe even become one of them. He learned that the east and west banks of the Mississippi River from Tennessee to Arkansas to Mississippi, were controlled by a Texan, Bingo Baxter. Alan Smith, the man who worked the Baxter circuit, met with an unexplained accident shortly after he introduced Sam to Baxter's collector, a little man with thinning brown hair and a pockmarked face who everybody called "Weasel". Weasel was accompanied by Hatch, a big mule of a man whose left hand generally rested on the pistol in his pocket. Weasel told him Baxter needed a replacement for Smith and Sam signed on. He had never met Baxter, but that didn't bother Sam. Weasel handed over the bankroll Sam needed for his start and Sam signed the receipt in bold, confident letters. The bankroll, Bingo's "stake" in his venture and the route Bingo assigned to him was all he needed. His business had always been making money off people he didn't know.

Sam traveled a circuit, starting from Fort Adams in southern Mississippi, along the Eastern banks of the Mississippi River, north to Memphis, stopping on the way at Natchez, Vicksburg, Greenville, Rosedale and Helena. That was the good side. The Memphis sheriff was more reasonable than most, letting him stay two months for five per cent of the take. "So long as I don't get no complaints about y'all." Then he had to head down the Arkansas side. At the Louisiana border he had to double back to Natchez to cross the river back into Mississippi. Louisiana was out of his territory. Setting up a tent in Cajun Country meant serious trouble for Sam and Bingo Baxter. Louisiana was controlled by the Chicago mob, Baxter's competitors.

Baxter ran the Mississippi/Texas/Arkansas/Tennessee gambling network from Dallas. A person might think Dallas was a long ways from Fort Adams, but somehow Bingo knew exactly what was going on in every town in his territory. Sam suspected Bingo had his own spies among the local sheriffs. Perhaps the very sheriffs who extracted money from Sam were getting bribes from Bingo, too. People who double-crossed Bingo usually ended up dead like Alan Smith.

Weasel and Hatch waited for Sam at prearranged stops along his circuit. The routine was always the same—Weasel sat at a table in some secluded spot at their meeting place. Sam put his lockbox on the table and took a seat across from Weasel. Hatch stood behind Weasel, sipping whiskey while his companion reviewed the daily drop sheets and counted the cash and bankroll. Then Weasel cut out Bingo's share of the take and stashed it in his battered briefcase. Next, Weasel and Sam signed duplicate statements, one for Sam and one for Bingo. The whole process usually took an hour. Sam was proud that his tally always balanced to the penny but Weasel never commented. He deposited Bingo's copy of the tally sheet in the briefcase and closed the lock. Then he and Hatch headed for the door without so much as a "See ya later". Once, early in their relationship, Sam invited them to stay and share a bottle of whiskey. They looked at him like he was crazy.

"We got other bidnuss to tend to," Weasel mumbled.

"What's the harm in a friendly drink among friends," Sam asked.

"We don't make friends," Weasel said as he put on his jacket. Sam thought he saw a ghost of a smile flash across Hatch's face.

Bingo had a good idea what the take from one circuit around Sam's territory should be. He was willing to make accommodations for bribing the local officials and for extras like the liquor and girls for the good customers. But Sam was sure that if the take came in too much below Bingo's number, or if he lost Bingo's stake, there would be hell to pay.

Sam met the carny owner, Big Mike, two years after he signed on with Baxter. He joined forces with the large, gregarious older man to take advantage of the crowds who came to the carny, but he soon found that for the first time in his life he had met someone whose company he enjoyed. He loved swapping stories with Mike after breakfast most days, before they got down to business. Sam regaled Mike with tales of big games, colorful gamblers and folks who bet the farm, literally. Some men even tried to bet their wives. And some wives went off with the winner, happy to be rid of their lowlife spouses.

Big Mike told Sam about his start in the carnival business at the Chicago World's fair in 1893. The "Midway" had introduced America to games, freak shows and the first "Wild West Show" starring Buffalo Bill and a band of honest-to-gosh red Indians. People were captivated. Mike was still in his teens back then, but he was clever and hard working. He was hired by Otto Schmidt, the manager of the Chicago Midway as a roustabout, a general handyman and gofer. It was a perfect way to learn how the fair operated, which acts attracted the largest crowds, which performers were temperamental and who was slipping cash into their pockets when nobody was looking. When the fair closed, Schmidt tried to hire some acts from the Midway to tour the little towns in the North. He approached Buffalo Bill and his Indians but Cody had bigger things in mind. He was taking his troop to Europe for a grand tour.

Undeterred, Schmidt collected some of the remnants of the fair and formed a touring company, the "Chicago Midway Plaisance Amusement Company". He kept Mike on. Schmidt decided Mike, a large muscular boy with unruly blonde locks and smiling eyes, looked sort of like Buffalo Bill. And the real article had left for Europe anyway, so nobody was the wiser. Mike as the fake Buffalo Bill and his band of fake Indians were a big hit in the little towns, but Otto turned out to be a terrible manager. The show folded at the end of the first year. Mike had already decided to part ways with his boss. Otto's fiasco gave Mike the perfect chance to start his own Midway. He hired Otto's best acts and managed to reconnect with other acts and freaks he had met in Chicago. Otto's sharp practices and rude manners had burned bridges with most of the towns in Illinois and Ohio, so Mike decided to move south to Mississippi and Tennessee. By 1939 when he met up with Sam, he had the best carny show in the South.

Mike's carny was good for Sam's business. It brought in so many more people than he could get on his own and gave his gambling operation an air of good clean fun. Mike had assembled a joyful, talented ensemble of acrobats, jugglers, clowns, a strong man, a magician, a fortuneteller, a fat lady, a midget and performing animals. He contracted with local vendors like Harriet's father to add to his attractions. Booths sold ice cream, funnel cakes, roasted peanuts and cotton candy. Other areas had balloon-dart games, water gun games, weight-guessing games and duck shoots. Sam was happy to pay him a percentage of his take in exchange for the added revenue and comfort. And Mike was delighted to have Sam Wilson. He had no problems with an honest card game.

"I can't pay you what you're worth," Sam had apologized. "I've got to pay a big chunk of the take to the local sheriff." Mike offered to intervene on Sam's behalf but Sam knew it wouldn't help, and he didn't want Mike to get in trouble.

"I've got my position to uphold," the lawman had said officiously, hiking up his suspenders. "I got a lot of grief from the City Council after your visit last year. And thirty days means exactly that. I'll be at your place with my men on March second. You'd better be ready to leave by then."

Sam had wanted to tell the bastard that most of the City Council had visited his tent on more than one occasion, but it would do no good. He would have to part company with his new friends. For the first time in his life, he wished he could stay put. He would miss the companionship, the music and lights, the big plates of bacon, eggs and grits Lucy prepared for breakfast, the smell of roasting peanuts and cotton candy that always perfumed the air and the laughter around the dinner table. In three weeks he would be back on his own, just him and his lock box and his truck, he told himself ruefully.

At least Sam's first few days in Natchez had gone well. He kept the list of each day's winnings and expenditures in his count bag, stashed in a big lock box that held Bingo's stake. He kept the key around his neck. He slept by the box; he drove with the box in the cabin of his truck. He was sitting on the box as he surveyed the crowd.

Suddenly the tent got quiet. Sam's hand moved slowly to his pistol. Then he relaxed. It was the Lane girl. She looked exhausted and scared, but when she spotted him she broke into a brave smile and wove her way through the tables.

"Have a seat," he offered. You look like you could use a drink. Of water," he added as she backed away.

"Oh, thanks."

"Did your pa bring you?"

"No. I came on my own. I walked," she said proudly.

"That's quite a distance for a young lady. Were you alone?"

"Yes."

"That's awfully brave. Does your pa know where you are? I wouldn't want him to worry."

"Yes, I told him," she lied. "I'd like to apply for your dealer job."

"So your ma and pa are okay with that?"

"They changed their mind," she said, thinking of the empty road behind her.

"Do you have a place to stay?"

She hadn't thought of that.

"It's all right," he said reassuringly. "There'll be room in one of the carny tents. Mike and Lucy won't mind one more mouth to feed. Speaking of feeding, you look like you could use a meal. Go down to the first tent on the right. Tell them I sent you. You can bring your meal back here and we'll talk."

He figured she had run away. Her pa might be on the road to Natchez this minute with a shotgun to bring her back. But it was a risk he was willing to take. He looked her over as she wolfed down some of Lucy's stew. She wasn't beautiful. He had always been attracted to beautiful women; as a handsome man he assumed he belonged with one of them. But he had begun to believe that beautiful women were more trouble than they were worth. They were all about themselves, demanding attention, adoration rather than helping. Harriet was not homely. She was attractive in a friendly, innocent way. But there was more to her than that. She reminded him of Lucy, who he adored. Her eyes were brimming with intelligence; her mouth curved in a smile as she surveyed her new surroundings. He could already see the customers smiling back at her.

◆ ►◼◆※◆◻◄ ◆

Harriet went to work the next day. By the end of the first week Sam knew his instincts had been right. She learned quickly. She had a head for numbers and an instinct for pleasing the customers without encouraging the sort of unwanted advances that inevitably led to fights and lost business. She was way better than the mix of low-class women and hookers he usually had to corral to work at the tent. He liked to use women because they attracted the men and they were easier to manage. Most of them came, tried their hand at dealing for a couple of weeks and drifted off, more often than not trying to take some of the house money with them. But at least they didn't pack guns and he knew their tricks, thank God: where they hid the money, places they thought he would never put his hands. Of course he had no problem putting his hands where they needed to be. Otherwise he would have to answer to Bingo Baxter. Baxter and his little weasel collector were a thousand times more unpleasant than any dirty, screaming, clawing bitch. Even though they often bit him in the process.

Harriet was different.

By the last week of his stay he couldn't teach her any more. She understood the games, the strategy, how to protect the bankroll and the winnings. She worked from noon to midnight when the tent closed. She quickly developed a nose for "crossroaders" — cheaters who worked alone or in pairs using special devices to beat the odds. She even helped with the other dealers. He would tell her about a dealer stuffing money down her blouse and Harriet would go "have a talk" with the miscreant. Her strategy was simple: she told them they could either turn the money over to her or face Sam. It usually worked.

He walked her to and from her sleeping cot each day. She never complained about the hours or the work. She never complained at all until he told her he had to pack up and be on his way to Vicksburg on March second. "The sheriff only gave me thirty days."

Harriet started to cry.

"I can't go back home. I can't. Please take me with you. I'll do anything. Please."

Sam looked at Harriet closely. Was she asking to be his woman? He had never had a woman in his life. The ladies he knew were hookers, dealers and Lucy. He thought of Harriet as a sort of junior Lucy. He had never even tried to kiss her. At first he had treated her as a good worker. Later he thought of her as a sort of friend, but his life was too chaotic for real friends. If he took her along he was responsible for her. If something happened between them he couldn't just leave her by the side of the road. They would be together in his truck, in the tent all the time.

"Let me think about it," he told her. Her smile was so genuine, so enthusiastic he almost agreed right there.

"What should I do," he asked Mike the next morning. "She's the best worker I ever had. I trust her, I like her, but to take her with me...well, that's a whole 'nother thing."

"If you don't take her, what'll happen to her," Mike lit his pipe and took a thoughtful puff.

"Hell, I have no idea. But I didn't force her to come here. She decided on her own."

"I might take her on myself," Mike said. "She's friendly, cute, a hard worker. And bright. Real bright. People like that are hard to come by."

For some reason, he didn't like the idea of Harriet working for Mike. He thought about that as he walked back to his tent. He didn't want to part with his new worker. Why? He liked her. He really liked her. And she would be company. A real helper. He wouldn't have to be alone. As to what would become of her? Well, that was a gamble. But he was a gambler after all. So long as she understood that he wasn't making any promises.

On March second, when the sheriff showed up, Sam already had his tent, tables and chairs in the back of his truck and the lockbox under the front seat to make room for Harriet. He and Harriet had said good-bye to Mike and Lucy and their carny friends.

"We'll try to meet up in Memphis," Mike promised. He told Sam where the carny would be and said he'd save a spot for the poker tent.

The sheriff wasn't ready to let Sam drive peacefully out of town. He needed to put on a show for the townspeople who had followed his new official Ford automobile down Confederate Street. It was good for politics.

"What the hell do y'all think you're doin' in my town? Don't you know gamblin's illegal here? Y'all's nothin' but a goddamn grifter. Now pack up your things and git or you'll wind up a guest in our local hoosegow, understand?"

His voice carried over the crowd, who ignored the fact that Sam's truck was already packed. The Sheriff was as much fun to watch as the acts in the carny show. He pranced around yelling and brandishing his pistol while Sam pretended to be angry and intimidated. Even Big Mike got into the act, complaining loudly that he didn't know there was gamblin' and drinkin' going on in the middle of his family entertainment.

Harriet decided the delay gave her time to do something she had thought about since she joined up with Sam. She made her way quickly to the fortuneteller, Madame Zena. Madame Zena was a real Romani gypsy, not an old local woman with a turban like so many alleged seers that passed through Selma over the years. She parted the beaded strands at the entrance to her tent and motioned Harriet to enter. It was completely different from the other tents. The inside was draped with woven fabric that gave off an ancient musty smell. A little stick of something was smoking in a dish, giving off a pungent smell. The tent was lit with candles that flickered, with golden light that played on the fabrics. Madame Zena was dressed in a silk caftan. Her fingers dripped rings. She wore a necklace with an amulet that seemed to glow in the candlelight. But what had led Harriet to believe in her wasn't her tent or her dress or her jewelry. It was her low voice with its musical accent and the strange spell she wove around herself; watching her surroundings with large dreamy grey eyes that seemed to see through people. Harriet had tried to talk to her several times before but she always slipped away.

Harriet paid the nickel admission, took a seat on the upholstered chair and placed her hand, palm up, into Madame Zena's extended hand. She noticed that the hand, though it looked old and withered, was remarkably soft and subtle.

Madame Zena did not immediately look at Harriet's out-stretched palm. She looked into Harriet's eyes.

"You are a very special person," she said, rolling her "r's" softly. "You do not know how extraordinary you are."

"What do you mean?" Harriet's voice trembled.

"You have talent, you have wisdom, you have skill far beyond your years."

"But. But I'm just Harriet Lane from Selma, Mississippi. I'm just a dealer in a poker tent."

"That is what you are today, Harriet. Before the end of your life you will be a different person. You will live a different life in a different place, in a city like the Emerald City of your dreams."

Harriet had expected Madame Zena to tell her whether Sam loved her, whether she would be happily married. Now she was frightened. She pulled her hand back, but Madame Zena closed her fingers around Harriet's wrist. Harriet froze. Madam Zena bent over her palm.

"Yes, you will marry your Sam. Your lives together will be like the lives of most people, some happy some sad. Some very happy some very sad. But that will not be important to your place in this world, Harriet. You will have another life, a life of great accomplishment."

Harriet staggered out of the tent, temporarily blinded by the sunlight. For a few minutes she felt like she was entering a different world. She shook her head to clear her senses.

"Hat! Damn I've been lookin' everywhere for you." It was her pa.

"I come to see you off. I hear you're leavin' with Sam."

"Guess so."

"Your ma was real unhappy when you left, Hat. But I understand. We gotta do what we gotta do to survive. It's like the moonshinin'. We can either sin or starve. It's a fierce God that puts those choices to us. I guess we don't measure up, you and me."

He wrapped her in his arms, an awkward gesture. He wasn't given to hugs. She couldn't even remember when he had put his hands on her. She hugged him back, holding onto his worn shirt that smelled of sweat, searching for a way to say goodbye forever to this father of hers.

"I'll try to write," she promised. "You take care of yourself."

He nodded and turned to go. As she watched his tired shoulders weaving their way through the crowd, she called out. "I love you Pa."

The shoulders straightened, he stopped. She thought he might turn around. She might run to him, find a way to tell him he was right.

They were two of a kind, her pa and her. But instead the shoulders hunched forward again and soon he was gone.

"There you are! Did your pa find you?" Sam was standing by the truck, anxious to be on his way.

"Yep."

"He's a good man, Hat. He came to settle up for the liquor, said he figured you were goin' with me. He was at peace with that."

"I know."

"Are you ready? We need to get on the road. Damn sheriff really put on a show. Mike should have charged admission."

He finally looked at her face. "What's the matter, Hat? Did your pa upset you?"

"I'm fine. Let's go. So is everything okay with the sheriff?"

"Oh, hell," Sam chuckled. "The last thing he did was whisper 'See ya next year'. Somabich made a good bit of money off me. The send-off's just for the locals. Happens every year. You'd think they'd wise up. But don't you worry. We'll be back." He patted her shoulder. "You'll have a chance to see your pa again."

They headed north along the river road. The huge mansions seemed to follow their progress from behind the live oaks and magnolias.

"Have you ever been inside one of those," Harriet asked.

"Nope. You?"

"Oh, yes. They're beautiful. My grandpa was a doctor in Natchez. He used to take me around to visit. Someday I'll have a place like that. Even better."

"And how do you know that," Sam teased.

"I went to see Madame Zena. She told me."

"Madame Zena? That old crone?"

"She's not an old crone. She's a real gypsy. And she knows things."

"She's a clever old thing, and a good listener. She picks up on what people say about themselves when they don't know she's around. And she's been known to do a little snoopin' when nobody's watching. But she's just a grifter, Hat. More talented than most. But don't believe what she tells you."

Chapter 2: Highway to Heaven

The first few months, as they moved north along the eastern edge of the Mississippi, were like a dream. Every day was an adventure, a new road, a new town, a new set of customers and dealers, new problems, new solutions. Most nights she lay in her bed for hours, thinking about her new life, too excited to fall asleep.

The drives were spent teaching and learning. Each town's sheriff had his own style, but each of them demanded money in exchange for allowing them to stay for a month or two, after which their operation would be "discovered" by the very same sheriff, roundly condemned and run out of town with great show. The same act could take place year after year, Sam told her. With the same sheriff in the same town.

They discussed different card games. Harriet had no idea people could find so many things to do with a deck of cards. There was blackjack, of course. That was her favorite game. It was all about luck and a little bit of smarts—the person with the hand closest to twenty-one was the winner. But there was also poker, which was much more about skill. She spent a week learning Texas Hold-em, the different card combinations you could make from the two cards in your hand and the five the dealer would lay out on the board: first three, the "flop", then the "turn card" and finally the "river". Men shouted "all in" before they knew what the river card would be; then jumped in exultation or wept in humiliation as they were saved or doomed by the last turn of the cards.

There were other games, too. Seven-card stud, Omaha, and 5-card draw. She had to learn the rules for each one, the best and worst hands, how to calculate odds. She learned how to spot black-jack card counters, people who kept track of the cards that had been dealt so they could increase the odds of getting a good card. Then there were the cheaters who "palmed" aces or tried to disrupt the table so they could rearrange their hands. Sam told her she was great at encouraging the customers to bet. She also knew how to discourage betting.

"You're a prize, Hat," he said, and she beamed.

Sam. Sharing the tricks of his trade, buying breakfast, laughing at the day's events over late dinners. Finally, there was Sam looking into her eyes and kissing her. The kiss flicked on the carny lights in her heart. She put her arms around him and returned it with passion. There was no one to stop them. Even if there had been, Harriet would have ignored them. She was in love.

They spent two months in Memphis, reuniting with Big Mike's troop, but then they had to cross the river to the Arkansas side.

"Do people play card games here," Harriet asked as they passed through the mean, dirty towns. People watched them suspiciously, hidden behind storefronts. The stores were nothing but run down shanties. Some didn't even have signs in the windows. Pigs and cattle wandered through the dirt streets. People threw their garbage in the alleys. Everything stank.

"I thought Selma was poor, but this beats all," Harriet hugged her knees and looked straight ahead, ignoring the stream of tobacco juice an old man had aimed at their truck.

"This is the bad part of my territory," Sam said. He kept his pistol loaded and stuck in his underarm holster all the time. "If somethin' happens, you run for the sheriff fast as you can. Don't try to help, hear?"

"Shouldn't I learn how to shoot that thing," she asked, pointing at the bulge under his jacket.

"You're supposed to run like hell if there's trouble. Not try to shoot somebody."

"But what if I can't run? What if there's nobody around?"

Finally he relented, laughing. "Folks'll start wonderin' if we're Bonnie and Clyde."

There was nothing else to do before the poker tent opened. She stood in empty fields and practiced shooting at liquor bottles. When she could hit five in a row from thirty paces, Sam began calling her Annie Oakley.

There were no hotels. Harriet refused to stay in the so-called "boarding houses". She could see bug droppings on the sheets and cockroaches scampering across the floors. They slept outdoors, using the poker tent for a cover, curling up in sleeping bags. At least they had good food. They bought fresh corn, carrots, peas and beans from the local farmers and caught fish in the river. The games finished early in farm country, and they had time to cook their dinner over an open fire in the early evenings. Harriet washed the dishes in the river while Sam laid out the sleeping bags. The ground was cold and stony, but Harriet still had a lot to be happy about.

The first hard rain came on the wind, just as they were closing up for the day. Harriet heard the drops pounding on the canvas. Outside, they bounced off the bone-dry ground.

"Rain!" The last of the players ran to their wagons, disappearing in a cloud of dust. The rain turned chilly.

"Looks like a cold dinner tonight, Hat," Sam ran to the truck to get their bag of fresh vegetables. "I have some cheese and bread saved from lunch."

They sat inside the tent munching on raw carrots and beans, cheese and crusty bread, washed down with a local brew that made Harriet's teeth chatter.

"Christ!" Sam took a swallow and coughed. "I can't wait till we're across the river. Don't worry, Hat. We'll be back in Mississippi before the snow comes."

"Are you sure?" Harriet peeked outside the tent. The rain had turned to hail.

"Let's move our sleeping bags together," he said. "We can keep each other warm. And we'll forget about the hunger."

They made a cocoon and climbed in. Soon they were kissing. She flinched when Sam's cold hand slid under her shirt and touched her breast. His hand stopped.

"I won't hurt you."

"I know, Sam. I don't mind. I mean, I like it. It's just, your hands are cold."

"I can put them somewhere they'll be warm."

One hand left her breast and slid between her legs. Higher and higher it went until it reached her private place. No man had ever put his hand there. But Sam was gentle. One finger circled her nipples one after another 'til they ached. Another finger stroked between her legs, finding a tender wet place and touching it again and again. Soon it was on fire.

Harriet moved a little so the finger had more room. The sleeping bag rolled off. She tried to grab it and pull it over them, but Sam said "Never mind, Sweetheart. I'll keep us warm." He rolled on top of her and flicked his tongue across her lips. She swam in an ocean of new, wonderful feelings, the cold on her feet, Sam's warmth on her breasts, his tongue exploring the edges of her mouth.

Sam groaned. "Move your legs apart, Sweetheart. Let me inside."

Harriet didn't even have to think about it. She spread her legs and in an instant Sam was between them.

"I'll be gentle, Sweetheart," he whispered.

"I love you, Sam," she said.

The next thing she knew Sam was poking at her with his Thing. Harriet had seen animals give a poke, but it was always from behind. This must be how humans did it.

She felt her wetness running out of her, then Sam was inside her. Something tore, and she moaned. But it didn't hurt too much. Sam stopped and kissed her.

"Don't worry about the pain, Sweetheart. There'll be a little blood, too. But it's a natural thing. It only happens once."

Harriet remembered her mother talking to her the day she had her first period. Then there was a lot more pain, and cramps, too. This time the pain passed quickly, replaced by an itch deep inside her belly. Sam moved on top of her. The itch got worse but it felt better. Better and better until it released and she screamed.

She lifted her hips and rolled her tongue around Sam's tongue.

A few seconds later, Sam pulled out of her; he moaned and collapsed on top of her. She felt something wet squirt onto her belly.

"I don't have any rubbers," he said. "We need to be careful so you don't get pregnant."

She wasn't exactly sure what rubbers were or what he meant about getting pregnant. She had hoped he would say, "That was wonderful." But instead he pulled the sleeping bag back on top of them, rolled off her and turned his back to her. "Sleep tight," he mumbled. Soon he was snoring softly. The only other sound was the rain hitting on the tent.

"I love you, Sam," she said again.

But he was asleep.

She thought about the animals she had watched. After a poke, what did they do? They just walked off. She guessed humans must be like that, too. But she wished Sam had put his arms around her and told her he loved her.

When the sun came up the next morning she saw the mess they had made of the sleeping bag. It was still wet where her bottom had been. There was some blood, too. Embarrassed, she took the bag down to the river and rinsed it, scrubbing the stain with soap, hoping it would come out. It was like her first monthly, blood and cramps. But she had no mother to put her arms around her and make her chamomile tea. She sighed. Those days were over. She hung the bag over two chairs outside their tent beside the fire. Thank goodness the rain had stopped.

Sam came back from the river with two fish for their breakfast. He saw the sleeping bag. She looked at him and blushed. He laughed. "It's alright, Sweetheart. Sex is a messy business. Like I told you, it only bleeds the first time. The next time it'll be all fun. I promise."

She smiled. There would be a next time and he had called her Sweetheart and they weren't even lying down.

―•‣•※•‣•―

From that night on, Arkansas was a wonderful place. The rains came occasionally, but mostly during the day. Harriet didn't care, even if they had to miss dinner. She could hardly wait to roll out their sleeping bags.

They learned how to do their pokes without making a mess.

At first they were doing it every night. Harriet was so sore she could hardly walk, but she didn't care. She wanted Sam to do it like the cows did, from behind. She told him it was more comfortable being on her hands and knees instead of on her back on the stony ground. He was happy to oblige. After a few weeks, he told her if they did it standing up neither of them had to be on the ground, and they wouldn't mess up the sleeping bag, so they tried that, too. There were so many things to try, so many things to learn about each other. Sex was almost as intriguing as poker.

Sam introduced her to cigarettes. She felt very grown up. He told her they made him feel better after a poke, and she said she wanted to try. At first she would take a puff off Sam's cigarette, but soon she wanted her own. Sam taught her how to roll them.

"You have tobacco on your lips, Sweetheart. Give me a taste."

Life was perfect. Sam let her do whatever she wanted except

drive his truck. She begged Sam to teach her how, but he refused. She was sure it was because he didn't trust her with his precious possession. "That's not woman's work," he said.

"I can smoke. I can drink. I can shoot a gun. I should know how to drive. What if something happens, what if I need to start up the truck?"

He grudgingly gave her a couple of lessons, but she couldn't figure out the gearshift. It was big and heavy, and she could never get the right timing with the release of the clutch. After the tenth time the truck staggered to a stop she gave up.

"Just let me handle it, Sweetheart. It's too much for a woman."

⋅ ⟫◆⟩※⟨◆⟫ ⋅

Harriet was relieved and when they crossed back over the river at Natchez and headed south to Fort Adams.

"Can't we go down to Baton Rouge and cross there," she asked. "I've always wanted to see it and it's so close."

"Nope."

"But why, don't you have time?"

"I'd get shot. Not my territory."

"But we wouldn't have to set up our tent, we could just go as tourists."

"Trust me, Sweetheart, they would know we're there."

"And they would shoot us, just for visiting?"

"You better believe it."

They stopped at a boarding house in Fort Adams. She was thrilled when Sam asked for one room for "Mister and Missus Wilson", but Sam's next words brought her back to reality.

"It's cheaper than two rooms, and besides there's no reason for us to sleep separate now," he announced, matter-of-factly. She was too nervous to ask him about the Mister and Missus business.

In a big city hotel room with a regular bed their pokes were different. The mattress was much softer and the boarding house took care of the sheets. That was a nice change, but on the other hand, they didn't have as much time for play. The customers stayed late—sometimes 'til midnight. They usually took meals from the boarding house and ate in the tent. Many nights they fell into bed, exhausted. But that was nice, too. She would curl up next to Sam, and sometimes he would hold her against him while they fell asleep.

She was delighted to be able to shop for necessaries in Fort Adams. It wasn't as big as Natchez or Memphis, but it had several reasonable stores. As she made her mental list she realized that her monthly was late. She was never late. She counted the weeks to make sure. Her last monthly had been six weeks ago.

Harriet swallowed a cold stone trying to creep up her throat from the middle of her stomach. Could she be having a baby? She remembered Ma complaining that she had missed her monthly and that another little bundle was on the way. Shit. Sam had said he was making sure she didn't get pregnant, but she had anyway. What had gone wrong? What would happen to her? Would Sam throw her out, or just drop her off in Natchez to go back to her parents? She decided she would keep quiet 'til they were out of Natchez. That way Sam would have to turn back to drop her off. She knew he wouldn't do that.

At first it was easy to pretend. She wasn't showing and Sam didn't notice she had missed her monthly. The only thing was, she was so tired all the time. Sometimes she could barely keep her head up. And in the mornings Sam had to practically drag her out of bed.

"You're gettin' to be a lazybones, young lady," he admonished one morning. She told him she was enjoying sleeping in a real bed for a change. That seemed to satisfy him.

Next thing came the morning sickness. She remembered Ma running to the outhouse first thing, looking green. Now she knew why. Fortunately she didn't have the sickness bad like her Ma. Mostly she was able to keep it from Sam. Then her nipples got tender. She flinched when Sam touched them. She pretended she was just excited.

What finally gave her away was the drive to Natchez. She was fine 'til the car headed around the first curve. Then she knew she was going to upchuck.

"Sam, stop."

"What? Why?"

"Stop! Now!"

Sam pulled the truck over to the curb. She was barely out the door when her breakfast came back up, splattering her shoes.

"Jezus, Hat, are you sick?"

"Must be something I ate. I'll be alright now."

But she wasn't alright. They stopped, and stopped again. Sam told her she must have a touch of food poisoning. She was happy to agree. When they reached Natchez she went straight to bed. She was too sick to eat anything. She could hardly move. Sam left her and went to set up the tent. She closed her eyes and the next thing it was morning and Sam was standing over her.

"You're really sick, Sweetheart. I'll get a doc to take a look at you."

"No! No, it's just some food poisoning. I feel fine now."

She hauled herself out of bed and got dressed. Another wave of nausea hit her and she rushed to the washbowl. She heaved and heaved but nothing came up.

She was barely able to straighten up. When she turned around, Sam was looking at her closely.

"You need to see a doctor, Hat."

"No, please."

"Why not? He could give you something, make you feel better."

She started to cry.

"Sweetheart, what's the matter?"

Finally she told him, between sobs and begging him not to take her back to her folks.

"You're gonna have a baby? Are you sure?"

She managed a feeble nod.

"But…but we were careful. Every time. How could this happen?" She cried silently.

"Shit. I've gotta think."

He sat down on the bed. The room was quiet except for her sobs.

"How far along are you?"

"About two months."

"Do you…do you want to keep it?"

She hadn't expected the question. "I don't know. I don't want to lose you, I want our life like we've had it."

"It'd be tough with a baby. Hell, it's already tough. A baby, though… I need to think."

"What do you need to think about?"

"I just don't know how we can take care of it, Hat. I never wanted kids, never wanted to get married. I liked moving around. A wife, kids, they would be a drag."

Harriet couldn't breath. She couldn't even look at Sam. She was so afraid of what he would say next. Maybe if she left right now she wouldn't have to hear him say he didn't want her, didn't love her. She started for the door, smashing the tears out of her eyes.

"Harriet, come back, sit down. I'm just thinking. I'm not saying I've decided anything. I like you. Hell, I like you a lot. More than a lot. You're the best dealer I ever had. Best friend, too. My life is hard, that's what I'm tryin' to say. But on the other hand, it's not like you'd be getting' into anything you don't understand. And a man has to settle down sometime. And with you I'd be sorta settled but sorta not. I guess that's the best of both worlds. Well, I guess we could try it, at least for a while. You're only two months along? That'd mean the baby might come when we're back in Arkansas. Not sure how we'll handle that."

She stopped crying. He was thinking about keeping her, about keeping the baby.

"What if I stayed behind in Memphis? Maybe with Mike and Lucy. You could go on…"

"No, I don't want you to be a burden on someone else. I want to be there. I mean, if we're married, if we're gonna have a kid we stay together. Besides, it'd be hard to catch up. I have to keep up my route, you know." He sounded apologetic.

"Of course you do. I don't want to slow you down, Sam. I want things to be just like they are."

He smiled and hugged her. "Things are never gonna be just like they are, Sweetheart. We're gonna be parents. Mom and Dad. Jezus, what a shock." He stopped to light a cigarette and look out the window. Harriet held her breath.

Finally he said, "I guess it could work out, though."

"Of course it will, Sam. Of course it will. I won't be any trouble. The baby won't be any trouble. I promise."

"We should probably get married," he mused.

"Oh, Sam!" She was so relieved she started crying again.

They took the day off. They went to a dry goods store and picked out a wedding band. Nothing fancy, just a plain band.

"Go ahead, Hat, put it on."

"No! I mean, you need to put it on once we're really married." Harriet took the ring and put it in her pocket where she could run her fingers over it every few minutes.

"We need to get registered and find a justice of the peace to perform the ceremony," Sam said. "I'm not quite sure how they do it, but we have a whole month here. Hell, when I tell the sheriff my wife is pregnant he might even give me a few extra weeks!"

It turned out the marriage process was easy. The hardest part was putting her parents' names and address in the register. She hadn't thought of Ma and Pa all that much. Now she wished she could tell Ma about the baby; invite her family to a real church wedding. Sam put the ring on her finger. She remembered the Brussels lace dress and veil, the silver slippers in Ma's hope chest. Her ma had been saving them for her. Well, what had come to pass couldn't be changed. She loved Sam and she was going to be a mother and there was nothing Ma or Pa could do about it.

She wrote a letter to Ma. She had never done that before. She told her she was married now and expecting a baby. She didn't go into detail about what had come first. She and Sam, her husband, were back in Natchez for a month. She told them the address of the boarding house. She said she hoped they might come for a visit. Perhaps Pa could sell some more whiskey to Sam. She kissed the envelope and turned it over to the clerk at the dry goods for delivery to the post.

Sam had to list his parents' names and address, too. She watched him fill out the form. Maybe he was missing his people as much as she missed Ma and Pa? But he entered the names and address, a town in Illinois, just like he entered the money tally at the end of the day.

"Maybe we should write to your folks," she suggested as they left the office.

"Folks? Oh, I just made those names up. I have no idea who my pa is. My mother left when I was five, dropped me off at the local orphanage on her way out of town. I left there when I was old enough to earn my keep. Been on my own ever since."

"I'm sorry," she said, and gave his arm a little squeeze.

"I don't never think about it, Hat."

They left Natchez without getting a letter or visit from her parents. She had kind of hoped to see them again, but she didn't want to make a fuss about them. Not after learning about Sam.

"I guess it's just you and me," she said when their time in Natchez was up.

"And our kid," Sam said.

"Right. That's our family."

Chapter 3: Arkansas

They reconnected with the carny show in Memphis. Big Mike had arranged a place for their tent, though they still had to pay the sheriff. Lucy was delighted about their wedding and the coming baby.

"Sam, you need to give Harriet a day off. Me and her are going shopping. Things for the baby, you know. Now don't say anything, Harriet," Lucy waved off Harriet's protesting hands. "You need baby things. I've waited years to have a kid to spoil." Lucy and Mike exchanged quick, sad smiles. "So now I've got a baby 'bout to come into this world and I intend to spoil it."

The two women wandered through the row of stores along Beale Street. Harriet had hoped Sam might talk Bingo Baxter into letting them stay in Memphis with Mike and Lucy till the baby came. But Sam never mentioned it and she was too shy to ask.

"Why do you want to go to Arkansas," Mike wondered out loud. "Those people have nothing. I would never take my show over there. We hear terrible stories. Murders, robberies. It's a nasty place, and getting nastier every day this damn depression drags on."

"I don't really have a choice," Sam replied sadly. I don't have the right to stay here, and my boss wants me to move on."

Harriet thought of paying another visit to Madame Zena, to see if she could offer advice about going to Arkansas, but finally decided not to. She knew Sam didn't believe in Madame Zena and she didn't want to upset him.

"You don't need some gypsy woman to tell you what's gonna happen, Hat," Lucy assured her. "You've got a handsome husband and you're about to have a wonderful little baby."

Harriet promised to name the baby Lucy if it was a girl.

"I can't wait till we meet up next year. I'll get to hold her!"

When their thirty days was up the sheriff came and they had no choice but to say goodbye to their carny friends and take their leave. They agreed on a date they would meet up in Natchez. He and Lucy waved goodbye as Sam and Harriet crossed the bridge into West Memphis. It was early spring. The baby would be born in the summer. Harriet tried not to think about where it might come into the world. The truck bounced along the rough roads. The bumps bothered her more than usual. Apparently the baby didn't like them either. It kicked up a storm.

Harriet had forgotten how different Arkansas was from Mississippi or Tennessee. Even in West Memphis, which was the largest town on their Arkansas tour, the people were poor and mean-spirited. In Memphis the talk was all about the WPA and other programs President Roosevelt had spearheaded to end the depression, but relief hadn't come to Arkansas.

"I almost had to give up with the sheriff," Sam said after their first day in West Memphis. "He wanted twice the money for thirty days. I told him I didn't have it. He got downright nasty. Threatened to arrest me. We only have two weeks here. I have to call Bingo. I'm not even sure it's worth it. People are flat broke right now."

The two weeks passed too quickly. Harriet knew that for the next several months they would be in rough country. Sam called Bingo to explain what happened in West Memphis. She overheard snatches of the conversation. "Wife...baby...poor...risky."

He seemed a little happier after the phone call. "We'll meet up with Baxter's messenger in Lake Village. He's as worried as we are. He's afraid of us carryin' too much cash. Maybe we'll be lucky and the baby'll be born there. I hear it's a nice place, a resort town."

They hadn't stopped in Lake Village on their last trip. Harriet didn't know anything about it.

"It's about 175 miles south of here," he said. "It's a tourist town, so the take might be better. The people might be friendlier. We'll stop at Hughes and Helena, then drive straight through to Lake Village. After that it'll be two little towns, then back across the river. Baxter agrees with me, there's not much action in Arkansas outside of Hot Springs, which is not my territory. This part of the country's just a waste of time. I'm not sure what we'll do next year. He says things'll have to change."

"Maybe Bingo'll give you a different territory. What d'ya think?"

"Maybe so. I think he trusts me, but he's never given me one of his better territories. I know he has some good ones along the Gulf Coast, or around Hot Springs. I'm not sure why. I never crossed him; always kept good accounts. We'll just have to see, Hat."

Helena was no different than West Memphis. The sheriff was a greedy bastard. He let them stay for exactly four weeks, for twice what they had paid him the year before. The second weekend the action was good, at least. The tent was full on Saturday night. Sam was able to get decent whiskey from the locals and the players were pretty liquored up. They sold the moonshine for a dime a glass and gave free shots to good customers.

Suddenly one of the men stood up and turned his table over. Cards and money flew everywhere. People jumped up, chairs skittered across the floor. Somebody cursed. Others dived under the tables, looking for coins and chips.

Neither Sam nor Harriet saw what had caused the ruckus. "What the hell's goin' on," Sam yelled, standing up and firing a shot in the air.

"Yore dealer's a cheat," the big red-faced man snarled. "Goddam bitch! She palmed an ace on me. I had her beat."

The dealer, a young farm girl they had just hired, backed away, terrified, tripping over a chair. "I didn't do nothin', I swear."

"We run an honest establishment, Mister," Sam said calmly. "Are you sure she's a cheat? If she is we'll fire her."

"Fuck you! I lost all my money with that cunt. I want my money back."

"Let's gather up the cards and have a look. If she palmed an ace there should be five aces in the deck."

"She's done hid the card again. You'll never find it. I want my money."

"He's a damn liar," the girl finally got enough courage to speak up. She had gumption. Sam had no idea who to believe.

"Let's everybody keep calm," Sam said. "Harriet, why don't you pick up the cards and pat down the dealer here so nobody can hide anything. Harriet's my wife," he explained to the customer. "She's expecting, as you can see. She's too slow to pull anything on you."

He was trying to lighten up the atmosphere, but it wasn't working. The room had grown hot and tense and close.

Harriet picked up the cards while Sam straightened up the table. She had the dealer stay put with her hands out so everyone could see she wasn't trying to hide anything while she frisked her. Harriet laid all the cards face up on the table. There were four aces.

"She's hidin' one! Yore bitch wife is hidin' an ace." The man lunged for Harriet, and ran straight into Sam's pistol.

"She couldn't hide anything, Mister. Everybody in the room has been watching. It's time you take your leave."

The man stormed out. "You'll be sorry," he said on his way out. "Damn sorry."

The rest of the customers went back to their games, satisfied. They had watched every move.

"Ole Bart jest lost his grocery money, that's all," one of them confided in Sam, chuckling. "The missus'll hide him good once he gits home."

The terrified dealer left. Her card game broke up. Harriet went back to her table, still shaking. Sam came over. "You all right?"

"I'm okay. Thanks." She tried to appear calm, but her stomach was churning.

The rest of their stay in Helena was pleasant enough. They made good money for a change. Rumors of the incident with Ole Bart had spread through the little town, and apparently it turned into good advertising. Word was that Sam and his pregnant wife ran an honest game with good cheap whiskey to boot.

They were anxious to be on the road once their month was up, but they had to wait for the sheriff to show up to escort them out of town.

"It's funny," Sam chuckled. "They all want us to stay around so they can make a big show of driving us out. I guess that counts for entertainment."

The sun was setting by the time the sheriff and his troops had shooed them across the city limit sign.

"See ya next year," the sheriff whispered, grinning, as he waved his pistol at Sam dramatically.

"I just hope the damn thing wasn't loaded," Sam said to Harriet as they set off.

"It's no different than Natchez," Harriet said. She yawned. The delay had forced them to drive at night. Harriet wanted to stay in town but that wasn't possible. They headed for a place a few miles south of town where they had camped out the previous year. The headlights flashed on trees along the winding road. They could hear the river rumbling comfortably just to their east, hidden by trees. The air was fresh and sweet and the humidity of the day had finally dropped. Harriet relaxed and adjusted her position in the front seat, trying to get comfortable.

"I got some bread and cheese for dinner. Don't think we'll be able to fish this late," Harriet said as they rounded a curve. Sam's reply was cut off mid-sentence as they almost ran into a truck stopped in the middle of the road.

"What the hell?" Sam skidded to a stop and jumped out of the truck to inspect the problem. Immediately, two pistol-toting men stepped out from behind the truck. Ole Bart's contorted face leered in the headlights. He motioned for Sam to get out of the truck.

"Just turn over your money and there'll be no trouble," he snarled.

"Okay, fine. I'll get the moneybag." Sam turned back towards the truck, facing away from the men. Harriet saw his hand reach for his pistol, then everything seemed to move in slow motion. Sam unholstered the gun and turned back towards the men. One of them fired a shot and Sam spun around, his face a portrait of agony illuminated by the headlights. Without thinking, Harriet dived across the seat to the driver side, slid under the wheel on her belly and reached down through the open door to the running board, just above where Sam lay in a pool of blood. Sam must have been semi conscious because he had rested his pistol hand within her reach. Another shot shattered the windshield, spraying glass over her. She squirmed to the floor and grabbed the pistol. The thieves were blinded by the headlights; she was pretty sure they didn't know what she was doing. On the other hand she could see them clearly as they advanced towards the truck.

"Now you keep calm, little lady." They had their pistols drawn, pointed at the truck. "All we want's the money. Jest show us where it is."

"It's under my feet over here," she called, squirming back under the wheel to the passenger side.

"We're gonna open the door over here and git the money. You stay nice and quiet."

Harriet faked some sobbing sounds. "My husband, you shot my husband."

"He's jest wounded. He'll be fine."

They were in the dark now, behind the headlights, by the passenger door. She watched as it opened slowly and Ole Bart leered at her from the shadows. She smiled at him. His face contorted into a quizzical grin, then he saw the gun in her hand and lunged across the seat at her.

She shot him dead center in the chest. Blood and guts exploded across the seat, the ceiling and the window as he fell over, his face almost touching her lap. She swiveled, planted her feet on his shoulders, leaned against the door and pushed him out of the truck. Bart's partner was still outside. When he saw Bart's body slide to the ground he turned and tried to run for it. She opened the passenger door and staggered out of the truck. She could just make out his retreating form at the edge of the halo of light. She took aim and shot. He staggered and fell.

Sam groaned. Thank God he was alive. He seemed to have taken a bullet near his collarbone. His blood formed an ugly dark pool that seeped around the truck wheel. She ripped a piece of cloth from her petticoat and tried to lift him to wrap the bandage, but it was hard squatting on the ground. As she struggled to work get the bandage under him she felt something tear deep inside her belly. She sat down with a thump. She felt wet under her bottom. She was sitting in Sam's blood. She wouldn't cry. It wouldn't help. She got the bandage under him and tied it off but blood was already soaking through. Help was an hour back down the road in Helena. She was alone. What the hell could she do?

She was finally able to half-stand, half-squat. She picked up Sam's legs like the handles of a cart and staggered to the passenger side of the truck dragging him behind her. The pain caused him to regain consciousness and he moaned. She knelt beside him again.

"Sam, Sweetheart, can you climb into the truck?"

He seemed to understand. He grabbed hold of the running board with his good arm and pulled himself to a kneeling position.

Then he clutched onto the seat. He half-pulled and she half-pushed him into the truck. He moaned again and slumped over. She lifted his legs in and shut the door.

She staggered around to the driver's side as a rivulet of pain worked its way up her back. Something wet was running down her legs. The seat was wet, too. She stopped herself from imagining Bart's guts underneath her. She grabbed the wheel and pulled herself into the truck with the last of her strength.

The truck was still running, thank God. At least she didn't have to get it started. She pressed down on the clutch and shoved the gearshift into first the way Sam had taught her. The truck lurched forward towards the robbers' truck. She turned the wheel sharply to the right and felt a bump. The rear wheel must have squashed Ole Bart. She fought another wave of nausea and tried to focus on turning the truck back towards Helena. Suddenly she was off the road, heading in a wide, slow semicircle through the field. Then another bump and the feel of the smooth road under her wheels.

Finally she was facing the right way. She knew there was a faster gear but she was afraid to try the clutch again. Besides, bugs were already smashing into her face through the broken windshield. She gritted her teeth teach and kept her foot on the gas pedal. Pains shot from her foot up her back to her neck. She bit into the steering wheel, trying to keep her eyes open, focusing on the road.

It seemed like hours before she saw lights. Helena. She came to a stoplight. It was red but she couldn't stop. Every time she tried to lift her foot off the gas pedal her back spasmed and something wet gushed out of her. She almost swiped another car. A horn honked angrily. The buildings swam by. Suddenly she saw red lights flashing behind her. A siren. Police. The car pulled up beside her and she screamed "Help!"

"Take your foot off the gas," a man was shouting at her.

She tried her best to concentrate on what he was saying. She seemed to be floating outside of her body. Finally she realized. "I can't lift my leg," she moaned.

"Press down the clutch. Turn off the engine." The words drifted through her brain, disassociated from the world outside the truck, like a directive from heaven. She could muster just enough strength, just enough tolerance of the pain, to lift her left foot and step on the clutch. Then she reached for the key and turned off the engine. She felt the truck slowly coast to a stop. Then she felt nothing at all.

Chapter 4: New Life

She woke up in a bed. Where had the bed come from? She tried to remember what had happened. She closed her eyes and inventoried the parts of her body. Head, hands, feet, arms, legs, belly. Something was different. She cast around in her consciousness for what it was. There was movement by her bed.

"There you are." It was Sam. The memories, feelings all came back. The fear, the pain. Sam bleeding. The baby.

"The baby..."

"Sam Junior is doing fine. He's just a little small. Needs some help. Kinda like you."

He bent down and kissed her. "Sorry I can't hug you. They tied me up pretty tight." She focused on his arm, wrapped in white bandages that went all the way up and around his shoulder.

"Sam Junior? Is that what you want to name him?"

"Seems fittin'. Did you have another name in mind?"

She had thought about naming the baby Ray after her pa, but Sam had his heart set on having a Junior.

"No, that's fine, Honey."

He stood up. "You sure? 'Cause I owe you plenty. You saved my life. I can't believe you drove that truck all the way to Helena at night with no windshield."

"And bugs slamming into my face."

He laughed.

"You killed'em, Sweetheart. And a couple of human insects, too."

She remembered the faces in the headlights, the guns pointed at Sam, at her. The bump as she ran over Ole Bart. She felt sick again. Sam patted her hand.

"Don't think about it, Hat. You did what you had to do. You saved my life; probably saved yourself and little Sam too. Those two had a bad history in this town. The sheriff isn't interested in pressing charges, not after he had a talk with Bingo Baxter."

"And the baby? Sam Junior? When can I see him?"

"Next time he's hungry, I 'spect."

She stayed in the hospital for two weeks. She was something of a curiosity for the doctors, who had never had a woman give birth in their facility before. Women had babies at home. If something went wrong, they died. The hospital was for victims of gunshots and farm accidents. The staff had no idea what to do with her. Her room was a temporary area of the main ward hastily separated from prying eyes by screens usually reserved for surgeries. Sam thought it was funny. Harriet was embarrassed every time she had to go to the bathroom.

"I'm ready to leave," she complained to Sam on the second day. Ma had babies and got up to cook breakfast the next morning. But the doctors said she was hurt inside and needed rest and Junior needed to get a little stronger.

"And where would you go," Sam asked practically. "We can't put you in a sleeping bag under the tent. And I wouldn't want you staying in the local boarding house." Meanwhile Sam was calling Bingo Baxter every day. Sam said there were "things to work out."

Finally Harriet was strong enough to leave. "Where are we goin' Sam? I don't think I can face another one of these holes in the road."

"It's over, Hat. Arkansas, I mean. This was the last straw for Bingo. He's movin' us to Texas. A place called San Antonio. He says it's a lot nicer than here, but it's a long drive. Good news, though. I have a new truck, complements of Bingo. He said to tell you congratulations, by the way."

"You mean for the baby?"

"For the baby and for killin' those two varmints."

Harriet had to laugh.

Having a kid was good for another reason. The year was 1940. President Roosevelt and Congress were starting a draft. As a father, Sam would be exempt.

"I might get excused 'cause of my shoulder. But Junior is great insurance. Why the hell would they want to beef up the army, anyway," Sam complained. "The President says we're not goin' to war. Somebody's tryin' to bullshit us."

"How can they draft you if they can't find you," Harriet asked. "You don't even have a home address they could come to."

"Well, that's about to change," Sam explained. "Bingo's arranged for us to have a house in San Antonio. They're starting an army base there. He's setting us up. We can stop traveling, at least for a while. But meanwhile we have a long hard road ahead of us."

Sam was right. The trip was a nightmare. If Harriet hadn't known the road would end at a permanent home she would have begged to go back to Natchez. Junior was no problem; he slept quietly in her lap, lulled by sound of the truck. The trouble was, Sam was still in a lot of pain. They were constantly stopping so he could rest his shoulder. They were going to meet up with Baxter in Dallas, which meant they had to drive through the Ozarks. Harriett looked fearfully into the woods for robbers around every bend of the rutted road. It was really not a road, just a mud track. Sam winced with every bounce and he was constantly having to change gears, which caused even more pain. Then it rained and the road turned to a swamp. Many nights there was no place to sleep except the truck. Harriet and Sam Junior tried to sleep inside the cabin but it was far from comfortable. Sam managed to made a small sleeping space among the tent and chairs in the back and covered himself with the sleeping bags to keep the mosquitoes away but the insects always managed to find some naked arm or toe or ear to attack. Finally they reached Texarkana. Harriett saw something she hadn't seen for months.

"Look, Sam! A road sign. It's a hundred seventy-eight miles to Dallas!"

"We'll lite there for a day or so and meet up with Bingo Baxter."

Texas' highways were a lot better than the Arkansas roads but it still took two days to get to Dallas. They were exhausted by the time they reached Baxter's house late one evening.

Harriet expected a tough old character. She was shocked when a round, friendly face peeked through his front door and looked them over. The face folded into a frown for a minute, before Sam said, "It's Sam Wilson, I'm here to meet Mr. Baxter." Then it cracked wide in a grin.

"Sam. I'm Bingo. Come on in. We wondered when you'd show up. How the hell are ya? And you must be Harriett." He wrapped her in a big hug, then held her out at arm's length. "Let me look at you. What a feisty little thing. You drilled those two sonsabitches. Good girl."

All of this was said in the nicest possible way as he quickly patted them down for weapons (even Junior's diaper) and guided them through a massive entry to the living room. They were not alone. Men were lounging against the wall in the hallway, the entry, the living room. Guns bulged under their jackets. Sam recognized Hatch, who nodded. Sam smiled. Hatch didn't smile back.

"Don't make any sudden moves," Sam whispered. Baxter heard.

"He's right, little lady. But I'm sure you're both fine."

"We're just really tired, Mister Baxter. Junior here needs a change before he stinks up your living room. And since my husband has one arm in a sling, I don't think he can cause you too much trouble."

Baxter roared with laughter.

"You're a stitch, you really are. I like you. There's a room for you." He gestured down a long hallway hung with pictures.

"I'm goin' to bed. Hope you men don't mind."

More laughter.

"Bingo likes you, Hat," Sam said as he climbed into bed later that night. "That's good for us."

The next morning Bingo told them about their destination. "It's called Randolph Field. The army air corps is already settling in. There'll be plenty of action down there and I'm rounding up some of my best hookers to work the place. I think I've got a line on some decent liquor. We don't wanna make our fightin' boys sick, now," Bingo chuckled. "We should do good. Real good. I've got you a house next to the base. I'll be down in a few months to check up on things."

They stayed for three days so Sam's shoulder could recuperate and they both could get a real rest. They had a long trip ahead—almost three hundred miles. But when they finally left Harriet felt better than she had for months. The road to San Antonio was good; there were big towns along the way where they could stay in hotels and they had a house, a real house waiting for them.

Chapter 5:
A Day That Will Live In Infamy

They arrived in San Antonio on a cool afternoon in November 1940. The house was a run-down bungalow in the middle of a dusty fenced plot but it looked like a palace to Harriett. It had running water and indoor toilets, just like the rooming houses and motels where they usually stayed. It had a bedroom for the two of them and a pantry they converted into a nursery for Junior. The kitchen stove was clean and the gas oven worked. They even had an icebox. The previous tenant had left most of the furniture they needed and Baxter had given them money to buy necessaries. Harriett got sheets and towels, pots and pans and dishes. There was enough left over to buy a real crib and a stroller.

"It's perfect," Harriett pronounced.

They had a day to get settled in, then Sam went to check out the abandoned Elks Lodge that Baxter had obtained for them. Harriett was content to stay home with Junior and set up house for the first week but she soon got restless. She set out to explore. The base was just a block away from their house. Soldier's wives were doing just what she was doing, settling in. Junior was a great attraction.

"What division is your husband in," a woman asked, chucking Junior's chubby chin.

"Oh, he's not in the army," Harriet replied. "He was shot. A huntin' accident. In the shoulder. He can't serve, they wouldn't accept him. Such a shame." She didn't elaborate on what Sam actually did. She got to know other mothers while Sam Senior got to know their husbands. She learned the best place to buy groceries while Sam Senior was connecting with the whiskey sellers.

Sam's operation was up and running in a week. He didn't even have to bribe anybody. Bingo had already taken care of the base commander. Business was good from the start. He called Bingo regularly from a payphone at a gasoline gas station down the street from their house.

"Bingo says we'll be at war within a year," Sam reported one evening.

"What'll happen to us if there's a war?"

"We'll do great. Those flyboys will flood into here. They'll want gambling, sex and liquor. That's always in demand, especially if you're about to go get shot at."

Baxter's prediction came true a year later, on December 7, 1941. Sam came running home in the middle of the day.

"The Japs bombed Pearl Harbor."

The three of them and a crowd of half-drunk airmen gathered around the radio at the Elks Lodge to listen to President Roosevelt's announcement: "Today, December 7, 1941. A day that will live in infamy."

Sam put his arms around Harriet. "We're at war."

"Are you afraid," she asked. "What if they come for you…?"

"They won't. Bingo told me. I'm wounded. It's all fixed."

Baxter was right again. Sam never got a draft notice. He was also right about war making good business. Their place was always full. They got a cut of the winnings and Bingo gave them an extra piece of the action from the hookers and liquor. They were able to find good dealers: air force wives and camp followers were always looking for extra cash. And most of them were relatively honest.

"Should we put the money in a bank," Harriet asked.

"Hell, no. The G-men would find out about it. We'd have to pay taxes and all. And they could trace the action back to Bingo."

Eventually, Sam dug a pit in the back yard and lined it with cement. He covered it with a metal lid closed with a big padlock and shoveled dirt over the top.

"Our safe," he said, wiping his forehead.

Their only problem came from an unexpected source: the wives and children of the airmen who had discovered that Harriet's husband ran the local house of infamy. The "Devil's Lodge" as the wives referred to it. The Base chaplain, a frequent visitor, railed against it in his weekly sermons. Sam got regular reports from the airmen.

"What a damn hypocrite," they laughed. "Maybe we should tell his wife he's one of our best customers. That way we won't be the only ones catchin' hell."

Harriet tried to make friends with the families. At first they seemed nice enough. She ran into the ladies and their children at the grocery store all the time. She would greet them and even invite some of them over for coffee. But before long they began to refuse.

"You keep the hell away from me," one of the wives, a woman who Harriet had befriended, yelled when Harriet approached her with an invitation. "You and your damn husband took our grocery money. I can hardly afford to feed the kids."

Her yelling had attracted a crowd. Other women were looking angrily at Harriet. She thought about defending herself, but something told her it would come to no good. What the woman said was true. The men were spending their paychecks at Sam's place, on gambling and liquor and even hookers. She discussed the issue with Sam that night.

"What am I supposed to do," he asked defensively. "Tell them they can only spend part of their paycheck at our place? Make them save money for their wives and their groceries? That's their problem. The wives should be yelling at their husbands, not at us. We don't force those guys to come to our place. The wives probably make their lives miserable at home. They come to us for some fun and relaxation. Just try to ignore 'em, Hat."

But of course she couldn't. She had to grocery shop with them, and as Junior grew, she had to walk him in his stroller and take him to the playground. The other kids soon learned Junior, still small for his age and uncoordinated, was fair game for bullying. Even though she sat on a bench watching it was impossible to prevent a kid from pushing him, from "accidentally" hitting him with a ball, from punching him when he wandered into the middle of one of their games.

"What's a whore, Ma," Junior asked in his baby voice, with tears running down his face.

"It's a bad word those kids shouldn't use. Their moms should wash their mouths out."

"But what does it mean?"

"Those kids are low-class. Forget them."

"I hate them," Junior bawled. "I don't wanna go playground any more."

"It's not just a phase," Harriet tried to explain to Sam. "We're not gonna change what we do. We're not gonna make friends with these people. What will happen when he starts school? When we can't protect him?"

"I'll take him to the Elks Lodge with me," Sam said after weeks of listening to Harriet complain "That'll keep him away from the bullies."

The decision proved to be brilliant. "I wanna go Elk Lodge," Junior whined each morning. The dealers loved him and the airmen, some of them stationed far from their homes and families, played with him. Sam was delighted to let him hold decks of cards in his chubby little hands. Soon he was pretending to be a dealer. The men thought it was cute. They let Junior drink the whiskey in the bottom of their glasses. They laughed when he staggered around afterwards.

Harriet was happy for her son but she was left with nothing to do.

"I think I should go back to dealing, Sam," she said over dinner one night. "I need to keep busy, and I can keep an eye on Junior at the Lodge."

"Forget it, Hat. I've worked hard to make enough to support my family. How would it look if you had go work?"

"But airmen's wives work. And I wouldn't do it because we need the money. I'd do it because I enjoy it."

"That's silly. A woman belongs at home. You have plenty to do, cooking, shopping, cleaning."

Harriet didn't know how to tell him. She hated cooking, shopping and cleaning. And she had no friends. And with Junior away she had no company at all. She finally decided she needed to get out of the house or she would go nuts. She began exploring the city. Thank heavens it had good public transportation. She was able to walk a block and catch the bus to downtown. She took a tour of the Alamo, walked along the river and visited the little shops, where Mexicans sold pottery, jewelry and other trinkets. Perhaps she could set up a little shop of her own, she thought. But she decided that her life was too unsettled.

She discovered the library and quickly got a card and began checking out books. At first she was drawn to animal stories. She loved the Irish Setter Big Red's adventures in the wilderness. She read all the Black Stallion books and Justin Morgan Had A Horse and decided she would own a horse one day. She asked the librarian for recommendations and was introduced to John Steinbeck and George Orwell. And she rediscovered the Emerald City of Oz and learned the author had written fourteen Land of Oz books. She devoured every one, then got the librarian to help her order her own set. When Junior turned four she decided she would start reading to him at night, as her mother had read to her. She sat by his bed, showing him how to identify the words: "dog" "man" "Oz".

She remembered how she waited all day for the time her ma sat with her and her brothers and sisters in their big bed, a book spread on the covers between them, reading the stories; how she had learned to love the characters, the thrill she felt when she learned the words.

She started reading to Junior as soon as the books came, but she soon discovered her son was not interested. He let her do whatever she wanted but he never talked about what she had read, he never asked her to read, and when she asked him to pick out a word he responded "Don't know." No amount of coaxing could get him to pay attention. Many nights he fell asleep at the most exciting part of a story.

"When you start school you'll need to read all by yourself. And write, too. Let's see if you can pick out the word "dog".

"I don't want to go to school. I want to work with Pa. I bet Pa never went to school."

"That's not true, Junior. Pa did go to school. He learned to read and write and do numbers just like you'll learn."

That night Sam confirmed that he had indeed gone to school and that Junior would go, too, when he was old enough.

"You need to do what your ma says if you want to work with me," he confirmed. But he took no interest in teaching his son.

"He's only four, Hat. He's just a baby. Give him time."

She realized it was useless to make a fuss but she worried what would happen when Junior had to go to school. His life was hard enough with the kids bullying him. What if he was a slow learner, too? She tried to teach him to count to ten on his fingers. She held up two fingers. "How many fingers is this, Junior?" She even resorted to playing cards, asking him to count the spots. But though he was interested at first he soon got bored. "I want to play cards at the Lodge," he whined. It seemed that nothing she did or said made a difference.

By 1945, Junior was five and the underground safe was full.

"Bingo's one of the most important kingpins in the country," Sam confided. Baxter was raking in money and had been generous with Sam.

"You and your Hat are my favorites," He confided on one of his visits. The first few visits were unannounced. He was checking them out.

If you let us know you were coming I could make a meatloaf and a chocolate cake for desert," Harriet joshed after the third time he appeared unannounced.

"Well that sounds just about perfect, Hat. I'll call ahead next time."

After the first dinner the visits became more friendly. Harriet enjoyed Bingo's company. She made a point to read the newspaper every day. They discussed the economy and politics. Unlike Sam, he was interested in the books she was reading.

"I raise quarter horses, you know," he told her after she confided her love of the Black Stallion books.

"I would love to see your operation," she replied enthusiastically. "I always wanted a horse. When I was little, we lived on a farm but we just had a mule.

"One of these days I'll take you to my ranch and show you around," he promised.

Occasionally he took them out for a "night on the town" even paying for a babysitter for little Sam.

"But I'd rather enjoy your cooking, Hat," he admitted. "I eat out all the time."

They talked about what would happen after the war. He loved to brag about how much his "people" were making, but he was evasive about what would happen to Sam and Harriet.

"We'll have to make some changes," he said. "I think Mississippi might pick up again when the soldiers come home. But I hear there's more opportunity out west. Let's wait and see."

Chapter 6: The Meadows

As it turned out, things did change after the war.

"The goddamn Chicago mob wants a piece of my action," Baxter complained.

"But how can they horn in," Sam asked. "I thought you had a lock on things."

"Rumor has it Capone made a hundred million a year during Prohibition. That's a hell of a lot more than we made with our gambling operations. I shoulda got into the liquor business, but I was too late to the game. Capone and the wops had it locked up in our part of the world."

Harriet thought about her pa's moonshining operations. How much had he made during Prohibition? She hoped he had done well. Maybe he sold out to Capone.

"But word is Capone's dying of syphilis," Sam said. "They let him out of jail back in '39 so he could die at home, but he's still around. They say he's got a whole organization behind him with enough dough to buy the entire fuckin' state of Texas. The state's not particular where they get their juice."

"They couldn't be interested in our little piece of the action, could they," Sam asked in a worried voice. But before long he knew the answer.

At first Sam blamed the officials at Randolph. "The city won't renew our lease on the Elks Lodge," he reported in September 1946.

"They say they're gonna demolish it. They won't tell me why."

Then their business slowed to a trickle. They learned a new place was opening up on the other side of the base.

"Is it Bingo," Harriet asked. "Have you done something to piss him off?"

"Hell, no. It's something else, I'm sure. I need to talk to him."

Bingo sounded a little resigned on the phone. "I may have to leave, Sam. The damn Lone Star State is gettin' too hot for me. Capone's boys are movin' in. Let's see what happens after the local elections here."

"But where will you go? What about us?"

"Well, you can stay put in San Antone and deal with the damn wops or you can move on with me."

"Move to where?"

"Las Vegas."

Sam had heard the name; some of the airmen at the base had been stationed at the army air base outside of Vegas. They talked a lot about the great times they had there.

"It's wide open," they said. "They've legalized gambling so we don't have to worry about raids. Prize fighting's legal too. Even prostitution. If you can put up with the desert heat, it's perfect."

"The desert? But the name, Las Vegas, I do believe it's Spanish for the meadows," Sam observed.

"Somebody must've been drinkin' a lot of tequila," his friend replied. "The place is nothing but sand. It's hot as hell."

"Maybe it means a good place, like in the Bible," Harriet said. They were discussing the move over dinner. She thought about Junior. He would start school next year. If he had to attend classes with the same bullies he met on the playground, if his parents were detested by his classmates' parents, his life would be hell. She remembered how she felt running home to her ma after school, crying from the teasing. The moonshiner's daughter. But she was different, far different from her son. She knew that now. She had a thick skin and a bright mind. There was no hiding the fact, Junior was not bright. He didn't have the talent to make friends or impress people. And behind all his bravado Junior was a sensitive insecure child. The teasing, the punches and shoves had already left a permanent mark on his spirit. She couldn't let him face the taunts, the attacks alone. Junior needed a new place, a fresh start. "He maketh me to lie down in green meadows." She looked at her husband and smiled. "Maybe it's a sign."

The call came in November 1946.

"The fuckin' wops bought the local elections here, Sam. It's time to move on. You comin'?"

"Hat and I have talked about it. We're with you, Bingo."

"That's great. I was hopin' you'd come along. The rest of my guys want to stay put and take their chances. They're all settled in with families and local connections. I'll be at your place in a week. Get ready to move out."

They decided to take their clothes and their money and leave everything else behind. "We've built up quite a little nest egg, Hat. Let's make this a brand new start."

They thought Bingo Baxter would show up in a truck packed to the rim with his longhorn furniture, the Remington sculptures he was so proud of and his collection of Western art. But he surprised them, arriving in a gold Cadillac with nothing in tow. Inside the car, wearing suits and ties and sitting much too straight for guys on a holiday, were Hatch and Weasel.

"Do they want to move to Vegas, too?" Harriet asked.

Bingo chuckled. "They might. But for now Hatch here's guardin' the goods and Weasel's keepin' the books."

They took off an hour later, driving fast to keep up with Bingo. They stopped every few hours to fill up the cars and empty their bladders. They managed to find decent accommodations each evening. Every morning, Weasel opened the trunk and removed a wad of bills for the day's expenses. Moneybags filled the entire trunk. He counted the bills and wrote some numbers in a black journal.

"Why's he have to do that, Bingo?" Harriet's curiosity finally overcame her.

"Cause I got podners, Hat. And they'll wanna know what happened to their stakes. And Weasel here's gonna tell 'em. Right to the penny. Eh, Weasel?"

Bingo slapped the little man on the back, which almost sent him to his knees.

"Right." He responded in his thin shaking voice.

"Just like you guys. I'm startin' clean," he smiled. "But I gotta keep good accounts. There's a million bucks in that there trunk. More or less. Right, Weasel?"

Weasel nodded, backing out of Bingo's reach. Harriet and Sam's stash was just over a hundred thousand, also in cash. Also in the trunk of their car. She decided Hatch was a welcome addition.

The weather was cool and dry. They followed the gold Cadillac, like a setting sun, northwest to Amarillo. There they caught the new highway, Route 66, heading west. Soon the flat prairie gave way to mountains.

Along the way Harriet learned Hatch had another talent. He was a great baby sitter. He and Junior hit it off right away. Junior begged to ride in Bingo's car so he could play with his new friend. The big man was happy for the company. When they got out at rest stops he tucked Junior under his arm like a football, carrying him from Cadillac to restaurant, to toilet, to sleeping accommodations as needed.

Bingo assured them Junior would be much better off in their new home. "Hell, the whole town's full of folks like us. Glass houses, as they say. Ain't nobody gonna throw stones at your boy."

"Vegas has mountains," Bingo told them. "You're gonna love it.

It's high and dry and busting with potential. We'll cross over the Boulder Dam on the way in. That's what really started the place growing–all the workers they brought in to build the dam. They liked the city. They never left. While the rest of us was fightin' the hard times, Vegas was boomin'. Still is. Some Hollywood boys built permanent gamblin' joints there. No more tents or Elks Lodge operations. No more havin' to please a landlord or local sheriff either. We'll own our place free 'n clear."

Route 66 wound west to Flagstaff then turned towards the Arizona/Nevada border.

"We got to go see the Grand Canyon," Harriet said. "It's so close. We may never get the chance again."

Sam was reluctant to stop but Baxter thought it was a great idea.

"I've never seen it," he confessed. "And the little guy should be able to tell folks he was there. I hear it's a wondrous sight."

They drove to the edge of the famous gorge. Even Sam was impressed.

"I never thought it'd be like this, so big."

"See that river down at the bottom," Baxter asked, pointing to the tiny silver ribbon below. "That's the Colorado. It flows into the Boulder Dam. That's the river that made Vegas."

Harriet stood still and silent, gaping. She let her head fill with images of the rocks in all their colors and formations, the pinion pine-scented air, the great birds circling overhead. She thought of all the descriptions in the books she had read, all the pictures. No words, no pictures could ever capture this place.

"What'd you think, Hat?" Sam must have been reading her thoughts. He put his arm around her and gave a little squeeze. He felt it, too. She could tell.

"I think it's as fantastic as our lives are gonna be." She squeezed him back. He didn't have a way with words but he felt things. And in his heart he was a good and adventurous man. She was a lucky woman.

They stopped again along the Virgin River, just east of the dam, so Junior could run around and use up some energy. He was getting more and more restless sitting in the car day after day. Even Hatch had a hard time controlling him.

"You must be sick and tired of his whining. Give him some beer," Sam suggested. "He'll fall asleep."

Harriet thought that was a bad idea, but Hatch loved it. Junior loved drinking from his friend's bottle and promptly dozed off. But when he woke up he was in such a terrible mood that Hatch swore he would never to do it again. Bingo said Junior would have to ride with his parents if he didn't shut up.

"We'll be at the dam tomorrow, anyhow" Bingo said. "Then we'll cross over into Nevada. We're almost home."

The next evening Baxter pulled off the road and pointed to a glow on the horizon. Sam pulled in behind him. Hatch carried Junior to the side of the road and pointed his head west.

"That's lights from the dam," Bingo said. "The Nevada border's in the middle."

"So we drive across it," Harriet asked.

"Yep. It's one of the great wonders of the world. Don't you go to sleep now, young man." Baxter ruffled Junior's hair. "You're about to see a sight you won't ever forget. Just about as impressive as the Grand Canyon."

He was right. They came up over the crest of a hill just as the sun was setting. Sam was so distracted he almost ran off the twisting downhill road. Ahead of them was what looked like a different planet. Huge metal towers stuck out of gray and brown cliffs at crazy angles. The place was lit up like a thousand carny tents. Below the towers a blue lake glowed with a surreal reflection of the lights. Water shooting out from huge tunnels roared so loudly they had to roll the windows up to hear themselves talk.

"I don't see any meadows," Harriet yelled to Sam over the noise. The lake and river were surrounded with solid rock as far as she could see.

They stopped on the Arizona side first. "Those towers carry 'lectricity all the way to Los Angeles," Baxter explained.

"It's amazing," Harriet sighed. "But it's so dry. There's not a sign of life anywhere."

"Oh, there's life all right. There's big horn sheep and coyotes and snakes, some of 'em actual reptiles, back up in those rocks. You just have to know where to look."

"At least the rocks are beautiful in their way," she continued, inspecting the surroundings. "And look at the sculptures. Somebody put a lot of love into this place."

Baxter harrumphed. "A lot of money, you mean. The dam meant full employment for Roosevelt's cronies. Six construction companies, two engineering firms, dozens of artists, sculptors. Millions of dollars in bribes probably changed hands. And they call us grifters!"

"It was worth it," Harriet replied earnestly, peering over the edge of the walls around the dam. Hatch toted Junior, holding him horizontal so his head stuck over the wall into the vast gorge below.

Junior looked over the edge. "Big," he said.

"Yep. Big," Hatch agreed.

They stopped at the Nevada side as well, to look at the memorial to the workers who had given their lives to build the awesome structure. Baxter pointed out the inscription, "They died to make the desert bloom..."

"You see," Harriet replied, smiling. "It really is the meadows. Las Vegas."

Baxter nodded. "It's gonna bloom for us, Sammy boy. That's for sure."

Chapter 7: LA Highway

They pulled into a motor court in Boulder City, just across the Nevada border. "It's too late to get to Vegas," Baxter explained. Harriet was happy to stop for the night.

"Tomorrow we'll see our own new home," she whispered to Junior as she tucked him into one of the twin beds and slipped in beside him. Sam Senior took the other bed. The bed was so small she had to hang off the mattress, one leg resting on the floor. The springs squeaked every time she moved but she fell asleep almost immediately.

What seemed like a minute later, she opened her eyes. She had to shut them right away. The sun was so bright. And the light was white, not yellow like she was used to. Sam was already up. "Come on lazybones. We're late for breakfast."

"Welcome to the high desert," Baxter said as they scarfed down plates of bacon and eggs.

"The light. It's so different." Harriet had to squint to look out the window.

"The air's like champagne. No humidity. Nights can be chilly this time of year, but the days'll kill you unless you stay in the shade. Then it's tolerable so long as there's no wind. It'll kick up the sand. Flies at you like bullets," Bingo warned.

"We'll head down over Railroad Pass. Vegas started as a railroad town. It's still laid out like one. It was a waterin' hole. Yep," he smiled at Harriet's incredulous stare. "That's right, there was real meadows down there. There's still cottonwood trees. Them's the water markers in the west. You wanna find a stream, look for the cottonwoods."

"Anyhow, downtown was originally owned by the railroad. They sold off the lots and now you have a town. I'll show you around. We'll have plenty of time before you get settled in tonight."

Baxter led the way as they wound down the hills into the valley. Harriet saw a little strip of road emerge in the distance, and at the end of the road, stretching along a railroad track; she could make out buildings surrounded by cottonwood trees. It looked promising from a distance, like a real town with regular buildings. It was bigger than Selma, bigger than any of the towns they had passed through in Arkansas. As they got closer she could even make out a church. Harriet was relieved. The way Baxter talked she had thought there was nothing in Vegas but gambling joints.

They passed a sign "Las Vegas, population 9,302". Finally, they reached the center of town. Baxter pulled up in front of a rather ordinary looking brick building with a sign in front "Westerner Club". Sam pulled in beside him.

"This is it," Bingo said, gesturing to the door.

Harriett got out just as a gust of wind came up. Before she knew it her teeth were coated with sand. She had sand in her hair, in her eyes.

"Get inside," Baxter said. Sam grabbed her hand and dragged her through the door. Hatch followed, shielding Junior with his body. Weasel ran for the door just ahead of Bingo, his body almost blowing away in the gusts.

Inside was dark and cool. Once Harriett's eyes adjusted she saw the tables and chairs. It looked just like the inside of Sam's tent except it was a building with a bar at one end.

"Here's where we're gonna put a big mirror on the wall," Baxter explained, waving his arms around the room. "And here's where I'm gonna have my big fuckin' horseshoe. And it's gonna be covered with real thousand dollar bills. It's gonna be worth a million bucks, that horseshoe. I'm gonna have it covered in glass or somethin'. It'll be the fanciest place downtown. C'mon, I'll give you a tour of the town."

Weasel said he wanted to make a closer inspection of the club. Hatch volunteered to stay behind and keep Junior, who was already busy with his own inspection. Sam, Harriet and Bingo climbed into the Cadillac. There were other gambling halls, some a lot fancier than the Westerner. Harriet wanted to see the school where Junior would go. She learned there were two kinds of schools. The Catholic school was next to the Catholic Church. The church was built of stone and looked very permanent and impressive. It had a huge bell tower that caught the sun. The Fifth Street Elementary School was a few blocks away. It wasn't nearly as nice.

"Are most of the folks here Catholics," she asked.

"They's all kinds of folks here, Hat," Baxter replied. Catholics and Mormons and Baptists. Probably even a few Jews. And of course, us heathens." Harriet had never heard of Mormons and, when she asked, Baxter didn't know much about them.

"I'll take you out the LA Highway, where the town is expanding." They drove to what seemed the edge of town. Ahead of them, a highway stretched to the edge of sight across the desert. "That's it," Bingo said, turning onto the highway. "Lots of new building out here." They passed several impressive ranch-like compounds along the way. "Casinos" Bingo said proudly. "Real ones, not little tents you have to pick up and move every damn month. Not gambling halls either. These are damn establishments!"

Harriet tried to look knowledgeable about gambling establishments but she didn't have a clue what he meant. "They have bars and dancin' girls and even rooms like in hotels. And they serve up steak dinners, too. It's the future of gambling," Baxter continued.

He pointed out the Last Frontier, owned by a famous Hollywood film producer D.W. Griffith. "See, it looks kinda like a set of one of them western movie sets. It's got corrals and horses and even fake gun fights."

One casino hotel was under construction and looked much bigger than the others. It had a fancy adobe front with a big pink flamingo sign. "That's Siegel's place," Baxter scoffed. "He's poured a shitload of money into it. Got it from the LA mob. It's supposed to be finished later this year. He's invited all the Hollywood boys and movie stars to come to a grand opening. He says it's the future of Las Vegas. It fuckin' better be or Siegel won't have any fuckin' future."

"How many people come here to gamble," Harriet asked dubiously. "Are there enough for all these places?"

"Hell, people come here from all over," Baxter boasted. "Folks from California. And the flyboys at the Base. They love it here. This place is gonna explode." He made an exploding gesture with his arms, waving towards the dusty lots all around them. Harriett tried to envision the LA Highway full of buildings.

"Where does it lead to?" She pointed down the road.

"Los Angeles. It's a direct route."

The wind had died down by the time they returned to the Westerner to pick up Junior.

"I don't wanna go. I wanna stay with Hatch." Junior squirmed away from his mother and ran to his friend, wrapping his arms around one giant leg.

"I'll see you soon." Hatch gently unwound the skinny little arms and pushed Junior towards his parents.

"I do believe I saw a tear in Hatch's eye," Harriet said as they followed Bingo. A few minutes later they pulled up to a wrought iron gate surrounding a large patch of green grass. Inside, a row of small houses lined the road.

"This is a new community," Baxter explained. "It's built around an old stream. That's why things are so green. It's pretty nice."

They drove through the elaborate gate and stopped in front of the bungalows.

"Pick one," Baxter said.

Harriett couldn't believe it. "Any one?"

"They're all the same, "Baxter laughed. "Whichever you pick, it's yours, complements of Bingo Baxter. They all have three bedrooms, tile floors, modern kitchen and bath. And a swamp cooler. 'Cause it's hotter 'n hell here most of the time."

Harriett picked one on a corner: "One Hundred Country Club Lane". Harriet looked around. There was no clubhouse in sight. "Why would you call this a country club?"

"It's an exclusive community, Sweetheart. There's gonna be a golf course and swimmin' pool and clubhouse, too. Before you know it."

Once again Bingo's arms waved across the empty space in front of them. Harriet hadn't seen anything resembling a golf course since they left San Antonio. She couldn't imagine what she would do with one. But she was excited about having a swimming pool. "And at least we have some grass," she grinned. " There's my meadow."

Chapter 8: Presents

Christmas Day, 1946. Their first Christmas in their new home. Outside a winter chill had set in, but it was different from anything she had experienced. The air was cold but there was no hint of snow. The wind brought a vaguely mineral odor.

"Devil's breath," Sam laughed. The wind gusts had picked up and everything that was not inside was covered with sand. The grass in their subdivision protected them from direct hits, but sand still dusted the back patio and Junior's new swing set.

Harriet's favorite present was a Christmas card from her family. She recognized her ma's beautiful curlicues on the envelope, spelling out her name. She hugged the precious paper to her face, hoping to breathe in a piece of home. Finally she opened it. Inside was a card.

"Dear Harriet. Merry Christmas to you and your family. We are all well here. Love, your mother."

That was all. Harriet held the envelope open, sure it must contain a note. But there was nothing. No news of how her family was celebrating the holiday. At least she knew they were still on the farm. Had they put on their boots and stomped through the woods looking for the perfect tree, blowing on their mittens to keep their hands warm as Pa sawed it down? Had they made popcorn strings and paper stars? She shook her head to clear away the tears.

Inside her new house the temperature was cozy. Everything was new and clean and bright. She stepped outside her front door and tested the air. No sand today. She took a deep breath. It was dry and light. It made her lips tingle. She loved these mornings. She would write home and tell the family all about them.

Back on the farm the nights had been still and moist and inky dark. Here the lights came on at dusk. Some lights never went out, like the signs that lined Fremont Street. They sent up a glow she could see from her kitchen window, powered by the electricity from the dam. She learned they were special, filled with neon gas. They were much more colorful than ordinary lights, pink and green and red and blue, spelling out words or drawing colorful characters against the sky. The street was nicknamed "Glitter Gulch."

This Christmas morn she looked up, beyond the pink and brown desert to the mountains ringing the valley. She could see hints of white on the peaks. The first signs of snow. She would have to go up there to see.

"I will lift up mine eyes to the hills," she recited the ancient psalm to herself. Then she chuckled. The Hebrews probably never imagined mountains capped with snow that glowed bright pink in the sunset. "Like neon," she told Sam, who laughed.

"It's not a reflection from Glitter Gulch," he replied. "It's some sort of glow from the sun. It bounces off the pink rocks onto the snow."

Her thoughts turned to her family in Las Vegas. Junior was still a problem. They had enrolled him in a local preschool program at a converted home run by the Service League. The women's group was working hard to improve life in the city. Harriet was delighted to learn Las Vegas had several women's organizations: members of Beta Sigma Phi, the American Legion Auxiliary and the USO Club were frequently in the news. But she discovered she couldn't join any of them. Sam hadn't been drafted and she had no social connections. It was funny, if you had been in Las Vegas for twenty years you were a "native". She was a "newcomer" and would probably always be.

She didn't want Junior to feel like an outsider in his new home.

Las Vegas would be a fresh start for all of them, especially her son. The first day of class, she and Sam drove him to the preschool and introduced him to the teacher. The place was small, but that was good. There were fifteen kids in the program. The teacher, a bright young woman with a bubbly voice, was friendly and all the kids seemed well mannered. They all said hello to him and the teacher conducted a tour of the room. The preschool was mostly about play, she said. Coloring, playing with blocks, singing. And every child had to take a nap. They were to pick up their son at two.

He was standing at the door with the teacher when they arrived.

"I don't think he's ready for preschool," the woman said, avoiding their eyes. "He doesn't get on well with the other children. You should probably wait 'til he can go to kindergarten."

"Couldn't we give it a week or so to see if things get better," Sam asked.

"Well, he hit another boy and threw a toy at a girl. I'm afraid he'll hurt somebody. I gave him a good spanking and made him sit in the corner, but it didn't help."

"I'll take the belt to him," Sam said, jerking his son down the sidewalk. Junior was wailing so loudly that people on the street turned to watch, which only made his father more furious. "I'm gonna beat you 'til you can't sit down, you little brat."

Harriet trailed behind her husband and son trying to think of some way to help.

"Please, Sam. Let's just get him home and discuss this. I'm sure Junior's sorry, aren't you, son?"

"I hate school. I hate it. I wanna go to the club with Hatch."

The big man and her son had remained close. The two would go for rides in Hatch's car and he always seemed to turn up when Junior was in trouble.

Sam laughed. "Well, that's pretty funny. I'm about to beat the tar outta him and he'd rather go with me than spend the day in that nice school."

"He adores you, Sweetheart. Please don't punish him. He just wants to be around you. Isn't that right, Junior?"

"I hate school. I wanna be with Hatch."

Junior sat sullenly between his parents in the truck, but at least he had stopped wailing. And his father had calmed down. Harriet hoped the trouble was over for the night. In the morning maybe Sam would take Junior with him. Maybe that was best for now.

It wasn't like Junior didn't have the best of everything. They were rich now. Baxter had sold them an interest in his Westerner Club and they were raking in money. Their biggest problem was finding a place to keep it. Sam had dug another pit in the back yard, but it was already half full of cash.

Junior's room was also full. He had trucks, a rocking horse, a toy train and a set of tin soldiers. He had a bright red Schwinn bike with the latest invention—a kickstand. They had bought him a puppy, a purebred cocker spaniel, but Harriet caught him pulling the ears on the little thing. "You can't have a puppy if you're not nice to it," she had scolded. He ignored her. So she gave the puppy away.

She was even more worried about Sam. She was afraid they were growing apart. It seemed the more money they had the less she had of her husband. He was busy all the time. And the things he had shared with her when there were just the two of them he now shared with Baxter. Sam was proud the older man had made him a partner. He looked up to Baxter as a sort of father figure. There was no way Harriet could compete. And what did she have to talk to Sam about? She spent her days at home. The most important thing in her life was Junior, and she rarely had anything good to tell Sam about Junior. She asked if she could work at the club but both Sam and Bingo said that was a terrible idea.

"You belong at home, Sweetheart," Sam said. "That's what I'm working for. So you can be a real wife and mother. Only poor women have to work."

She had put her energy into getting ready for Christmas. She bought a huge artificial tree and made ornaments. She tried to get Junior to help but he wasn't interested, so she popped the corn and made strings, cut out paper stars and even found some bulbs at the local department store, though they weren't near as beautiful as the ones she remembered.

Junior wasn't interested in the tree or in the pile of presents that greeted him Christmas morning. He opened each one and threw the contents into a corner. Then he threw a tantrum because the presents were gone. Sam spanked him and sent him to his room.

Harriet couldn't even enjoy the gold necklace Sam had bought her. It was delicate and had a diamond pendant, a heart with a ruby in the middle.

"It's wonderful, Sam." She kissed him and he hugged her back. "Are you sure we can afford it?"

"I won it off a rich guy from LA in a poker game," Sam explained with a straight face. He laughed when she looked at him, aghast.

"Just kidding, Hat. I told you, we're rich. And this is a way to spend our money so we don't have to bury it."

That wasn't much more romantic than the poker story. She had hoped he would say she was worth it, or that the heart was a symbol of his love, but he didn't. He thought of the necklace as an investment. She tried not to show her disappointment. She didn't need any more trouble spoiling her holiday.

When Junior was finally let out of his room he went back to the present pile. Sam was in the bathroom getting ready for work. She watched her son from the kitchen, hoping he would pick up one of the new toys and begin playing with it. He grabbed his new truck, stood over it and jumped on it with both feet. Its wheels popped off as it squashed with a crunch. Junior laughed. Harriett started to say something but some instinct kept her quiet. Suddenly Sam came up behind her.

"I'm off to the Club. We're gonna be packed today. I'll probably be home late. Merry Christmas."

He headed for the door. Harriet was terrified he might see what his son had done to his new truck, but Sam was thinking about other things. He didn't even say goodbye. Junior watched his father go, then turned his attention to destroying his new toys. For once something had distracted him from going with his father.

The following night was the opening party for the new Flamingo Resort, Siegel's new place.

"We're not invited," Sam joked. "We're just not glamorous enough, I guess. Maybe I need to buy you a more expensive necklace."

As it turned out, they didn't miss anything. Baxter did get invited and he spent the next day telling Sam stories about the place – the gaming tables had to shut down, the air conditioning didn't work, the lobby was draped in construction cloths. It poured rain and hardly any of the Hollywood celebrities Siegel had bragged about showed up. Baxter thought it was hilarious. "They should have called it the Duck," he said. "You know, water just rolls off a duck's back. But Bugsy, Jezus. He was angry as a pit bull in the ring. He even threw some guests out. The place is a flop. He'll never live this down."

"Let this be a lesson," he told Sam and Harriet. "Don't spend beyond your means. What people want when they come here is to gamble. A good meal, good whiskey, maybe a little entertainment and a nice clean room. Sure. But they don't need some damn French chef or a luxury suite. Just give 'em a fair game and honor their bets. No matter how high. That's my rule. Sure, we might lose big some of the time but they'll keep coming back. And in the long run the house always wins. The other casinos call my customers high rollers," he laughed. "They think that's an insult. Horseshit. That's what brings the gamblers to me. But we cover our bets with our own money. We don't borrow. You spend more then you make and you're gonna get in trouble. 'Specially when you borrow from the mob."

Chapter 9: Opal

"I wanna go to the club. I wanna go to the club with Hatch." Junior's nagging wail had finally gotten to Harriet. She grabbed him and gave him a swat on the bottom.

"Shut up, you little brat!"

It didn't help. The wailing continued.

"If I take you to the club will you be a good boy?"

The wailing stopped. How could he turn it off like that? Like a faucet? He was all smiles. "I'll be good, Mama. I promise."

She thanked her stars that Sam had finally bought her a car. "Otherwise I'll be trapped in this place all day. I'll go nuts," she pleaded.

The car was a beautiful red Ford with a huge chrome bumper. She fell in love with it on the spot and insisted Sam buy it for her.

"I'm gonna learn to drive this thing if it kills me," she said.

"As opposed to the last time when you killed those varmints?" Sam grinned.

He teased her but he was happy to oblige. They still had plenty of money buried in the back yard. They brought it to the auto dealer in bags. The guy didn't even blink.

"We need to think of something big to spend our money on," Harriet said as Sam stuffed car money into a bag.

"Like what?"

Harriett said she would think of something.

"Not more jewelry, Hat," he joshed.

"I'm serious, Sam."

"My little genius." He tousled her hair. "Maybe we should buy our own club. Think that'd piss off Bingo?"

"I'spect it would. But maybe there's some other kind of property we could buy."

She was thinking about the money as she bundled Junior into the car. Maybe she should start a school for young kids. Then Junior would have a place to go where they couldn't kick him out. She was terrified what would happen when he started school in the fall.

When she pulled up in front of the club she discovered that her parking space was blocked. A woman was standing in the space facing away from her, looking at the door. When Harriet honked she turned around, startled. At first Harriet thought it was June Allyson, the movie star. She had the same hourglass figure and long, curly blonde hair. Her eyes were huge and blue. Harriet laughed at herself. No Hollywood actress would be standing in front of Baxter's club.

"Are you okay," Harriet asked as she tried to hold on to Junior who had jumped out of the car.

"Sure. I'm fine."

"Mama, I want to go in. I want to go IN."

"My son wants to go in," Harriet laughed. "Were you looking for something?"

"I was actually looking for work. Do you know if they're hiring?" She nodded towards the club.

"I don't know, but we own the place. At least we're co-owners. What sort of work did you have in mind?"

Junior was pulling at her arm.

"Why don't we go inside so Junior calms down," she said.

"Can Ezekiel come in," the woman asked.

"Who's Ezekiel?"

"My son."

Harriet finally noticed a little toddler curled up against the wall, head resting on his arms. He lifted his face to look at them. He was the most beautiful child Harriet had ever seen. His eyes were huge and dark blue like his mother's, framed by long curly lashes. His hair was thick and black. He stood up.

"This is MY club," Junior said, as if Ezekiel had challenged him somehow.

"I like it," the child replied. He couldn't have been more than three, but he spoke very clearly, like an adult.

Junior looked at him, cocking his head as if he were making some sort of judgment. "You can come in," he announced finally.

Sam was in the middle of a conversation with Bingo when they walked in. Sam appeared to be irritated at the interruption.

"What are you doing here," he said. Then he noticed the woman. "Well…hello! What have we here?"

"Sam, this is…what was your name, dear?"

"Opal. Opal Cullen."

"Opal is looking for work. Do we have anything?"

She had assumed Sam would say no and send the woman on her way. But instead Sam walked around her, inspecting her like their new car.

"For someone as good looking as you we can probably come up with something. You married?"

"No. No, I'm not." She looked at the floor, then at the small figure holding her hand.

So the child was a bastard. Interesting. Harriet remembered how worried she had been when she learned she was pregnant and unmarried. She wondered what sort of man could have sex with such a gorgeous woman and then desert her.

"His father was in the army. He was killed. In Germany," Opal said, as if to dispute Harriet's unspoken conclusion.

"Who's gonna take care of him?"

"I'll find someone, I swear. I'm willing to do anything. I just need a job."

Bingo and Sam looked at each other as tears formed in Opal's wondrous eyes. Some unspoken message appeared to pass between the two men. Finally, Bingo spoke.

"If you can find someone to take care of the kid you can have a job as a hostess. But I hope you meant what you said about the hours. We stay open around the clock. You'll have to be here from six pm to two am and from twelve to two during lunch. That's when our customers come in."

"Oh thank you!" She threw her arms around Bingo. He grinned at Sam.

"What about the kid?" Sam asked as she unwrapped her arms from Bingo.

Harriet looked from her husband to his partner. It was amazing what a beautiful woman could get with a few tears. Oh, well there was nothing she could do to stop them. She looked at Ezekiel. He was looking around, his bright, curious eyes seeming to make some sort of judgment.

Junior interrupted her thoughts. "I wanna show him my place," he said proudly, holding out his hand to the little boy. Ezekiel took his hand and the two walked away, with Junior explaining what the poker tables were for and what was served at the bar. Harriet had an idea.

"What if I took care of the kid while Opal works? He might be good company for Junior."

She held her breath, waiting for Junior to complain. Having another child around would mean her son would no longer be the center of attention. But he'd be asleep for part of the time she'd have to keep Ezekiel. And Ezekiel would probably take naps for part of the time Junior was awake. It would be easy, she decided. And a good way to make friends with Opal. Which was a good way to keep tabs on what was happening at the club.

"Oh, thank you so much!"

Harriet noticed that she did not get the same hug.

"How can I pay you?"

"I'm sure Sam and Bingo here can come up with some way to make it up to me," she said wryly, looking at the two men. They looked down.

"Besides, Junior should learn to get along with little kids. It's not good for him to play with Hatch all the time."

Harriet heard a grunt. Hatch was standing behind her. "I'm sorry, Hatch. I know you love Junior and he loves you. I didn't mean to hurt your feelings."

Hatch didn't look at her. He turned and walked out the door without a word.

Chapter 10: Ezekiel

Harriet and Opal sat at Harriet's kitchen table sharing gossip and coffee. In the past year, Opal had made herself indispensable to Sam and Bingo, at least according to Sam.

"She's the key to our future, Hat," he told her. "Vegas is gonna grow, there's gonna be lots of competition. We need a secret weapon just to keep up. She's our secret weapon."

Harriet thought of the sleepy town she had come to know, its dusty streets lined with motels to attract the people traveling to Los Angeles and the soldiers on holiday. She had a hard time understanding how Las Vegas was going to "explode" much less how one woman would be the key to competing if such an explosion were to occur, but she kept her mouth shut. And she went out of her way to make sure her relationship with Opal was comfortable.

They developed a routine. Opal dropped Ezekiel off at Harriet's before her lunch shift and picked him up after. She brought Ezekiel to work at six in the evenings when she started her shift and Sam brought him home to Harriet.

At first it was perfect. Ezekiel played with his food and Junior enjoyed the mess the toddler made of things. He acted like an older and wiser big brother. Ezekiel worshiped the bigger boy. But lately things had changed. Or rather, Ezekiel had changed and that had destroyed Harriet's peaceful domain.

It began innocently enough one evening. She had never given up trying to interest Junior in reading. She knew she couldn't force him to listen to her before he went to bed. Anyway, the eight-year-old had outgrown the nightly tuck in. Undeterred, she decided to see if Ezekiel would enjoy her Oz books. She brought one to his bedside one night after he complained about Junior getting to stay up later.

"Why can't I stay up and listen to Sky King like Junior," Ezekiel asked.

"You're a little too young to stay up late, but if you'd like I can read you a story."

Before long she was reading to Ezekiel every night. He loved it. "I want OZZZZZ," he would say as she put on his jammies.

A few weeks after the readings began Junior poked his head through the guest room door as she was beginning a story.

"Want to join us," she asked, hopefully.

"Reading's for babies," he scoffed, backing out quickly.

Before Ezekiel was four he could identify simple words. He would shout out "Ozzzz!!!" whenever he saw it on a page, his huge eyes sparkling with joy. He sought out the books the minute he arrived at the house, looking at the pictures while Harriet made dinner.

"He's so bright," she bragged about him to Sam as they ate. "He even knows his numbers."

Ezekiel proudly counted to ten. Harriet was constantly amazed that he spoke like a grownup, with perfect diction. If he didn't get a word the first time he would repeat it until it came out right. One of Junior's favorite tricks was to teach the young protégé a dirty word so he would demonstrate it to the grown ups.

"I have a penis," Ezekiel announced over dinner. "You have tits," he pointed at Harriet's breasts. Sam laughed until he cried. Harriet worked hard to redirect the child's efforts.

"How many cups are on the table, Zeke," Harriet asked.

"Three."

"That's right!" Sam and Harriet clapped their hands.

Junior watched sullenly. "Bet you can't do this," he bragged, performing a handstand in the middle of the kitchen. He lost his balance and tumbled over, his feet knocking against Harriet's chair.

"Junior! For heavens' sake, you're so clumsy," Harriet complained. Junior's face fell.

"We know you're a fine big boy," she said, patting his head. "You didn't hurt anything. It's just that you should do your tumbling tricks outside. Okay?"

"Your mother's right, Junior," Sam said. "Do your stunts outside from now on."

Junior ran outside. Harriet heard a "thunk".

"He kicked the fuckin' door," Sam said.

"Leave him be, Sam."

From that day on the mornings and evenings were battles in a war between the two boys.

"I'm so sorry, Opie," Harriet apologized for the latest offense as she pored them a second cup of coffee. Opal had arrived earlier than usual that Saturday morning. Harriet was up but Junior and Ezekiel were still asleep. Sam was still at the club. The two women had chatted about Opal's job as a combination hostess, cocktail waitress and fill-in dealer. Harriet listened with interest. She had entertained Opal with many stories of life in the traveling poker tent, but her companion rarely discussed her past. Despite the passage of time, their relationship was still a little guarded. Harriet assumed Opal was simply reluctant to open up to her boss's wife. She didn't know how to break the barrier.

Harriet had lived alone, just her and Sam and Junior for so long, she realized. She had never had a woman friend. She always kept her distance from the dealers and hookers Sam worked with. And the wives in San Antonio hated her. She had made a few acquaintances in her new home but she felt closest to Opal. She learned

Opal came from a farm outside Bakersfield, California. From what she could tell she believed Opal's farm was not so different from the place Harriet was raised.

"Is Bakersfield close to Hollywood," she asked.

"Shucks, no. It's in the farm belt. My daddy grows carrots. Lots and lots of carrots."

"I just ask 'cause you sure look Hollywood."

Opal blushed.

"Nope. Never been. I wanted to go. Plenty of folks told me I should try for the movies. But....but then Ezekiel came along. Nobody'd take me in the movies knowin' I had a kid. But thanks for saying that." A lock of golden hair had fallen over her eyes. She pulled it back, tugging it behind her ear.

"So how are you makin' out? At work, I mean," Harriet added quickly.

"Great! I really like meeting the customers. And I'm making a lot right now..." She stopped herself mid-sentence, taking another sip. "It's more'n I coulda ever made in Bakersfield. And Mister Baxter says he has big plans for me."

"Is that why you moved here? I mean, movin' far away from your folks like that with a young baby to raise. That's a hard choice. Your ma and pa must've been real worried about you." Harriet thought of her own departure from her family farm. She was so lucky that Sam was such a nice man, that he had decided to marry her when she got pregnant. She wondered what was behind Opal's choice to leave.

"Sometimes the Lord moves in mysterious ways," Opal looked away. Harriet thought that was a strange thing to say. Opal wasn't religious as far as she could tell. But on the other hand she had named her child Ezekiel. Harriet knew that was from the Bible.

"Bingo has big plans for Opal, you know." Sam and Harriet shared a rare moment alone. Harriet made pork chops and mashed potatoes, Sam's favorite. She wanted to talk about Junior's problems at school, but Sam wanted to discuss Opal. She had become a constant topic of conversation. "She's a real hit with the customers."

"Yeah, that's what she was saying. What sort of plans?"

"Bingo wants to buy the place next door and expand—make the club into a real casino with a stage, restaurant, the whole shebang. Even wall-to-wall carpeting."

"Why?"

"To compete"

"With what?"

"Look around you, Hat. Cliff Jones just opened the Thunderbird. It's a goddamned palace compared to our place. And the new Nugget even has a damned swimming pool and a covered entrance. And there's more like that on the way. We need to change with the times."

Sam drank his coffee slowly. "Question is, do we want to stick with Bingo or open a place of our own?

"What do you think, Sam? Maybe it's a little early to go it alone." Harriet knew Sam would do what he wanted regardless of what she thought but she was interested in his decision.

"I'm not sure. I think we might want to stick with Bingo a while longer, learn a little more about the business. But eventually I'd like to move on. A lot of people are involved in Bingo's deals. I haven't even met most of 'em. If it was just him and me it'd be one thing, but he's got relatives investing too. And blood's thicker'n water, you know."

"How much will we have to put up in this new place he wants to build?"

"We're talking about that. Probably a million." He'd have to pay more than that to buy us out of our interest in the Westerner. I'm pretty sure it's worth at least that much."

"Frankly, I'd like to spend some of our earnings on a real business," Harriet said. "It makes me nervous having all that money buried in our back yard."

"I thought you were gonna look for other places to put it." He tousled her hair fondly. Harriet was delighted with their chat. It was the first time in ages they'd had a real discussion. As a matter of fact, she had been looking for places. She and Ezekiel had become tourists, driving along the LA Highway to the edge of town, watching streets being built and lots being cleared. And on her free days Harriet loved to walk along Fremont Street. She poked her head into the new Golden Nugget that had opened in August, though she got such hostile looks from the security guards she left right away.

"I'd like to get out of the house more, Sam. But I'm pretty stuck here takin' care of Ezekiel. There's only so much I can do, even with Junior in school. So what would Opal's role be? Will she make enough to afford a babysitter? I'm tired of working for no pay."

Chapter 11: School Days

Three years later Bingo's new casino opened, renamed the "Horse-shoe". It was doing well. They were still partners with Baxter.

Harriet wanted Sam to ask Bingo to buy them out, but she didn't want to nag. She talked about the new casinos opening on the LA Highway, now renamed "The Strip" and reminded Sam of how they had dreamed of building a place of their own, but Sam seemed to have lost interest in moving on.

It seemed she was stuck in a rut. She couldn't change her life no matter how hard she tried. Ezekiel had started school but Harriet still kept him from three in the afternoon until Opal picked him up and for part of the weekends. Opal hadn't gotten around to finding substitute childcare and Ezekiel was happy spending his time with Harriet. She was sure that was the reason Junior spent most of his time at the club. He and Hatch were still buddies. She tried to talk to Sam about Junior but he wasn't interested. Sam wasn't interested in talking about most things.

"What's Bingo doing with Opal these days," she asked her hus-band over dinner, trying to start a conversation. Opal was the one topic Sam was always eager to discuss.

"She's a combined hostess/head showgirl. She's doin' great. The customers love her. No more dealing for Opie. It's surprising," he continued, leaning back his chair and lighting a cigarette, "there used to be a lotta girl dealers, especially during the war years. Now there's hardly any. But she's too pretty to be dealing anyhow. We'll use her to get some good publicity for the new place. There's gonna be a contest next year for Miss Atomic Bomb. Bingo's gonna enter Opal. He wants to have atomic bomb parties and she'll be a real drawing card if she wins."

Harriet had heard about the parties. The government had started nuclear tests in the desert outside the city. The explosions created huge mushroom clouds that glowed in the dark. They drew thousands of spectators. Las Vegas was being marketed as "Atomic City USA". Since the blasts usually went off around four am people stayed up late gambling, waiting for the big kaboom. Casinos were having parties, a lot like New Year's Eve parties but they were held every time the government set off a blast.

"So when will Bingo put up that million-dollar horseshoe he keeps bragging about?"

"Pretty quick. He's already bragging about it."

"You mean he's really gonna plaster real money on a fake horseshoe?"

"Yep. Ten thousand dollar bills. And you know what's funny... He's borrowin' the money."

"What? He's the one who kept harpin' on spending your own money. Not livin' beyond your means..."

"Well, Bingo don't always practice what he preaches. And he's convinced a million dollar horseshoe will bring in ten million of business. Like Opal. Worth the investment."

Harriet laughed. "I can't imagine Opal wanting to be compared to horseshoes and atom bombs."

"I'm not sure she has a lot to say about it, Hat. And for that matter, she'll be makin' so much money she won't care."

Harriet suspected Opal was already making a hell of a lot of money. She knew her friend's hourly pay had increased from eight dollars to forty dollars a week. But she was obviously bringing home a lot more than that. And not all of it serving drinks. Harriet's first clue was when Opal arrived in a 1950 maroon Buick Roadmaster complete with automatic transmission. It was nicer than Harriet's Ford.

"Pretty soon clutches will be a thing of the past," Sam said when she mentioned Opal's new car. He seemed a little nervous. "What a difference it would have made when we were cruisin' the roads, huh, Hat?"

"Those cars are expensive, even second-hand ones," Harriet said, looking closely at her husband. "She must have saved forever."

Sam was quiet for a minute. "It was a tip. Opal made one of our high rollers real happy. He's a car dealer from L.A."

"When does she have time?"

"Bingo makes time. Like I said, she keeps his high rollers real happy."

"She would keep me happy if she took care of her son."

"Ezekiel loves you, Hat. Opal tells me he thinks of you as his aunt. He talks about you all the time."

"I love him, too but we need to let him go, Sam. He needs his mother. And I need to stop playing nursemaid."

"Can I have some more coffee, nursemaid?" Sam pecked her on the cheek, a sign the conversation was over.

The next morning Harriet inspected Opal closely. She looked like the same sweet, innocent girl that arrived at their doorstep. How could she be so different inside? She had become a prostitute, albeit a part-time one. Harriet didn't even like to think about it. But prostitute or not, Opal had to take care of her kid.

"You know, Sam says you're really popular in Vegas now. You could probably work anywhere."

Opal looked at her sharply. "Why would you say that? Is Sam tryin' to get rid of me?"

"Oh, hell no. He thinks you're the best. I just meant, well, you don't have to do everything Bingo tells you to do if you don't want.

You could even get a regular job where you could spend time with Ezekiel. After all, he's in school now. He doesn't need as much care. You're not tied to using me as a babysitter. At least you could get somebody to watch him after school till you get home. Maybe I could just watch him on weekends if you have to work."

Opal turned scarlet. "Thanks, I'll think about it. I've got to be on my way." She corralled Ezekiel and left in a rush.

Chapter 12: The Wages of Sin

Harriet waved cheerfully at Junior's glum face peering at her from the window of the school bus. The city had finally sprung for the busses so all she had to do was make sure he got to the bus stop and stay there until the doors closed behind him. Every school day was a challenge, demanding her full attention to cope with Junior's temper tantrums, passive resistance and constant complaints. But finally the bus pulled away.

She went back to the house and poured herself another cup of coffee. Something was tickling the back of her brain and she needed to figure out what it was. There were so many possibilities. Was it Opal? Sam? The new club? Some piece of the picture was out of focus. What was it?

She washed the dishes and put in a load of laundry, still unable to solve the puzzle. She made the beds and decided to vacuum. When she pushed the switch the machine made a buzzing sound but it had no suction. Something was broken. Damn! On the other hand she had wanted a new vacuum. She would just go to the safe and get some cash. Thank goodness they had plenty of money stashed away. Suddenly she realized what had troubled her. It was Bingo borrowing money for his horseshoe. Bingo not wanting to buy Sam out. Bingo was in trouble. But why? The club was making good money. It must be something else.

She decided not to ask Sam. He worshipped Bingo. He was

obviously blind to any problem. Opal certainly wouldn't know. She would have to get it out of Bingo herself. That would be hard. She rarely saw their partner. But perhaps she could invite him for dinner, or maybe visit the club.

"Sam, I'd like to invite Bingo over for dinner," she met his questioning look with her sweetest smile.

"What's put that idea in your head, Hat?"

"Well, if we're thinking about staying in business with him I'd like to learn about his plans."

"I've looked at his plans. The casino is going great."

"Whatever, Sam. It's our money."

"Are you saying you don't want to stay in business with Bingo?"

"Sam, I'm not saying anything. But you were nervous about Bingo and his relatives, as I recall. What's changed?"

"Don't you trust my judgment?"

"All I'm saying is I want to invite Bingo over for dinner and learn a little about what's going on. This has nothing to do with judgment. His family still isn't here; maybe he'd like a good home cooked meal for a change, like we used to do in San Antonio."

That was another thing that bothered Harriet. Why were Bingo's wife and kids staying in Texas?

Bingo was delighted to come. She made her favorite recipe–pot roast, mashed potatoes, peas and carrots, buttermilk biscuits and a chocolate cake for desert.

"That was a meal and a half, Hat," he said, leaning his chair back, patting his belly.

"You should come more often Bingo," she smiled. "At least till your family gets here. When are they coming?"

Bingo patted his jacket for a cigar and lighter. He unwrapped the cellophane, bit off the tip and spit it on his plate. He lit it and took a few puffs, still rocking on the back chair legs. He looked at Harriet through the smoke. She saw something in his eyes, suspicion, perhaps. Or concern?

"It's hard for a family to pull up stakes, Hat. My wife Elda Mae has her family there. The kids like their school and their friends. Hell, little Bonnie even has a boyfriend. But I'm sure they'll get here in good time."

"You must miss them a lot. I don't recall you've been back to Texas for a visit since you've been here."

Once again her words hung over the table as Bingo rocked and puffed.

"Tell the truth, Hat," he said finally, "I'm not welcome back there. Kinda burned my bridges as they say."

"Why, what'd you do?"

Sam was squirming in his seat. She ignored him.

"Killed a man. Strictly self-defense. Just like you, Hat. But now, with the Chicago mob runnin' Dallas, folks don't see it that way."

"Oh, Bingo. I'm so sorry." Harriet's sympathy was genuine. She liked Bingo's quick humor and easy smile. The older man was a hero to Junior and an indulgent partner to Sam. And he had always been good to them. "What're you gonna do?"

"Don't know yet, Hat. Right now my lawyers're tellin' me to build up a war chest."

"War chest?" Sam, finally worried, was looking at Bingo.

"A pot of money. I might need it for expenses. Legal bills and such." Bingo was still looking at Harriet.

"So that's why you need us to stay put in the casino?"

Bingo smiled like a kid who'd been caught stealing. He looked at his feminine interrogator and chuckled.

"Damn, Hat. You're a clever one. Well, the answer's yes, at least for the time being. I thought you and Sam wanted to be partners in the new place. But I confess I couldn't buy you out right now if you asked."

"How many other people are investing?"

"Just a couple of cousins. It's not like I have to go ask for investors. People come to me. This is a good business, Hat. But I don't have to tell you that."

"Of course, Bingo. And I'm real sorry you've got a mess on your hands. I know how it feels to kill a man. It stays with you. Even if you didn't have to cope with the law."

"I appreciate that. I really do. I hope this trouble passes. But if it doesn't, well, it's best to be prepared."

"Jesus, Hat. How'd you figure that out?" Sam was helping clear the table. Bingo had left, thanking them again for the great meal; acting as if they had nothing to digest except dinner.

"What?" She smiled to herself. It was amazing what a woman could get out of a man with a little chocolate cake.

"You know what? I would never have guessed what he was up to."

"You're too close to it all, Sam. But when you told me about him borrowing money I just got worried."

"What should we do?"

Harriet smiled to herself. It had been a long time since Sam had asked that question.

Chapter 13: Birthday Present

The party tent was up, decorated with multi colored balloons. The ponies had arrived, three shaggy little beasts ready to carry the children around the patchy grass that Bingo Baxter had identified as a future golf course. The cake had been delivered; Opal had splurged on a custom decorated chocolate fantasy with a lion, scarecrow and tin man made of colored frosting. It was Ezekiel's tenth birthday. He had grown into a good-looking, popular boy.

Their city had grown, too. Bingo had been right about the sleepy town. By 1955 the population had exploded to fifty thousand. The "Strip" was lined with new casinos. The motel era was over for good. But Harriet was worried. The city was full of rumors of casinos going bust.

Harriet loved each new casino opening. She and Sam were invited to most of them. They were flashy events, with fountains of free champagne, live music and local celebrities. But lately there had been more closings then openings. She wished she could understand how the city worked; how experienced business people like Bill Miller could overestimate so foolishly the money his new Dunes would bring in. She and Sam partied at the openings of the Hacienda, the Riviera, the Moulin Rouge and the Royal Nevada. Then just a few months later she read in the paper about their shrinking business and the problems with so much competition.

Every week the local paper was printing stories from the national news about the "funeral" of Las Vegas. It was only a matter of time, they said.

"Ezekiel made straight A's again," Opal said proudly, interrupting her train of thought. Harriet ignored the statement. The bragging had begun to wear on her nerves.

The casinos weren't the only failures she was worried about. Junior had failed math. And he had been doing fairly well in the subject to Harriet's surprise. She had suspected something unusual was behind the improved performance but she was too pleased to enquire about the reason. She finally learned what happened. Ezekiel had been "helping" her son.

The help consisted of doing Junior's homework. By copying Ezekiel's work, Junior got every problem right until the final exam. Then he got almost every problem wrong.

"He made me help him," the younger boy explained with an innocent look in his blue eyes. "He always makes me. Maybe I made a mistake. I don't know."

"You didn't make a mistake, you creep." Junior was ready to attack. She stepped between the two. "You did it on purpose. You told me the wrong answers. You made me fail. I hate you. You're a stupid, nasty little piece of shit."

Ezekiel looked at Junior, then at Harriet.

"I'm sorry, Aunt Hat," he finally selected the best audience. "I was trying to help. Junior kept telling me he'd beat me up if I didn't. So I did. But I must have made a mistake. I didn't mean to."

"So you did Junior's math homework?"

"Yeah. I'm sorry. It's just that…" the eyes turned to his rival. "He's so….so stupid."

The eyes locked on Junior's. They were not angry, not accusatory, not defensive. They pronounced judgment. The effect was more brutal than all of Sam's beatings, all of the bullying. The look on Junior's face broke his mother's heart. Her son was facing a future where he could never compete, never succeed. He made a point to be away from the house the day of the birthday party.

Harriet realized with a shock she had seen that look twice before. The first time was from Bugsy Siegel. She had met him at one of Bingo's cocktail parties after the Flamingo's grand opening. Bingo was ribbing him about the fiasco.

"Looks like you're under water," Baxter chuckled. The rain-soaked opening would be forever linked with financial disaster. Siegel had looked at Bingo in that vacant, haunted way. A few months later Siegel was shot dead in Los Angeles.

The second time was Bingo Baxter. He thought staying away from Texas would save him, but the feds came to the Horseshoe to arrest him—not for murder but for tax evasion. At first he had laughed it off: "I guess I should be flattered," he grinned. "They wanna treat me like Capone." The Chicago kingpin had served time for the same reason. But as the trial progressed and witness after witness turned on Bingo in exchange for favors from the government, he began to look haggard. He lost weight. The famous smile turned to a grimace. By the time the guilty verdict came down he was an empty sack, sucked clean of his money and his confidence.

"I've got to turn things over to you, Sam. Looks like I'm gonna be taking an involuntary vacation in San Quentin for a while. Take care of the Shoe for me." Though his voice was normal his eyes were fixed on a hopeless future.

She returned to the present. Opal was looking at her. "That's nice, Opal," she said dismissively as she arranged the paper hats, the little cups filled with M&M's at each carefully decorated place. Every chair would be filled with one of Ezekiel's friends. Everybody wanted to be his buddy. She took a deep breath. "I really think its time you bought a house, Opie."

Opal backed away like she'd been slapped.

Harriet continued undeterred. "I mean it. Ezekiel needs a yard where he can play and a real room of his own."

"Who would take care of it, Hat? My hours are so crazy. I can't imaging coming home to face a big place with rooms to clean, grass to mow, faucets to break, roofs that leak."

"You can hire people. You make lots of money."

Opal looked at her with concern. "Is everything all right, Hat? Has Ezekiel done anything wrong?"

"Of course not. It's me. I think I need a break from childcare. But let's discuss it tomorrow."

Harriet was sure Opal would tell Sam what had happened. She prepared herself for a dinner confrontation with her husband.

"What's up with you and Opie?" Sam seemed more curious than angry.

"What do you mean, Sweetheart?"

"She said you want to have a discussion about taking care of Ezekiel."

"That's right."

"So what's up?"

"I want to do other things with my days, Sam. I don't need to be at Opal's beck and call all the time. I've had it with being an unpaid baby sitter. And Ezekiel's bad company for Junior."

She refused to sound defensive. Beneath Ezekiel's good looks and brilliant mind lurked a calculating soul. Ezekiel loved to read. He excelled at math. He got along perfectly with everyone. But he didn't seem to have an emotional connection with anyone. He was a beautiful, cold child. Even worse, he was cruel. No one but Ezekiel could have studied Junior's weaknesses, played on them and used them to humiliate him. That was scary.

Opal was scary, too. She had the same split personality as Ezekiel. The face and voice and manner of an angel hid the calculating mind of a hooker.

"Hold on, there, Hat." Sam held up his hands. "I didn't mean to upset you. If you don't want to take care of Ezekiel that's your business.

Opal can afford to pay somebody. I thought you enjoyed it."

"That was back when Junior needed a playmate. He's outgrown Ezekiel. It's time Opal and her son went their own way."

"Sure. Sure. I'm not gonna force you to do something you don't like."

"What don't you like, Ma?" Junior came out of his room to sit at the dinner table.

"I don't like spending my days taking care of Ezekiel."

Junior treated her to a huge smile. "What's for dinner?"

The next morning Opal came early. Harriet sent Ezekiel out to play so the two women could talk.

"You know I love Ezekiel, but I need to have time for myself. You have the money to hire a live-in caregiver. Things are going well for you. And your son should be able to invite his friends over to his place, not be cooped up with me every day after school. He's growing up."

Opal took her hand and squeezed it. "Of course you do, Hat. I should have thought about how you might feel. I've been so selfish. I'll take care of it."

"I've been driving around the city lately, Opie. I've found three houses I think you'd love. Why don't we take a look at them tomorrow?"

A month later Opal and Ezekiel had moved into their new house.

"I'll miss you, Aunt Harriet," Ezekiel said on his last day. He kissed her cheek softly and she wrapped him in a hug. He had brought grief to her and Junior. She was pretty sure he didn't care a fig for either of them. But he was such a precious little boy, and she did care about him, after all. She wrapped her arms around him. "Come see me any time, Ezekiel."

Chapter 14: Promotion

Bingo was tucked away in San Quentin. His gaming license was revoked. Sam held the license and was technically in charge but Bingo's family called the shots. They had finally moved to Vegas after Bingo's conviction. His wife Elda Mae worked in the cage and his oldest son Jake, just eighteen was learning the business from Sam.

"I'll take over soon as I'm old enough," Jake bragged to Junior. Jake had replaced Bingo in Junior's esteem. He tolerated the hero-worship.

Harriet was desperate for Sam to leave the Horseshoe but he felt he owed it to Bingo to stay. And against her better judgment they had invested another million dollars in the place just before Las Vegas began to crash.

"I have to match his family's contribution, Hat," he explained. It wouldn't look good for me to stand by and watch Bingo's relatives put in all the money."

"What if we lose it, Sam? Bingo's not family," Harriet complained. "We're locked into business with a convicted tax dodger. And what are we gonna do if one of the mob guys hanging around the Shoe wants you out? Have you thought about what's buried in the yard that you never paid tax on? We're no different than Bingo."

The various mobs from LA, St. Louis, and Chicago had become a real worry. For years they had focused their Nevada operations in Reno. Bugsy Siegel's failure had convinced them Vegas was going to be a flop. But the new casinos going up on the Strip had lured them back. They moved into town with a vengeance, spending fortunes updating the Flamingo, the Desert Inn and the Dunes, betting the city would continue to grow. But it didn't. As the economy tanked the competition turned deadly. Rumor had it that the desert northwest of town was filling with bodies. At least the mobs committed their crimes outside of Vegas. They didn't want to scare the tourists or bring down the heat from the locals.

"What do you want me to do, Hat? Desert Bingo? I owe him a lot. So do you. And he'll be free before too long."

"He'll be free but he won't have a gaming license. He's not gonna let you go, Sam. You have to break away."

"He'll figure it out somehow, like he always did."

"I don't understand why you're not more worried. People are moving out. The Strip looks like an atom bomb went off in the middle. The casinos out there are closing. There's one that looks like the owners just walked away and left it half finished. The building materials are all stacked up, drying in the sun. It's a mess."

"The newspapers aren't helping," Sam replied sadly. "People all over the country think Vegas is dying. The press never liked gambling in the first place and they're spreading rumors about cancelled reservations, bad food, mob shootings. Every lousy story they can think of, even if it's not true. And folks are buying it. There's not enough business to support all those new places. And I hear the owners borrowed a lot of money to put up those fancy buildings. From the Teamsters. They're just a front for the mob. Now they can't pay it back. There's gonna be a lot more bodies planted out in the desert before long."

"What are you gonna do about it?"

"Me? Well, the downtown places are doing a lot better than the Strip. We've got our loyal customers from LA and the locals still come to Glitter Gulch. And we didn't borrow any money. Except for the damn horseshoe, of course. But Bingo's partner can come and jackhammer it out any time he wants. So we don't have a mortgage to pay.

We might have to cut back on some frills but we'll make it. It's the places on the Strip that are in trouble."

Sam was right. So far their casino was holding its own, though it wasn't making the profits they had expected. The million-dollar horseshoe was enshrined at the entrance. Bingo's extravagant parting gesture attracted hundreds of visitors each week. They came to see the "Shoe" and to meet "Miss Atomic Bomb" formerly known as Opal. They enjoyed the carpeted floors. They loved the buffet. But most of all they loved to gamble. They poured their nickels and dimes into the one armed bandits, dropped their quarters and dollars at the blackjack tables and ran up markers for thousands of dollars at the craps tables as they chased their losses. They stayed 'til four am for the "Atomic Bomb" parties, ready to cheer the glowing mushroom-shaped cloud with a "nuclear" martini, serenaded by Dean Martin and other celebrities. But they were slowly deserting downtown for the newer flashier places on the "Strip". Even though the new casinos were failing, they had spoiled the tourists. Harriet suspected the downtown business would never come back.

Harriet had come up with an idea but wanted to do a little more research before she ran it by Sam. She had gathered all the facts she could from driving around and reading the Las Vegas Review Journal. She needed to learn what was happening behind the scenes. She decided to see if Junior had any ideas. She hoped that he had learned something from all the time he spent at the Horseshoe.

"Junior, can I talk to you?" He was on his way out the door.

"What is it?"

"I wondered if you've heard anything at the club about, well, about problems the city is having."

He reentered the kitchen. "You want to know what's going on?"

"Well, you spend a lot of time there. I thought you might have heard some rumors, people talking."

He sat down. He was thinking. It occurred to Harriet that this was the first time in years the two of them were having a real conversation.

"I think I heard Dad say something about some sort of committee."

"Committee?"

"Yeah. Some committee to promote tourism and stuff. They want Dad to join. He's not that interested."

"Thanks, Junior."

He looked at her to be sure she wasn't joking.

"Sure, Mom. Any time." He pecked her cheek and headed for the door.

That night she talked to Sam.

"Are people going to do anything about the casinos closing?"

"Oh, there's talk about this and that but I doubt it'll amount to anything."

"What are they saying?"

"Some of 'em want to form a committee to promote the city. They're trying to get all the casinos to send representatives to a meeting. It's probably a way to try to get money from us."

"Sounds like an interesting idea. Who are you sending?"

"Me? I don't want to get involved, Hat. We're doing fine. I don't want to get tied to those Strip operations."

"Not even to promote the city?"

"Anyhow, I don't have time. I'm trying to keep the Shoe running. Elda Mae watches me like a hawk. She second-guesses everything I do. I've got my hands full."

"What if I went? As your representative?"

"You? What would you do on a committee?"

"What's the matter, Sam? You don't want me to learn about the city? You think I'm too stupid?"

"That's not what I meant, Hat. I just don't think it'll accomplish anything."

"Then I'm the best person to send. I can learn what they're thinking about and report back to you and if you don't like it I can just drop out. Nobody'll notice me."

"Look if you want to go to a meeting I'm not gonna stop you. But don't get your hopes up and don't commit the Shoe to nothin.'"

Harriet learned the Committee met in the boardroom of the refurbished Flamingo Hotel. She had never been inside the Flamingo. She put on her best dress and bought a small notebook, which she tucked in her purse. She parked at the front entrance and slipped inside. The interior looked busy. A line of guests had queued up at the front desk. Lots of people were milling around. Valets were toting luggage. She looked for someone to ask directions. Finally she saw a man in uniform who looked helpful.

"Can you direct me to the Board Room?"

He looked her over suspiciously. "You mean the back of the house, little lady?"

"I'm here for the promote Vegas meeting," she informed him. "I represent the Horseshoe."

He directed her through the unmarked double doors and up the stairs to the executive offices. She could feel his eyes inspecting her retreating back. When she got to the Board Room her heart sank. It was empty. She must have had the wrong day or the wrong place.

"Can I help you, Miss?"

A man had come up behind her.

"I was looking for the promote Vegas meeting." Seeing his skeptical frown she added quickly "I represent the Horseshoe."

"Well, you're in the right place. We're the first to arrive."

"I thought the meeting started at four."

"Well, that's four Las Vegas time. Which means sometime closer to four thirty. I'm Jack Hartman, by the way."

"Harriet Wilson. Pleased to meet you." She stuck out her hand. He looked at it, then decided to shake it.

"Are you Sam's wife? I didn't know he was interested in our work."

"Did he tell you that?"

"Well, no," Hartman smiled. "I just heard it through the rumor mill."

"So you believe all the rumors you hear? "

He chuckled. "You have a point, little lady."

"My name's Harriet."

His eyebrows lifted in surprise.

"Yes, well, Harriet. So Sam delegated this job to you?"

"Yes. You have a problem with that?"

He backed away and raised his hands in mock defense. "Hey, just asking. I think you're the only woman on the committee."

"I worked with Sam for years before we came here. I'm familiar with the business." She figured it was just a little exaggeration. "I think everyone should work together to bring more tourists to the city. It's clearly having problems, especially the Strip casinos. But I don't think you can say one part of the city is having problems but the other parts are okay. It's just one city, right?"

"Right. Great observation. So you have any ideas?"

"Ideas about what?"

He smiled again. "About how to help the city."

"Oh. I don't have enough information yet. Has anyone done any studies?"

"That's a good idea, uh, Harriet. Studies I mean."

"So have they been done?"

"Well, no. Not yet. We're just getting started."

"I'm happy to help."

The room was filling. Almost every casino had sent someone. She was the only woman. Jack introduced her as "Sam's wife from the Horseshoe."

She took a seat in the back to listen to the discussion. Jack conducted the meeting. People wanted to talk about new signs, new headline acts, new improvements to the casinos. She raised her hand, trying to get Jack's attention. He ignored her. Finally she decided to stand up and shout.

"Could I say something?"

Thirty pairs of bemused eyes turned towards her.

"I'm as new at this as the rest of you, but I read the papers. Seems to me what we need is to convince folks from outside the city to come here. Till people stop being scared to come here there'll be nobody to see our signs or visit our shows no matter how great they are."

"And how would you propose to change their opinion, Mrs. Wilson?" Jack's smile was amused but not hostile.

"Maybe we should send people, like goodwill ambassadors to other places. Maybe we run adds in national papers, or get interviews with some famous reporters. We could even invite them to come here and learn about us so they could write some good stories for a change. Maybe have some of our entertainers appear on national radio shows and talk about all the great things we have here. There's more here than just gambling."

"So how would you go about this?"

"Do I have to come up with all the answers? I just got here."

"Well, little lady, you're the only one that's got a plan."

She looked up at Jack Hartman. "First, I'm not a little lady. Second, I'm happy to work on a plan but I'll need help. And probably money. A lot of money."

Chapter 15: What I Like Best

"What do you like best about Las Vegas?" Harriet had finally found something she could discuss with Junior, something that he was excited about and able to discuss. "I mean, other than the casinos?"

Junior reflected for a minute. "Well, there's the boxing. And golf."

"Boxing? Golf?"

Junior smiled. "I guess you didn't know about those?"

"I had no idea. I know the field outside our house is supposed to be a golf course one day and that's all. I did read something in the paper about a prize fight."

"You need to read the whole paper, Mom. We're gonna have a heavyweight prize fight here. You ever hear of Archie Moore?"

"Nope."

"If he wins he gets to fight Rocky Marciano. How about Sam Snead?"

Harriet laughed. She was delighted to give her son the chance to show he knew more than his mother.

"I don't have a clue, Junior. Is he another boxer? I'm so happy you keep up with these things."

"Sam Snead is a famous golfer, Ma. He's playing in a tournament at the Desert Inn golf course, for a wheelbarrow full of silver dollars."

"So do you think people would come to Las Vegas for a boxing match or a golf game?"

"I guess you'd have to ask. But yeah, I think so. I think they're a heck of a lot better than some stupid atomic bomb explosion in the middle of the night."

"I wonder how much people in America really know about this place," Harriet mused. "The papers want them to believe it's a sin pit where they're likely to get robbed or shot at any minute."

"You gotta tell them," Junior said.

Harriet decided she would pursue the idea of a national advertising campaign at the next committee meeting. They should get all the casinos to kick money into a pot for ads in major newspapers. People should learn about the golf the boxing, maybe other things as well. Junior was still sitting next to her. She needed to think about advertising another time. She turned to him: "Would you like to learn golf, Junior?"

"Nah. Golf's for pussies. I would like to learn about boxing, though. I wanna go to the Archie Moore fight, but Hatch said no."

"Will there be other fights?"

"Well, sure. There's a guy named Doc Kearns who puts 'em on over at Cashman Field."

"Why don't you find out when the next one will be. I'd like to go."

"You, Ma?"

"Sure. If your dad can't go, that is. Do you want to become a boxer?"

"I don't think so. But I'd like to see a fight, just to know what goes on."

Chapter 16: Fight Night

Before the month was out Harriet was so busy with her committee work she forgot all about her talk with Junior. She was cutting out newspaper articles and reading books. She had heard about Palm Springs, another desert community. Why did people flock there and avoid Las Vegas? She read a book by George Wharton James describing "The Wonders of the Colorado Desert" extolling Palm Springs as having "great charms and attractiveness". Palm Springs had its own Desert Inn, a "hotel and sanatorium". Movie stars loved to go there, and there was a lot of building going on-fantastic new hotels. It seemed to Harriet that tourism was like a snowball; you had to start by convincing people to visit. Then the more people visited, the better things got. What had happened with her city?

She thought about it a lot. What had convinced her and Sam to come? Of course, it wasn't the great hotels or wonderful climate. It was the gambling, the prostitution. They had gotten off on the wrong foot, given people the wrong impression and now the snow-ball was melting.

Maybe she could get some famous writer to write about the virtues of Las Vegas? It had fresh air, after all and beautiful moun-tains. Perhaps they could ignore the sandstorms. There were plenty of attractions that had nothing to do with gambling. Not just golf and boxing, but the fabulous Boulder Dam, which people now called the Hoover Dam.

She shared her ideas with Jack Hartman. He was skeptical at first, but he finally began to listen. "Nobody else has come up with anything, Hat. In fact, it seems you're the only person who's really interested in this project. People are willing to chip in a little money but that's about it. Everybody's just sitting around thinking things have to get better."

Sam was also interested. They finally had real discussions.

"I had lunch with Johnny Meyer at the Flamingo the other day," Sam said over dinner one night. "He mentioned he knew you from the promote Vegas project. He said you were doing a great job."

Harriet blushed. "So now you think the Committee is a good idea," she teased.

"I think it's good for you," he replied. "By the way, you didn't make Opal very happy."

"Should I care about Opal?"

"She's making a fuss about having to come up with the money for a live-in maid."

"Oh, for Christ sake!"

"Now don't get all upset, Hat. I'm just sayin'. I think its part jealousy. People are talking about you. You have some good ideas, apparently. Opal's just a pretty face. You're a brain."

"Ick! What a thing to say. Don't you think I'm pretty too?"

"Jesus, Hat. Don't put me in the middle between you two. You're my wife. Opal's my special employee. You're both important to me. You need to get along."

"Did you tell Opal that?"

"Matter of fact, I did. Her reaction was about the same as yours. I know she made your life difficult–she probably took advantage of you for a while–but that's over now. She has her place and you have yours. You two were friends for a long time. You need to make peace."

Harriet adjusted her new scarf around her neck and secured it to her jacket with a new pin. She loved paying special attention to what she wore. She spent an hour choosing her outfits each day. Today her color theme was blue and white.

"I would have lunch with her or something, but I'm really busy right now, Sweetheart." Harriet treated Sam to an imitation Opal smile.

He just shook his head.

Harriet was delighted that people were talking about her for a change. She was good and tired of Sam's constant raving about Opal's latest triumph, she thought as she fastened pearl clip on earrings. She tucked a pert little pillbox hat in place and inspected herself in the mirror. She was pleased with the effect. She promised herself she would work even harder, learn even more about her city.

"When can we meet with those public relations people you mentioned," she asked Jack Hartman over lunch the following day. "I have so many questions about advertising and promotion. I think we need to hire a consultant like you were saying. Somebody from LA, hopefully."

They lunched at Piero's, the place to see and be seen in Las Vegas. It was a known hangout for the mob but the food was so good people ignored the reputation.

"People should learn about Piero's," she said, after ordering the spinach ravioli and a glass of Chardonnay. Most diners drank hard liquor with lunch. Jack was nursing a whiskey with his osso bucco. She had taken a liking to wine, and Freddie Glusman, the owner, told her that in Italy everyone drinks wine with meals. Wine made her feel Italian and slightly glamorous. "We have some wonderful restaurants. Let's add that to our promote Vegas list."

"We need more money." Jack put down his fork and looked at her, ending her thoughts about taking a trip to Italy. "We're trying to do a first-class promotion on a shoestring budget. It's just unrealistic."

"Right. But how to get it? Have you asked again? How many casinos have contributed?"

"Not enough." He paused. "Your husband's casino hasn't chipped in yet."

"I know. I'll get Sam to approve a contribution," she promised. After lunch she remembered how she had promised Sam she wouldn't ask him for a donation.

That night she tried to direct the conversation to the Committee but Sam was too wrapped up in the latest crises at work.

"Opal's threatening to quit."

"She's not serious, Sam. It's just a ploy to get more attention."

"That's what I thought but she says she's had an offer from the Starlight, with better pay and better hours."

"After all we've done for her!" Harriet was furious. "What an ungrateful bitch."

"She's got to look out for herself, Hat. I'd pay her more if I could but the casino's not doing that well. It's slow, just like the places on the Strip. Thank God we don't have a bank loan to pay. But we can't give raises to the staff. It's hurting us. Opal's not the only one."

"Can you get some more money?"

"From where? Bingo's still in jail. I talked to Elda Mae about it. She says every dollar that's not necessary at the Shoe is tied up in legal fees. Bingo's appealing the verdict and trying to at least get out early. It's costing a fortune."

"So what will you do about Opal?"

"I'm gonna have to let her go, I guess. That's gonna hurt our business. I'm thinking of maybe paying her something out of our own stash."

"I can't believe you'd say that."

"Now don't get all pissy with me, Hat. I just mean, well, I think we need her and the place can't afford her."

"First I take care of her kid for free, then I have to pay her out of my own pocket. What's she ever done for me, Sam? Except take advantage of me."

Sam patted her shoulder.

"I know. I'm sorry, Hat. I'm proud of you. And you're right. We need to think about ourselves, stop helping people like Opal and

Bingo. But I wish to God it was easier."

The next morning Harriet watched as Sam left for work. She sipped her coffee thoughtfully. She hadn't asked him for money. It wasn't the right time. On the other hand, she had no intention of seeing any of her money go to Opal. She knew the Committee needed the funds for a real public relations push. A great publicity campaign would help the Horseshoe as much as it would help the casinos on the Strip. She was sure. And the money was needed now.

Junior came in rubbing his eyes and sat down for breakfast.

"How's it going, Ma?"

"Just fine, Junior. Do you have time to join me for breakfast?"

He looked at her quizzically. She laughed. "I was just joking. Lately it seems you go from your bed to that jalopy of yours. We've hardly had a chance to chat."

Junior nodded and sat down. She poured him a big bowl of corn flakes, which he doused with sugar before adding milk.

"Opal's quittin'," he said suddenly. "Goin' to the Starlight."

"Where did you hear that?"

"The club, of course." He still spent his afternoons at the Horseshoe. He was old enough now to help around the place as an unpaid busboy. Sam told him it was payback for the car, a second-hand Plymouth that he worshipped. Harriet had meant to talk to him about demanding some kind of actual salary, but she couldn't discuss it till the casino was doing better. And she knew Junior made good tip money, though she suspected he was dropping it in the slots when Sam wasn't around.

"What do you think about Opal?" She put down her coffee cup and looked at her son.

Junior looked away. "Opal? Who knows? She brings in a lot of folks, I guess. They spend their money at the Shoe. I guess they'll follow her to the Starlight."

"That's not good for our business."

He was still looking out the kitchen window. "Maybe there's other girls. Lots of girls at school want to work in the casinos. They ask me about it all the time. Some of them are real good lookin'. I tell 'em they can make great money in tips. They don't really care about the money, though. They think it's excitin'."

"Did you tell your father?"

"Na. He's busy." Junior looked at his feet.

"Well, why don't you talk to him, get him the names of some of those girls? Maybe the Shoe can run a contest, a beauty contest to pick the next Miss Horseshoe. That could get them some good publicity."

He looked at her, finally, and grinned. "You really are something, Ma."

He scooped up the corn flakes, slurped the last of the sweetened milk from the bowl, ran his sleeve across his mouth and bolted out the door before she could kiss him goodbye.

Publicity. It was the key to success. She had learned so much about it in the Committee meetings. She looked at Las Vegas with new eyes. The city was just a big business–the tourist business. They had to work together to build the business, then they could argue about how to split it up.

The safe was nestled in the back yard under the doghouse, a reminder of the long-gone puppy. She pushed the doghouse aside and lifted the squares of grass to reveal the steel cover of the concrete vault. She smiled as she spun the combination lock: 6-29-39. Their wedding day. The door creaked open. She looked into the hole filled with piles of wrapped hundred-dollar bills and Sam's old pistol. She wrapped her fist around the pistol's cold handle, remembering the night Sam lay in the dirt, helpless. She had taken control of their fate at that moment. And she had won. Sam had said he owed her his life. She had as much right to the piles of hundred dollar bills as her husband. Anyway, she could easily take one bundle of hundreds – that would be five thousand dollars. Sam would probably never notice. The money would be enough to buy all the publicity they would need for a while.

The donation would give her new status in the Committee members' eyes. Jack Hartman would think she was a hero. It would help Sam, too, she decided though he might not appreciate it right away.

◆◄►◦❈◦◄►◆

"This is terrific!" Jack smiled as he tucked the package of hundred-dollar bills into his briefcase. He didn't even comment on the means of payment. "This will get us all the help we need and then some! And I hope it'll finally get those other casinos to take this seriously. I'm buying lunch. And please thank your husband for me."

"Oh, it's nothing," Harriet said, pulling her kid gloves back on her hands. "What's the next step?"

"We'll meet with Roper & Gray. They're the best PR firm in California. Ask them for a marketing plan and a budget. Thanks, Harriet!"

He wrapped her in a big hug and kissed her on the cheek. She pulled away quickly, almost falling over backwards. He grabbed her to stop her fall. "Hey! Careful there."

"I'm fine." She straightened her skirt, avoiding his eyes.

"So would you like to meet them," he asked.

"Who?"

"Why the PR guys of course. Since you're paying for them you should get to know them. Shall I invite them here or shall we meet them in LA?"

"How much will we have to pay to get them to come here?"

Jack laughed. "I expect they'll do it for free if they know they have the job. On the other hand, a face to face in their office is always the best way to start off. They won't be worried about catching a plane and we'll get to see their operation."

———◄━☼•⚹•☼•☼•►———

"I need to go to LA next week." Harriet had made Sam's favorite dinner: pork chops, mashed potatoes and gravy. She smiled sweetly as he devoured it. She had switched her suit, gloves and hat for a shirtwaist dress and sandals, spritzing some Joy cologne into her cleavage. She had hoped Sam would notice, but he focused his attention on the pork chops. "We're interviewing a PR firm for our Promote Vegas campaign."

Sam was lifting a forkful of potatoes to his mouth. She watched closely, checking for any hitch in the movement.

The fork hesitated, but only for a second. "Fine."

"I'll probably stay overnight. Think you can manage without me?"

He put the fork down and finished the bite. He looked at her and cocked his head. She felt her stomach turn.

"Wellll....I guess I can have dinner at the club. Breakfast, too, for that matter. Don't worry about me."

She hurried to another topic. "What's Opal's status?"

This time the fork stopped. He took a long swallow of water.

"She still needs a raise."

"Well, of course. That's what you said before. So nothing's changed?"

"She'll stay if I...if we agree to pay her the five grand."

"Why five grand?"

"How the hell would I know, Hat? I can never understand the crazy bitch. That's what she wants. She says her clients spend that much at the casino in a week. And she's right. If she gets the money she'll promise to stay for three years."

"Then what?"

"Then....then I'm not sure I care. By then Bingo'll be out of the pen and he can decide what to do. By then Opal may be over the hill. Question is, how to get the money. The casino doesn't have it."

Harriet's eyes traveled out the window to the doghouse, then quickly turned back to look at her husband.

"What were you thinking?"

"We have the money." Sam looked out the window.

"But that's our money. For our own plans."

"I can loan it to the casino."

"Are you sure they can pay it back?"

"I don't know. I don't know what choice we have."

" I was talking to Junior...." Sam looked at her sharply. "He said there were some beautiful girls in his school who want to be show-girls. Maybe you could have a contest for the next Miss Horseshoe. It would be great publicity..."

"NO! I mean, no, that's crazy. An untrained high school girl can't do what Opie can do. I need her. We need her."

Harriet changed the subject. "Where's Junior?"

"I don't know. He left the casino around five. I thought he was on his way home."

"I haven't heard from him."

"He's probably with his friends, or Hatch. Just forgot to check in."

"I'll save him a pork chop and some potatoes. He'll probably be starving when he gets home."

◆ ▸⊰◆❋◆⊱◂ ◆

The last time Harriet had felt this much excitement was the day she left her parents' farm to run off with Sam. Now she was running off with Jack Hartman. Well, not really running off. Just going on a business trip. Overnight. Jack was probably married, she figured, though she had never asked. She wondered why his marital status had never occurred to her. The mirror reflected her blush. He didn't seem to have any problem going away with her for a night. Maybe he hadn't told his wife he was going with a woman. She hadn't exactly told Sam she was going with a man.

"Get over it, Hat," she told her reflection. "This is about a meeting with a PR firm." But she couldn't stop smiling. She pirouetted in front of the mirror, checking the way her new dress clung to her hips. She slipped on the matching bolero jacket and fastened her favorite three-strand pearl necklace around her neck.

The drive would take most of the day. Just her and Jack alone in the car. The Roper people were entertaining them at dinner that night. The business meeting would be the following morning. They were staying at the Beverly Hills Hotel. Jack had made all the arrangements. They wouldn't return until late tomorrow night. She really had tried to explain the details to Sam but he seemed distracted. She left a note on the kitchen table with her hotel phone number, securing it with a coffee cup. The gesture caused another attack of déjà vu. "It's not a rock," she reminded herself. She hadn't even had a chance to tell Junior her plans. She had hardly seen him since their breakfast chat. She didn't think that much about it. He was a teenager, after all. With a car of his own. Hell, he was just the age she was when she left home for good.

The doorbell rang. That was Jack. She took one last look. At the last minute she took off her pillbox and fluffed out her hair. She would save the hat for later.

———— ◆·▷◆※◆◁·◆ ————

Harriet had gone on occasional shopping trips to Los Angeles with Sam, but seeing the city through Jack's eyes was different. He was a native "Angelino" as people from LA called themselves. He told her all about the city and the place he grew up. He came from a middle class family in Pasadena. He had gotten a degree in journalism at USC. He started working with the Los Angeles Times out of college. They sent him to Las Vegas to cover a story and he fell in love with the new city in the desert. He left the Times to take a job with the Las Vegas Review Journal, but the salary was small.

He worked with the Publicity Committee and did public relations consulting for several of the casinos to earn extra money. His work gave him access to all the casino managers, and all of them wanted to stay in his good graces. The Review Journal had the power to make or break a casino.

Jack was also an insider in Los Angeles. He had learned LA's secrets as a young reporter. He knew all the local dirt: who the Hollywood directors were having affairs with, what stars were secretly pregnant or married; who was turned down for the most juicy movie parts because they had gotten too old or had "let themselves go"—a phrase that generally referred to alcoholism or drug abuse. Harriet was surprised to learn that LA had problems with the mob just like Vegas. Only the problems weren't so noticeable because the city was so much older and bigger. But the mob was trying to take over the studios, just like they were infiltrating the casinos.

"They've already bullied their way into some of them," he told her. "The studios get a lot of their money from the Teamsters Union. The bosses tell them what stars to promote. Actresses do special favors for the bosses to get ahead. It's pretty sick."

Harriet told him about her life on the road and how they had come to Las Vegas.

"You mean you actually shot two men? And drove a truck with your wounded husband to get help? I better stay on your good side, Lady."

She laughed. She laughed a lot the whole trip. She hadn't had that much fun for years, not since the days she and Sam cruised the roads in his big truck. Sam had taught her about gambling on those trips. Jack talked about himself and asked about her. She learned he didn't gamble. She told him how she loved the Wizard of Oz books but had never seen the movie. He told her how Shirley Temple was supposed to play Dorothy but the studios couldn't make the deal work; and how Bert Lahr and Ray Bolger had tried to upstage the newcomer Judy Garland.

She learned he wasn't married.

"Just never found the right woman, I guess."

They arrived at the Beverly Hills Hotel at five. She had never stayed there. He told her about the famous guest list—from the Duke and Duchess of Windsor to John Wayne.

Jack had reserved separate rooms for them. Harriet requested, chastely, that the rooms be on separate floors. She had time to take a quick shower and change into her best outfit before meeting Jack in the lobby for the short cab trip to Chasen's.

She had never sipped a Brandy Alexander at Chasen's. She had never been treated like her own person instead of Mrs. Sam Wilson. The experience was more intoxicating than the liquor. Mr. Roper loved her ideas.

"You have great common sense, Harriet. Sometimes people who aren't in our profession can see things better than we do. I had never thought about it before but Las Vegas does have a lot in common with Palm Springs. It just got off on the wrong foot. Let's see if we can't lure some movie stars to your city. Though I bet they actually spend time there. They just don't want to admit it." He laughed. "It'll be a challenge, alright. But as you say, Vegas has a lot to offer. And it can have a lot more. We need to work on this from both ends, you need to give me reasons for people to come and I need to let people know about them."

After dinner Jack suggested they have a nightcap at the Polo Lounge, the famous bar at their hotel.

"It's a great place to people watch," he added. "This is the most famous watering hole in town."

They chatted about their meeting with Roper. Harriet was going to have to put in even more time coordinating the publicity campaign from the Las Vegas end.

"Call for Mr. Stewart. Call for Mr. Stewart." A dapper little man in a smart red jacket and white cap walked through the lounge holding a telephone on a silver tray. Everyone followed the man as he found his recipient and made his way to a secluded table carrying a telephone.

"See the people at that table? That's Jimmy Stewart and his agent, I believe."

Harriet craned her neck to get a better look. The pageboy carried the phone to Stewart's table grinning broadly.

"Lots of the stars hang out here," Jack continued. "See the phone jack by our booth? People arrange to have phone calls here – they think it makes them look important."

As if on cue, the pageboy entered the lounge again. Everyone turned to look at him.

"Call for Mrs. Wilson. Call for Mrs. Wilson."

Harriet looked around the lounge to see who the call was for.

"It's for you," Jack said, waving at the pageboy.

The pageboy plugged the phone into the jack, dialed the operator and handed the receiver to Harriet, who took it under the watchful eyes of the diners.

"Hat. It's Sam. I've been tryin' to reach you for hours. Where the hell you been?"

"Sorry, Sweetheart. We had dinner with the PR firm and it ran late. I just got back to the hotel."

"Junior's in the hospital. He's banged up pretty bad."

"Oh my God. Is he…will he be okay?"

"I expect so, but he's in a lot of pain right now. I thought you might want to come home."

"I'll be there as soon as I can. Tell Junior…tell him I love him."

She hung up and looked at Jack. "I have to get home. There's been an accident."

"We can start back first thing tomorrow morning. I'll call Roper and let them know. I'm sure they'll understand."

"So what happened?"

They had left LA at seven that morning. Jack was making small talk, trying to be cheerful but Harriet was too worried to pay attention. Jack's question interrupted her thoughts.

"I don't know. Some sort of accident."

"Kids....it never fails."

Harriet realized she was not the only person whose day had been ruined. She searched in vain for some sign of resentment in Jack's voice.

"I'm really sorry, Jack. This was such an important meeting. You went to so much trouble. Such a waste..."

"Don't even think about it, Hat. These things happen. Roper understands. And anyhow we got a lot done over dinner last night. They're delighted to get the work. The fee is good and it's a great introduction to all the Vegas casinos. I'm sure they expect to get lots of future business from this. I think the important thing was that you got to meet them. What did you think?"

"What?" Harriet's mind was on the hospital.

"What did you think of Roper?"

"Oh, they were nice, I guess."

"I can tell you're not ready to concentrate on this. Never mind. It's not important right now. Let's just get you home."

He pushed the accelerator up to eighty-five.

They arrived at the hospital at three. Jack asked if Harriet wanted to go home first but she was too worried.

"Let me take your suitcase," he said as he parked the car. "I'd like to meet your son. Maybe there's a story there. Has the Review Journal reported on the accident? I'll get the first interview with the victim," he joshed.

Harriet tried to laugh but she couldn't. She told him it wasn't necessary, but he insisted, taking her elbow and escorting her and her luggage through the hospital lobby.

They arrived at Junior's door, Jack holding Harriet's suitcase; Harriet dressed in the same new dress she had worn what seemed like years ago. She had no idea of the impression the two of them made until she saw the look on Sam's face.

She stumbled through an attempted introduction but Jack intervened.

"Mr. Wilson, I'm so happy to make your acquaintance. I just wish it was under better circumstances." Jack extended his hand.

Harriet tried to interrupt, realizing too late what was coming next. She was unsuccessful.

"Thanks so much for the contribution. Don't worry, the PR firm understands about your son. They're completely on board with our Committee."

"What contribution? What PR firm?" Sam was looking from Jack to Harriet.

"Sam, sweetheart. Don't you remember the contribution we made to the Promote Vegas Committee?"

"We are so grateful, Sam. Five Thousand Dollars will cover all the costs of the PR firm. The other casinos should be ashamed of themselves. We're all very excited about the campaign, by the way. We had a chance to discuss it over dinner last night. I'll make sure they give the Horseshoe a special place in their promotions. They're the best firm in California. I'm delighted they had time to take this on. But they're thinking long term, if you ask me. I'm sure they're angling for lots of future business from the casinos...."

Jack continued enthusiastically, apparently unaware of the looks shooting between Harriet and Sam.

"Thanks for dropping Harriet off. We'll be in touch." Sam cut Jack off mid-sentence and shouldered him out the door. Jack cast a puzzled glance at Harriet, who smiled helplessly. Sam didn't even offer to shake Jack's hand.

"Well.....alright then..." Jack backed away. Sam slammed the door behind him.

"What the hell was that about? What five thousand dollars..."

"Mom...."

Harriet had forgotten all about her son. She scurried away from Sam to sit on the side of Junior's bed.

"What happened, Junior? Are you alright?" She kissed his cheek and stroked his hair, ignoring Sam.

"I'll tell you what the hell happened." Sam joined them at the bedside.

"Me and Hatch was helping out Doc Kearns," Junior continued, refusing to look at his father.

"Doc who?"

"You know, Ma. Doc Kearns, the boxing promoter. The guy I told you about."

"How were you helping?" Harriet ignored Sam scowling at Junior. She took Junior's hand.

"They built a ring for a fight. Over at Cashman Field. But they discovered at the last minute it didn't have enough support."

"You mean not enough money?"

"No." Junior tried to laugh. He winced in pain.

"He means they didn't build the ring according to specifications. It didn't have enough support beams," Sam interrupted. "So Kearns decided to enlist this blockhead and his idiot friends to crawl under the ring and hold the boards up during the fight. And the damn thing collapsed on top of him. He has a concussion and a broken collarbone. He's damn lucky he didn't break his back. If Hatch hadn't lifted the boards off him he'd probably be dead from suffocation."

Sam was pacing around the hospital room. "My son is a fuckin' moron. He's just a stooge for Kearns. And you!" He turned on Harriet. "What the fuck do you think you're doing? Takin' five grand of our money? Runnin' off to Los Angeles with some guy? How much did you pay him to escort you to the big city for a good time, Harriet? How much?" He was screaming. He raised his hand. Harriet leaned back, expecting a slap.

"Don't you touch my Mom!" Junior was trying to sit up in bed. He fell back, yelping in pain. The sound stopped Sam in his tracks.

"What about you? You took five thousand dollars to pay Opal." Junior's voice came out a whisper. "You think I don't know? You think I'm stupid, that I don't see things? That I don't know what's goin' on? I know what you paid her for. I know."

Sam had turned white.

"Is it true, Sam?" Harriet tried to stay calm.

"You little shit!" Sam shook his fist at Junior. Junior just stared at him. Harriet felt a fundamental shift in the bedrock under her feet. She slumped onto the foot of Junior's bed.

"So you and Opal? While I was taking care of her kid? Being a good little nursemaid so you could…." She couldn't finish.

"He had to bribe her to keep her mouth shut," Junior continued smugly, ignoring Sam looming over him. "Opal threatened to tell you. She said if she didn't get the money she'd leave the Horseshoe. When Pa told her he didn't have it, she said if he didn't get it she'd tell everything."

"That's enough, Junior." Harriet used up the last breath in her body. She looked up at Sam. He turned and walked out.

Chapter 17: Split Decision

Harriet lived in a strange new world. Half of her inhabited an unfriendly house with a cold and alien husband. She found she could do all the things she had done except speak to him or touch him or talk to him.

Half of her thrived during lunches with Jack Hartman, in meetings with people from LA, casino bosses and airline representatives arranging promotional campaigns. For this other half of her life, her personal shopping assistant at I. Magnin's Beverly Hills store sent her four chic navy dresses, spectator shoes and white kid gloves. Jack had introduced her to the store.

"I. Magnin's is the best store in California. I know you're going to love their clothes. They carry all the best lines, as well as their own label. And they're famous for their service. Oh, yes," he looked at her feet. "And you'll love their shoe and handbag selection."

Harriet felt an immediate bond with Sherry, the personal shopper, even though they had never met. They talked on the phone often, discussing fashion trends, colors and accessories. The telephone bills were outrageous. Harriet dared Sam to criticize her, or to block her access to the safe. He clearly noticed everything but never said a word. He came home at 5:30 each night, sat at the dinner table, wolfed down his dinner and left. She assumed he was going back to the casino or to Opal but she didn't care. He returned sometime during the night after Harriet was asleep. He slept in the spare bedroom. He was gone before she got up. They organized their lives to assure as little contact as possible.

Junior wasn't much better. As soon as his shoulder recovered enough to let him drive he was off with his friends. She heard rumors that he had a girlfriend, a fast girl, daughter of the Starlight manager. She tried to talk to him about his social life but he just mumbled and blushed and left.

"What happened, Hatch?" The big man had stopped by to chat a month after Junior was released from the hospital. They hadn't spoken since the accident.

"They just got careless, is all. They shoulda built the thing better, but they just threw up the boards on some sawhorses. Then about the third round they saw the boards startin' to slip, the sawhorses began tipping over. They were afraid the fighters would fall through. So between rounds they had us crawl under there and hold the thing up. But it was too far gone."

"Sam said you saved Junior's life."

Hatch lowered his head.

"I don't know how to thank you. You've always been a friend to him. He needs you, Hatch."

"Yes, Ma'am." Hatch thanked her for the coffee and bolted out the door before she could ask him about Junior's girlfriend.

In time, Junior recovered completely. Las Vegas was recovering, too. Harriet's efforts finally convinced the airlines to have more weekday flights. By April 1957 weekday departures had ballooned to thirty-three on Western, United, TWA and Bonanza.

The only thing that hadn't recovered was her marriage, but she was too busy to worry. It seemed she woke up every morning with a new idea. And the Committee listened to her.

"Why don't we ask the city to get involved with our committee," she suggested. "After all, the tourists spend money in the city, too."

Within a month the mayor's office appointed a representative.

A few weeks later, Clark County and McCarran Airport signed on. The committee's role expanded to promoting Las Vegas and the surrounding area.

"Has anyone thought of building a convention center?" Harriet had listened for weeks to the city representatives complaining that the only reason people came to Las Vegas was to gamble. "The airline people always comment that Las Vegas doesn't have a place for big conventions. It's all about gambling. Conventions would bring businesses here, and visitors who wouldn't even think of coming to gamble."

"Think of what it would do for the hotels," Jack added. "Especially during the slow months. And it would give us a chance to promote the city in a whole different way."

"I just don't see how we can do this," Mayor Baker interrupted. "We have so many other problems in this city. Our water system is a nightmare. It hasn't been repaired since the Railroad installed it. The sewers…I don't even want to talk about them. We need a whole new infrastructure. And there's only so much money to go around. We just spent a fortune to build Cashman Field."

"And Cashman Field has paid for itself, Mayor," Jack replied testily. The discussion quickly turned from debate to argument. Mayor Baker wasn't shy about expressing his opinion. Neither was Jack. They were getting nowhere.

"Can I ask a question, Mister Mayor," Harriet interrupted in her softest, sweetest voice. Both men stopped yelling to look at her. "Is the issue just money? Is it how we pay for the center?"

"I suppose that's what I'm sayin'." The mayor had calmed down.

"Then could we at least do a study on where the center could be and how much it would cost? And then you could decide how you're gonna pay for it?"

Harriet was delegated the job of scouting locations, not because she had any idea how to do it. She was the only one who had the time and interest. She was delighted. She had another excuse to get out of the house and drive around the city. She drove by acres of land and learned what was for sale and what the sellers were asking. She looked for a site that could accommodate traffic and parking, that was close to the Strip so the visitors could spend money in the casinos and hotels. And she had to find something cheap.

Three months later she had a plan. It was unorthodox, unexpected. But it was the best idea in her opinion. She drove Jack to the site to get his reaction. He laughed.

"Why would you pick a place like this, Hat?" They stood at the entrance to a dilapidated racetrack. A sign still hung over the entrance but the paint was so faded they could hardly read it: "Las Vegas Park Speedway".

"It's perfect," Harriet gushed. "It's less than half a mile off the Strip, it already has great access and parking. And we should be able to get it for a song."

A gust of wind blew sand into their eyes, forcing them through the former entrance to the dilapidated concourse inside. Harriet hoped her friend could see the run-down stands as she saw them: a beautiful new building with places for conventions, entertainment, meetings. A place that would bring people to the city from all over the world. And once here....well, it was the Committee's job to give them a reason to come back.

She had never put together a proposal for a convention center. But she figured nobody else had either. She didn't have to describe the Speedway, everybody knew about the eyesore on Paradise Road. The issues were whether, how much and who would pay.

"I like it..." Mayor Baker was smiling at her. Other Committee members were excited, too.

"But it's not your money we're talking about here," Baker looked at each member. "I have to think about the how much and the who will pay. Let me talk with my people and get back to you."

"We have to lock up that racetrack as soon as possible," Jack said as they left the meeting.

"Don't we want to wait for Mayor Baker to make a decision?"

"Hell, he's already made a decision," Jack responded.

'How do you know that?"

Jack chuckled. "You have a lot to learn about politics, my dear. I could see it in his eyes. He needs a big idea, something to inspire the voters to keep him employed. What better way than to remake their city into an international convention venue? And you just showed him the way."

"But why do we have to do something now?"

"Do you know the Wells brothers? The guys who own that dump?"

Harriet shook her head. "I mean I know who owns it but I don't know anything about them."

"They're old Nevada. They claim to be miners but they've made more money speculating in penny mining stocks than digging ore. If they find out their dump of a racetrack is about to become the site of a new convention center they'll decide it's the most valuable piece of land in Nevada. They know how to put lipstick on that pig, trust me."

"So we have to lock it up before the mayor goes public." Harriet nodded. "But how?"

"Well, somebody needs to take an option to buy it for a reasonable amount. That takes…"

"I know….."Harriet laughed. Money." The two said the word in unison.

"And it has to come from someplace that won't raise their suspicions, he continued, looking at her intently.

◄►✣◄►

Harriet had almost forgotten she was a woman. The Committee members, the casino executives, Jack Hartman, even the mayor treated her like an equal. Her husband ignored her. She was an asexual being. Until she and Hardy Wells eyed each other across his desk.

"You wanna do what, little lady?"

"I want to reopen the Speedway. Redo it. Maybe have horse races there as well as cars."

"What would put an idea like that in your pretty little brain?" Wells thought she was a little lady with a pretty brain. Good. She attempted to bat her eyelashes. She decided it looked silly. She looked at him and smiled her most innocent, brainless smile.

"Well, I just like racing's all." She managed her sweetest southern drawl. "I could do, say, Seventy Thousand.." She saw his pupils expand. "But I'd need, ya know, six months to raise all the money."

Wells smiled back. "Well, little lady, my brothers and I just discussed selling this property but we couldn't do it for less than a hundred twenty-five thousand. So what'll you pay me now, for an option, say six months to raise the rest?"

She had taken ten thousand dollars from the safe and put it in her handbag, just in case. She excused herself, went to the ladies room, stashed half the wad behind the toilet and returned to his office.

"Well, Five Thousand's all I have right now," she said disarmingly, sliding her open bag across the desk so the money was right under his nose. "And I couldn't do more than a hundred thousand."

He reached in, removed it and counted it out on the desk, fanning the c-notes out in front of him.

"You willin' to pay the whole amount in cash assuming we do the deal," Wells asked.

"I guess so, if that's what it takes," Harriet replied as innocently as possible. She pulled out two copies of the option. Jack had printed it out carefully on yellow lined paper with a carbon copy. Harriet had no idea what an option was until Jack explained it to her. She wrote in $100,000 and Five Thousand in the blanks. She and Wells signed their names at the bottom of each copy and initialed next to the dollar numbers. He scooped one copy and the bills into the desk drawer. Like most people in Vegas, he asked no questions about wads of c-notes that would never have to be reported to the IRS.

She hurried back to the toilet to "powder her nose" and retrieve the extra cash. She decided she would keep it at the bottom of her underwear drawer, a place Sam would never look, so she wouldn't have to remove more money from the safe.

"A bold new agenda…" She marveled at the headline in the Review Journal less than a month after she signed the option. Jack was dead right. The mayor couldn't wait to premier his view of the city's future. He proposed to float new bond issues to raise more than three million dollars to revitalize Las Vegas. They would underwrite a fire alarm box system, a railroad underpass and expansion of the overtaxed sewage treatment plant. And a spectacular convention center on Paradise Road.

"I hope you have that option in a safe place, Hat. It may be the most valuable piece of paper in Las Vegas." Jack looked at her seriously over their turkey sandwiches. They were grabbing a quick bite at a sandwich shop off the Strip.

"Meaning what?"

"Look around you, Hat. What do you see?"

"A sandwich shop with a few slot machines in it?" Harriet looked around for something unusual.

"This place is a few blocks from what's about to be a multimillion dollar convention center. What do you think that's gonna do for this area? Think of the restaurants, the shops, the new casinos that will spring up all around here. Think of the people who would give anything to control that convention site right now. And it's you." He sat back in his chair and looked at her.

"You have the right to buy the Parkway for a hundred thousand dollars. It's now worth much much more. It could even be worth more than a million if the mayor's bond issue passes."

Harriet thought she was doing a favor for the City. She hadn't figured that she had just made a great investment. She wondered if the owner of the sandwich shop would be interested in selling.

"So what do I do?"

"Well, you could hold onto it. Or you could sell it to the city for the new convention center. What does Sam think?"

Sam... she would have loved to tell him about her investment but of course he had no clue what she was doing. She couldn't find a way to start the conversation. And just when she thought of something to say he was out the door.

"Oh, he's really busy at the club these days. We haven't discussed it."

——◆◦▸◦✵◦◂◦◆——

Sam was shoveling food in his mouth, looking at his plate. She wondered how he would look if she were to put her arms around him and say she missed him? Or tell him about the option.

"Sam, can I talk to you..."

"Sorry, gotta run." He was out the door.

It was only six thirty. The sun was still bright. Junior was out. She decided to go for a drive. She had been thinking about a piece of land on the Strip; she had come across it while she was looking for places for the convention center. The owner had some bills that were coming due. He needed cash fast. She had never bought real estate before, but she didn't think it would be too hard. She still had the five thousand dollars in her underwear drawer. If necessary she would get more money from their safe. Sam would probably notice the missing wads of bills but she didn't care any more. In a way she almost hoped he would get upset. A least they would have something to talk about. Maybe she could buy the sandwich shop, too. And some of the adjoining property.

Harriet turned onto the Strip. The tourists were braving the last of the day's heat, walking from the Flamingo to the Starlight.

Casinos lined both sides of the highway all the way to Desert Inn Road, then the road stretched out to the horizon bordered only by a couple gasoline stations and the entrance to the airport. Close to the airport, a local businessman, Ted Rogich, was building a beautiful new sign "Welcome to Fabulous Las Vegas".

The sun had just disappeared behind the ragged edges of the horizon. The sky was changing from day to night. She could almost feel their world changing as well. People were ready for some excitement. The newspapers were all abuzz about a young man, Elvis Presley, who had appeared on the Ed Sullivan show swiveling his hips seductively. There was even a television show featuring young people dancing to live entertainment, American Bandstand. Ford introduced a sexy new car, the Edsel. An author named Vladimir Nabokov had written a novel full of explicit sex, Lolita. America's leader was an elderly war hero, but a handsome young man, John F. Kennedy, was running for President. The country was flirting with glamour and youth and sin. That was what she knew Las Vegas could stand for. Roper & Gray were promoting it as a cool place for the younger set, the "war babies", to see and be seen.

The city was growing by enormous leaps. It had more than sixty thousand residents with more coming every day. She decided to bet on the future.

The empty land on the Strip would be filled with casinos one day. She could feel it in her bones. Just like the land around the convention center would fill with pricy shops and other businesses. Many of the lots were held by undisclosed owners, waiting for something—a buyer, a loan, something to start building. One lot, the one she was about to visit, was in the middle of the block just south of the Desert Inn. The road in front was paved and there was even a stoplight at the corner. It was ready for development.

She parked the car and got out, walking around the plot. The dirt under her feet could be her dirt, her little piece of the future of the city. She was sure it was a bargain. And owning it would be so much more exciting than owning a dress or a car.

Suddenly she remembered where she had first heard someone talk about owning land. It was her father, kneeling at the edge of their barren fields and grabbing a handful of dirt on the day the bankers foreclosed. He clutched the earth between his hands and watched it fall back to earth. Like his own blood.

"Land, it's the most important thing, Hat," he said. "It's permanent."

Now she knelt down and picked up a handful of desert grit. She laughed. It wasn't the rich topsoil of the Mississippi Delta. What would her father think about these little grainy bits running through her fingers? About what she planned to plant there?

She had written to her parents several times. Once just after Junior was born, telling them they had a grandson. Once from San Antonio, letting them know she had a permanent address. And each Christmas after she settled in Las Vegas, describing her new home and her new surroundings, so different from the farm in Mississippi. She got a Christmas card each year. Once in a while her ma wrote to tell her about a marriage, a baby, a death in the family. But aside from that she heard nothing. Maybe she would write them today and tell them about the land. They would know she remembered about the farm, about what her pa had said.

She looked at her dirty palms. Without thinking, she dusted her hands together. The gesture summoned her father's image, dusting his hands together as he walked from the fields. She watched him retreating into the past and was overcome with an unexpected sadness so strong it bent her double. Her life was an hourglass, the fine tough grit marking her own passage. Her relationship with Sam would never be the same. Opal had left the Horseshoe for the Starlight but her departure couldn't erase what had happened between them. Her son was becoming a man. Someday he would leave her, just as she left her farm in Selma.

Land was permanent. She would buy the lot.

Chapter 18: The Carny Show

Harriet returned to the house one day to find a "TV" in the living room and Sam sitting in front of it, adjusting the rabbit ears. Las Vegas had gotten three television channels. Soon the TV became his best friend. He took his dinner to the living room and stayed there until the screen went blank and the Indian head pattern came on. Harriet listened from her bed. The new acquisition kept Junior home more, but soon the TV gave Sam and Junior something new to fight over—what show to watch. They jumped from their chairs, turning the channel knob so many times it came loose. Harriet couldn't help but laugh at the struggle, conducted without words.

Junior usually lost the battle, but won the war, locking himself in his room and playing *Jailhouse Rock* and *You Ain't Nothin' But A Hound Dog* full blast on the phonograph until his father gave in or stomped out of the house.

When the fights got too loud, Harriet retreated to her piece of land. She had bought it for less than she expected. The owner was desperate. When the fights got too loud she got in her car, drove to the Strip, parked and sat, watching the sunset, the stars and the lights.

She was sitting at the kitchen table, smoking, the TV was blaring. She was trying to decide whether to go to her room or drive down the Strip. Suddenly Sam was standing in front of her.

"What the hell are you doin', Hat?"

She was so shocked she almost dropped her cigarette. Maybe

she was hallucinating?

"What the hell are you doin?"

Nope, he had really done it. Said something to her. Started a conversation. She took a deep breath, just to calm herself.

"What do you mean, Sam?"

He sat down next to her and put his head in his hands. His shoulders were shaking. She put her hand on his back.

"What is it, Sam?"

"I don't know what the hell's goin' on. I don't know what to do. I....I..just...don't...know."

The words came out like a gurgle. Harriet had never seen Sam cry. She patted his back helplessly.

"It's okay. It'll be okay."

"It'll never be okay. I fucked up. Now you're off doin' things, I don't even understand. It's like you're a different person. The way people talk about you. I don't even know what's happening, what to say or do."

"Nothin's wrong, Sweetheart. Nothin's goin' on except I think I made us some money. That's all. And, well, I bought us a piece of land. Out on the Strip. I tried to tell you about it but you bolt outta here every night. If you'd stayed put for a minute I would've told you."

He looked up, blew his nose and wiped his eyes.

"I don't know what to say, Hat. I'm sorry? Ashamed? I just didn't know. I couldn't sit at home and face up to you. I guess I thought if I did you'd have a chance to tell me we were through. But I was angry, too. I mean, with what you were doin', going to LA with that man? I thought there was somethin' between you and him. And I kinda deserved it, I suppose. I thought you'd be leavin'. Every night I come home thinkin' you'll be gone. But you're still here, fixin' dinner and all. And then people started talkin' about you. How you were helping the Committee, and then that idea about the convention center, and the deal with the Speedway. Even the goddam mayor talks about you. People think you're some kinda genius. Even Bingo's wife. Every time she gets a call askin' her to make a donation to the Committee she comes in and raves about what a great job you're doin'. And you bein' a woman and all. I didn't even know what to say."

"Well, I'm not going anywhere. And you're here. So let's talk. There's things we need to decide, Sweetheart. I didn't mean to shut you out. I've got this option, and Jack says it's worth a fortune…"

She saw him recoil at the mention of Jack.

"Look, Sam. Jack's a friend. If I wanted him to be somethin' more do you think I'd be sittin' here tonight?"

"I don't know. People talk about you and Jack like you're partners or somethin.'"

"I guess we kinda are. But not in that way, Sweetheart. We're just friends, trying to come up with good ideas for our city. We were never anything else. I'm not sure Jack even likes women in that way."

Sam began to laugh. "Holy shit, Hat. Don't spread that rumor around. People think Hartman's a great guy. They talk about you and him and then they look at me kinda like…like what's between the two of you?"

"Jack had some ideas and I had some money and we put the two together. So now I have this option on the Speedway and the mayor thinks the voters are gonna approve the bonds and it'll be worth a fortune. I paid five grand for it…well, for an option to buy it for another ninety-five thousand," she explained. Sam's eyes got huge. He sat collapsed back into his chair.

"You're dealin' in that kind of money, Hat? Good God in heaven, I don't know you any more. You'd put our money at risk like that? Without tellin' me?"

"It's not like I didn't try, Sweetheart. Anyhow, the Wells brothers have already offered to buy it back for a hundred fifty. We could close the deal and donate it to the city or sell it for a hell of a lot more than I got to pay the Wells brothers when the time comes. I didn't buy it to make money. I bought it so Las Vegas could have the convention center. But I didn't figure on it being worth so much. So what do we do?"

"We?" Sam looked into her eyes.

"Of course we , Sweetheart. It's our money I used. It's our future. And then there's this other parcel I bought. Not an option, just a piece of raw land out on the Strip."

Sam's eyes got bigger still. "Let's take one thing at a time, Hat. It sounds to me like you took a big gamble and came up with a winning hand. Don't go givin' it away. If the Mayor's really gonna do this convention center thing the city should pay a fair price for the property. There's nothin' wrong with that. Now, about that other land the piece you bought, let's discuss it in the bedroom."

"You haven't even had dinner, Sweetheart. Aren't you hungry?"

"Yes," he said, pulling her up from her chair. "But not for food."

They had so much to talk about. The Committee's plans for the convention center and what it would mean for the city. The promotional campaigns she was working on. The piece of land she had bought.

"Where'd you say it was?" He was running his fingers through her hair.

"On the Strip south of Desert Inn. Its just raw desert land with a little diner on it but its gonna be something in the future."

He sat up. "Jesus."

"What?" She sat up beside him.

"There's lots I have to tell you, too. Bingo's about to come home. He'll never be able to get a gaming license again. He wants me to stay on at the Shoe as his front man. Behind the scenes. But only for a couple more years till Jake can get his license."

"Well, that's what we wanted anyhow, isn't it?"

"Sure, Hat. But the thing is they don't have the money to buy us out. So Elda Mae was talkin' about some sort of land swap. Seems Bingo was never that thrilled about bein' out on the Strip with all the mob boys. But he has a couple of parcels on the Strip. I think she said the parcels were just south of Desert Inn."

They went back into the kitchen. When Harriet got out her plat map with all the notes written on it, Sam let out a gasp.

"Those are the parcels. Right there next to what you bought." They were sitting at the kitchen table over cold meatloaf and mashed potatoes when Junior walked in.

He looked at the two of them and smiled. Harriet offered to warm up some dinner.

"I already ate, thanks Ma. Are you two okay?"

Harriet and Sam looked at each other. "We're okay, son," Sam said.

Junior nodded and went into his room. They heard *Jailhouse Rock* blasting through the door. Sam shook his head.

❖

"So what about you and Opie?" Sam hadn't talked about it. They were back in bed, sharing a cigarette. It was past midnight.

"If we do Bingo's deal we'll have enough land to build a really big casino. It would hold its own against any of the others on the Strip. We could even build one of the new-style multi-story parking garages out back." Parking was a problem for the Strip casinos. The original structures were single story affairs, spread along the street with parking out front and in back. But as the casinos got bigger the car problem did, too. Cars were often parked two deep along the Strip and drivers got into punching matches trying to get to their rides. People had talked about building special parking structures but no one had done it yet. The time it would take to build a parking garage would interfere with the business. But Harriet and Sam could start from scratch.

"We could even rent space in the garage to some of the other casinos till we got goin'," Sam said.

"Yes…but what about you and Opie? Don't try to duck this, Sam."

"I wish I could explain it, Hat. It just happened one night when we were both tired and drunk. Somethin' came up, one of her customers got rough, I think. She was upset. I hugged her and one thing led to another. It was just one night. I swear to you."

She believed him. Even if it wasn't true, she thought, she would believe him anyway. Because of where they had come from and because they had something together; they would build something even better. She couldn't imagine doing it with anyone else. And she supposed that was what love was. She turned into his arms and he folded her close to his chest.

"I need you, Hat. You're my best friend. We've come a long way together, you and me. There's nobody could be what you are to me. Please, please say it's alright between us."

She sighed. "Of course it's alright, Sweetheart. And it's gonna be better. The best. We have so much to live for. Together."

She wished he had told her he loved her. She wondered for an instant if he had said that to Opie. She pushed the thought away as she pulled his head into her breasts.

❖

"So what's up with Junior these days," Sam asked. They had slept late. Junior was gone by the time they got up. Sam was looking into his son's empty room.

"Oh, God. I've been so busy I haven't really paid him much attention. And he seems to be off doing his own thing. I have to ask Hatch what's going on with him. At least those two have stayed friends, thank goodness. Hasn't he been comin' to the Shoe?"

"Not since…since we had our falling out. He's almost a grown man, I suppose. He's old enough to mind his own business."

"I asked him if he wanted a party for his high school graduation," Harriet said. He looked at me like I was crazy. I tried to talk to him about college, but it's no use. He hates school. I can't force him to go."

"When we build our place he can work for us," Sam said firmly. "Hell, he can start now. There'll be plenty of errands for him."

Harriet could hardly believe it. Suddenly they could be a family again. It seemed like such a long time ago, each of them went their separate ways. Could they knit themselves back together somehow? Could it be that easy? Just because of the money they had made, the land they would own? Could the little plots of dirt in the middle of the desert make them forget Opal and Ezekiel and all that had come between them? Just like that? Harriet remembered what her pa had said. "Land is everything."

Maybe it was.

They talked to Junior. Harriet made chocolate chip cookies and set them down on the kitchen table next to the plat and they showed him their parcels.

"What're you gonna call it, Ma?" Junior said, munching on a cookie.

"What?" Harriet was still working through her web of memories. Saying goodbye to her pa, the family farm, the day she left her life behind, the hope chest she had retrieved from under her parents' bed. Looking through the contents with her ma.

"I think we should call it the Silver Slipper," she said suddenly. She didn't even have to think about it.

"That's a great name," Sam agreed. "It's kinda classy. Glamorous. What do you think, Junior?"

"I think it should have a boxing ring," he said.

"What the hell!"

"A boxing ring. People like boxing. You should see the crowds that come to Cashman Field when there's a fight in town."

"Is that where you spend your time, Junior? Hanging around Doc Kearns and his crowd? I thought you'd learned your lesson."

Sam's voice was sarcastic. Harriet watched her husband and son face off. Her stomach tightened. She had seen so many of these confrontations. At school, in the hospital, over watching the TV. She didn't want their fresh start to begin with another fight. She looked at Sam. He was ready for a fight. Surprisingly, Junior wasn't interested in spoiling the mood.

"Boxing's a big deal, Dad. Ask Hatch. Sugar Ray Robinson was here. He's a friend of Doc Kearns. He put on a clinic for some local fighters. He said he'd come back someday. Maybe we can get Kearns to go in with us. He's looking to build a permanent ring. A real swell place. And we have a lot of land. There's room for a boxing ring. It'd be different. And you should have some other stuff, too. Stuff people can do if they want to take a break from gambling. So they stick around."

"Remember the carny show, Sam?" Harriet thought about Mike and his tents filled with games and shows, the peanut stands, the fortune teller, the crowds of people strolling along the sawdust paths, the men stopping by their poker tent. Sam loved to travel with the carny show. He said it was good for business.

"Maybe we can put a bit of the carny inside our casino," Sam replied thoughtfully.

"And a boxing ring." Junior added.

"We'll see," Sam said.

Chapter 19: Call In The Night

There was so much to plan, so much to do. Harriet had never realized how much work it took to build a casino.

"At least I have a gaming license," Sam said as they looked over their To Do list for the twentieth time. "That's the only reason Bingo kept me around so long."

"We have no quarrel with Bingo, Sam. He brought us here. He gave us our start. And he's agreed to keep you on till the casino's finished."

"I know, I know. But that's because he needs me. It's his wife, Elda Mae I can't stand. She's like a mother tiger protecting her own. She watches me like a hawk, double counts the take every night. Second-guesses everything I do. You'd think Bingo would have told her, I've been workin' for him for almost twenty years now. I've accounted for every penny, even when there were plenty of chances to take a little something for myself."

"Elda Mae wasn't part of all that. And she's alone in a strange city with a husband in the slammer. I expect she's just scared."

"Well, she's about to find out what it's like without me around."

"And we should be grateful she's happy to see you go. She doesn't mind that we're building the competition out on the Strip." Harriet went back to examining the list. Each of them had put the things they wanted for their casino. Junior had written "boxing ring, swimming pool, outdoor bar" in his square schoolboy script. Sam had added "newest slots, good lighting, nice floors, special entrance, hand-carved gaming tables, giant wheel of fortune, separate show room with upholstered seats, nice restaurant". His writing was not that different from Junior's.

"What are you doin' for the women customers," Harriet asked.

Sam scratched his head. "I hadn't thought of that. But now you mention it women are comin' to the clubs more 'n more nowadays."

"I think you're missing out. If you have a swimming pool and a nice restaurant men are gonna want to have their women with them. Or were you thinking they'd just hang out with showgirls and hookers?"

"Dammit!" Sam pushed his chair away from the table and started to get up. The chair started to tip backwards and he reached out to grab it, looking at her angrily.

"I'm not trying to start anything, Sweetheart. I'm just asking. Since women are goin' to be eating in the restaurants and hanging out by the pool, maybe you should have something for them too. How about a fancy ladies' lounge? Where they could get manicures? Even a beauty shop? So they can pretty up while their husbands or boyfriends are at the tables."

"That's not a bad idea, Hat." He smiled and sat down again. "How about a nice dress shop? Maybe by the pool, where the ladies could get some fancy bathing suits?"

The list filled up one page and spilled onto a second. They wanted some arcade games, pinball, grab-a-prize. A Keno parlor. Special booths that would sell ice cream, popcorn.

"Like the carny." Sam got nostalgic. "I loved the smell of roasted peanuts."

But how to put their ideas all together? And how to pay for everything?

"That's the problem with Bingo's deal, we're land rich but cash poor," Sam said.

"I thought we had plenty of money in the safe."

"If we want all the things on this list, it'll take a lot more, Hat. And we'll need start-up capital as well. The Gaming Board'll require us to have a certain amount of cash on hand to open. Cash for the slots, for the tables. They're getting real particular these days. They even changed their name-they're calling themselves the Nevada Gaming Commission these days. They think it sounds more official."

"What do we do?"

Sam looked at the list. "Let's get some drawings, some building estimates. I've talked to the Meeks brothers, the guys who built the Flamingo. They put me in touch with the best casino designer in the country. He's from New York. He did the Desert Inn."

Sam contacted Arthur Lessman the famous casino architect, but he said he was too busy for their project. He recommended an architect in LA, Barry Thalden.

"Thank God, Sam. We could never have afforded Lessman. Hopefully Thalden is less expensive."

"Let's make an appointment to visit him in LA. Take him our wish list and see what he comes up with."

"You mean you want to take a trip with me?" Harriet ventured a little sarcasm.

Sam half-smiled. "Just you and me, Babe."

"What about Junior?"

"We'll leave him at home."

"Can we stay at the Beverly Wilshire and have dinner at Chasen's? Maybe see one of the new movies? I really want to see Ben Hur, and it won't be in our theatre for months."

"Sweetheart, we need to save our money, remember?"

"I know, Sam, but just this once…"

"It's a whole new discipline," Thalden enthused. "Casino design is actually a science. Part psychology and part structural engineering. You need to know how to use your space to bring the crowds in and keep 'em in. Especially with a casino as big as yours. Space planning is critical."

They discussed the wish list over the phone. Sam wanted to be sure they weren't wasting their time.

"I love it, you're thinking ahead, looking at what casinos can be. Not just slots and tables in a box. A real entertainment venue."

They made an appointment and planned their trip.

"And we'll do some shopping for you while we're there, Sam. You need to start wearing slacks and good shirts, and some really fine ties and jackets. Boots and jeans are too cowboy. Las Vegas is changing and we need to dress the part."

Sam blew smoke rings at the ceiling.

◆◆◆◆✳◆◆◆◆

The call came at two a.m.

"What the hell? Shit." Sam stumbled to the living room in the dark, stubbing his toe on a chair. Their first thought was that something had happened to Junior, but Harriet checked his room. He was sound asleep in his bed. She turned on the lights and followed Sam.

"What's going on?"

Sam put his hand over the receiver.

"It's Opal."

Harriet sat down.

"She's in a clinic," Sam explained as they pulled on some clothes.

"A clinic? But why?"

"It's a place the Starlight uses for people who get hurt at the casino. So they don't have to tell the police. If they went to a hospital it'd have to be reported."

"But what happened?"

"She got beat up pretty bad, apparently. Some high roller chink from San Francisco took a belt to her."

"Why would she call you?"

"That was Mike, the Starlight casino manager. Opal's sedated. Mike knows we took care of Ezekiel when Opal worked for us. Apparently the kid's all alone. Somebody needs to take care of him."

"And that somebody is you?"

"Us, Hat. Who else is there? Opal's a loner, you know that. We're the closest thing she ever had to friends. And Ezekiel has nobody."

"What about her parents? Surely there's somebody."

"Let's just get there and see what's going on. Then we can decide what to do."

"Sam, Opal and Ezekiel are out of our lives. I can't believe her new boss would even call you after what happened. She tried to bribe you, tried to hurt me. Ezekiel tried to hurt Junior. I can't believe this..."

"Like I said, Hat, Opal didn't call. It was Mike. I couldn't turn him down. And we can't turn Opal and Ezekiel down. Could you sleep tonight knowing there's a young kid at home all alone not knowing what's happened with his Mom?"

"Shit. Oh, shit." Harriet pounded her fist on the kitchen table.

He patted her knee. "It'll be alright, Hat. I promise."

Chapter 20: Revenge

Harriet remembered something her ma told her when she came home from school crying one day. Sallie, the golden-haired, blue-eyed school sweetheart had called her a moonshiner's daughter and the whole class laughed at her. She held her tears until she walked through her door. Then, safe in a place where no one could see her, she bowed her head and cried.

"People like that, Hat, they get what they deserve in the end. Cruelty doesn't bring joy to folks. It comes back around to the ones who put it out. The Lord will take care of Sallie. You don't have to worry about her."

Harriet didn't see that happening, though. She had to go to school every day and watch Salle Mae and her friends smirk and whisper. She wondered what had ever become of her tormentor. Now she was looking at another Salle Mae lying in a bed with nurses hovering all around, her face all bandaged up, tubes coming out of her. Was it the Lord's revenge for what Opal had done?

"She'll be out for at least a day," Mike explained. "We've got a doctor coming from LA. He'll probably have to do some skin transplants on her back. It's pretty torn up. We're keeping her sedated meanwhile."

Mike looked at Harriet.

"Don't worry. She'll make it."

Thank God he couldn't read her mind.

"So, can you take care of the kid? He'll be scared silly."

Harriet was so involved in her own thoughts she didn't hear what he said.

"Sure," Sam said, before she understood. "We'll go over there right now."

"What are we gonna do with Ezekiel? We're about to go to LA. Who'll take care of him? We can't bring him to the house. Junior will have a fit."

They both said "Hatch" at the same time.

"He's not a baby sitter, Harriet."

"Exactly. He's Junior's buddy. And he'll keep Ezekiel in line."

Chapter 21: The Second Time Around

Why? The question hung between Harriet and Sam, though they were too busy to sit down and talk about it. They arrived at the Cullen house at four a.m. A sleepy Ezekiel came to the door. He and his cocker spaniel puppy, some clothes and his schoolbooks were bundled off to their house. Junior woke up the next morning to find his sworn enemy eating breakfast, sitting in Junior's chair as if he had never left.

"Opal's real sick, Junior." Harriet tried to explain. "It's just till she gets better."

Junior must have picked up on the insincerity. He looked at Harriet and Sam, shook his head and left without eating. Ezekiel finished his cereal.

"I need to leave for class," Ezekiel said, wiping his mouth with his napkin in an unconsciously elegant gesture.

"Have a wonderful day, EZ. We'll see you tonight."

"When can I see my mom?"

"I'm not sure, son. As soon as the doctors say it's okay. She's real contagious right now. We don't want you to catch whatever she has."

Harriet hoped the kid would buy it. She wasn't sure.

Hatch was happy to stay with the boys. "So we can still have our trip, Hat," Sam hugged her reassuringly.

But it wasn't the same. There was a third person in the car, one they couldn't see. Harriet couldn't stop thinking about her trip with

Hartman. They had so much to talk about. The time flew. With Sam the trip was too long. There was too much silence. Driving across the desert Harriet searched for a radio station, anything to create a distraction. There was nothing but static.

The visit with Thalden should have been exciting. He went through their list. He thought all their ideas were great.

"I love the boxing ring. Very unique."

Harriet smiled. "I'll be sure to tell our son. It was his idea."

"Let me do some drawings. I'll get back to you in a few weeks."

"Any idea how much this will cost," Sam asked.

Thalden looked at their list and checked the plat map. "I would say we can produce a good set of plans for less than ten thousand."

Sam took a deep breath. "I meant to build it."

"Oh. No. No idea. I can give you the names of some contractors. You should probably get several bids. This is a big project."

"About how much time do you think it will take? To build it, I mean," Harriet asked.

"Rough guess? If you want to do it right I'd say at least two years. And that depends on what's underneath the dirt. I'd say you're gonna have foundation issues. You're building on sand, you know. And you want to go twelve stories? That'll mean a lot of work just to get a stable base. You don't want to spend all that money on something that'll crumble."

"I guess that's why all the original casinos were single story," Sam said. "They didn't have to worry about the foundation."

"Right. But people are starting to build up. Though you're the tallest I've seen. I don't want to name names but you're not the only ones to come see me. Vegas is changing. I would bet in ten years you're gonna see a completely different Strip. And you're gonna be a big part of it. You have some wonderful ideas here. But there are problems, like I said. I look forward to working with you."

Two years. That meant two years with no income except what

Sam could get from Bingo. All their plans, their hopes, had seemed so simple. Harriet thought coming up with the ideas was the hard part. That was just the beginning.

The drive home was worse than the drive to LA. They talked about money. They decided to sell the Raceway option to the City for the most they could get.

"Maybe we should sell one of the parcels to raise some cash," Sam suggested. But Harriet was adamant. "That's our land free and clear. We're not partin' with any of it. We need to see how much it will cost and come up with some way to pay for it. That's all."

They had gotten a late start, lingering over a custom omelet and fresh-squeezed orange juice at the Beverly Wilshire. Harriet made a note to find out what brand of coffee they used. It was the best she had ever tasted. Maybe they could use it at the Silver Slipper.

"At least the sun will be at our back," Sam said. "Driving into the sun gives me a headache."

"And we have the wind at our back," Harriet tried to sound optimistic. "We're gonna make it, Sam. I can feel it."

But as she looked down the road all she saw were problems. And there was another problem waiting for them back at home. Harriet had called the house twice a day from the hotel. She was relieved that Junior seemed to be taking things well. Thank goodness he had his big friend to take care of him. He was excited that Thalden liked the boxing ring idea.

"I can't wait to tell Hatch. Is he coming to work for us?"

Harriet and Sam looked at each other. Hatch had become such a part of their lives they assumed he would go with them. But they hadn't asked.

"We'll talk to him as soon as we get back, son. I expect he'd love to come work with us but it's his decision."

They hung up and looked at each other. "How will we pay for him?"

Chapter 22: A Firm Foundation

"You're in luck," Walter Meeks removed his sunglasses and swiped his forehead with his shirtsleeve, collecting the beads of sweat about to drip into his eyes."

"What? What did you find?" Sam and Harriet stood in the middle of the lot full of machinery, trying to ignore the hundred and ten degree heat. Harriet silently thanked the gods that the wind hadn't come up.

"There's bedrock at twenty feet. We can secure the foundation. It'll save you a couple of hundred thousand."

Harriet had to laugh. Three months ago the idea of spending a couple of hundred thousand dollars would have scared her to death. Now they were talking about shaving that much off a budget of over two million dollars. And that was just for the construction.

"The build out will set you back another half mill at least," Meeks said. She was amazed that he could roll the numbers off his tongue without even cringing.

"Well, that's some good news," Sam took a puff on his cigarette. "I'll let the bank know."

The bank was represented by Percy Harris, their loan officer. Harriet had finally agreed to do what she swore she would never do, borrow money against their parcels to pay for construction. The effect was immediate. Now they had to report their progress to Harris every week. The meetings made her feel like an unruly child reporting to the principal.

Jack had introduced her to Harris, who had come to Las Vegas to set up a branch of Deseret Bank, the Mormon-owned lender headquartered in Salt Lake City.

"But they're Mormons, right? I can't believe they'd get involved in the casino business."

"There's where you're wrong, Hat," Jack replied. Harris contacted me just last month, looking for possible casino projects to finance. I told him you and Sam were his best bet. The Mormons aren't stupid. They see the future of this city. Your new convention center had a lot to do with that, by the way. You've made Las Vegas respectable."

The convention center was half completed. Compared to their casino it was simple. It was a big, spread out single story empty space with moveable dividers and seats. The city didn't face the problems Sam and Harriet had to cope with. The convention center would be finished long before the Silver Slipper. They city already had advance bookings for the new project that would more than pay for the cost of development.

"So the Mormons have money to lend so long as you and Sam are clean," Jack continued. "You have no ties to a mob-you're perfect candidates."

To her surprise, Jack was right. Harris was eager to proceed.

"Send me a proposal, a budget and the names of your architect and contractor. I'll forward it to our loan committee with my recommendation."

Within a month the loan, for a maximum of two and a half million dollars, was approved. Sam was delighted. Harriet was scared.

"They're Mormons, Sam. We're not."

"Yeah but Mormons won't want to dirty their hands managing the casino. They want to stay out of the business. They're not like the mob. We can work with them if we run into problems."

"There better be no problems."

Harriet didn't want to mislead the bank. "I've never borrowed money before," she admitted to Harris. "I thought we could build the Slipper using our own funds. I underestimated. I've never built a casino."

But Harris wasn't really interested in what she had to say. He and Sam discussed Sam's history with Bingo Baxter and how he had come to Las Vegas and helped start the Horseshoe. "But we want to start something of our own now," Sam added.

"You're the perfect borrowers," Harris told them. Actually, he addressed his comments to Sam. It was obvious to Harriet that she was nothing more than Mrs. Wilson. She wondered when Harris would learn she was anything but a typical housewife.

Harris explained about the reporting requirements, the goals they had to meet in order to take "draws" on their construction loan and the deadline for repayment.

"By the time the loan comes due you'll need to have permanent takeout financing," Harris cautioned. "In other words, you'll need another loan to payoff the construction loan we're making. That would be a typical mortgage you can pay over ten or fifteen years. Our bank may be willing to do the long-term financing, depending on how things go. We're prepared to be flexible on the repayment and I'll work with you."

Harriet was skeptical. She remembered the bankers talking to her pa about the mortgage on their farm. She didn't recall their being flexible.

Harriet and Sam left the bank with a thick folder of papers, their heads spinning.

"I don't know whether to celebrate or start running," Sam said.

"It's too late, Sweetheart. We've signed our names. They've got us. We're committed. But at least we got the money. And we have a good team. I mean, I think they're good."

She and Sam had prepared a construction schedule working

with Thalden and Meeks. Meeks said to add three months to the estimated construction time "so we don't get tight". Their loan would come due February 28, 1963.

That was two years away. But Harriet knew it would come too soon. They had so much to do.

"Let's do the garage first," Sam suggested. We can rent it out to the Desert Inn. They're dying for parking and we're right across the street. At least we can bring in some revenue while we finish the casino."

Now they learned they could build their six-story garage without having to spend a fortune on the foundation. That was good news.

"Looks like we drew an ace" Sam said, kissing her forehead. He had already talked to Wilber Clark, the Desert Inn's manager.

The mention of the "DI" made Harriet shudder. Clark had started building the casino using his own money. But he had run out of funds in the middle of construction. He had to borrow. The only available lender was the American National Insurance Company. There were rumors of ties to the Cleveland crime syndicate, but they had Clark over a barrel. He was desperate for money. The loan was a joke, there was no way Clark would be able to repay. The Insurance Company foreclosed on his dream casino. It was now owned by Moe Dalitz and the Cleveland mob. Clark was just their front man.

But that was almost ten years ago. Now, thank God, real lenders had taken an interest in Las Vegas. And now they had good news. They would be able to build on a firm foundation. That would save two hundred thousand dollars. Harriet took a deep breath.

❖──◈✦◈──❖

"We have to open a bank account, Hat."

Harriet stared at her husband. "Bank account? Why?"

"The Gaming Commission and the IRS. They want to tighten down control on the casinos. Hell, Bingo never had a bank account and nobody complained. But now the government is breathing down our necks."

"Just like the revenue agents," Harriet spat in disgust. "They get their hands in every damn thing."

Sam laughed. "Now, Sweetheart, they just want the casinos to do business like the rest of the world. Keep books, write checks for expenses. So we gotta have a bank account."

"So we have to take the money out of the safe? Do we have to pay taxes on it?"

"I have an idea. We can set up a separate corporation for the Slipper. The corporation can have the bank account. We can put the borrowed money into the bank. Hell that's what Harris wants anyhow. We put the money into the bank that loaned it so they can keep track of it. And that way we can keep our own money to ourselves."

"That's good, 'cause I have some plans for our money." Harriet smiled at Sam.

"Hat, you know when you smile like that it makes me nervous."

"What makes you nervous, Aunt Hat?"

Ezekiel had come into the kitchen. They hadn't noticed. He was so quiet around the house Harriet sometimes thought he was trying to sneak up on them. Sam said she was imagining things.

They were into their third month as Ezekiel's keepers. Opal's recovery was taking much longer than expected. Harriet tried to find out what was going on but it was hard to talk on the phone. For the first month Opal couldn't even talk. Their phone conversations consisted of Harriet asking questions and Opal saying Uh Huh or Uh Uh, followed by tears. The doctors refused to talk to her.

"We're just talking about the Silver Slipper, Zeke." Harriet made an effort to sound friendly. Her relationship with her little boarder was a constant strain. He was just a teenager, so why did Harriet feel so threatened by him? It was probably because he kept to himself so much. He came home from school and went to his room to study. He played with Spanky, his cocker spaniel, throwing balls in the yard for the dog to retrieve. He sat at the dinner table and ate his food quietly. He responded to questions. Then he went back into his room.

Sam invited him to join them watching TV. Sunday was their favorite night. Even Harriet loved the Ed Sullivan show and the Dinah Shore Chevy show. "See the USA in your Chevrolet" Dinah sang as the family gathered in the living room. Junior's favorite program was Maverick, which overlapped with the Ed Sullivan Show. He and his parents had worked out an accommodation. Every other week he saw Maverick. Harriet had to admit, James Garner was a handsome man. "He reminds me of you, Sam," she looked at her husband fondly.

"Yep, he's just like me, a gamblin' man."

And Junior always watched the Wednesday Night Fights. "See," he said. "It's even on TV."

"You convinced me, Son," Sam finally conceded.

But Ezekiel usually refused.

At first he had asked about his mother every day. When could he see her? When could he talk to her?

"She's real sick, Sweetheart. As soon as she can talk, she'll call you." Harriet knew she should try to comfort the youngster but something always held her back. And Ezekiel didn't seem to want hugs or kisses. He reminded Harriet of the guests on another show she enjoyed: "I've Got A Secret".

Things improved when Opal was able to talk. She and her son had long phone calls every evening. Ezekiel still had no idea what had happened to his mother. Opal told him she had gotten very sick and had to stay in a clinic in LA till she got better.

Opal and Harriet talked, too. "Please, come see me, Hat. I miss you."

Harriet didn't believe it. But she finally agreed to visit the clinic. She needed to know what Opal's plans were and she didn't want to discuss it in front of Ezekiel or Sam.

Harriet's first visit to the clinic had been in the dead of night. She was too tired and worried to pay attention to the details. But now she was able to study the place. It looked like a resort. Its exterior was not marked with signs. Its purpose, a place to hide victims of the violence that was part of the casino business, was a closely guarded secret.

Inside there was a handsome reception area with custom furniture (Harriet did a quick cost estimate) and an attractive young receptionist. She took Harriet's name and called for an "attendant" to escort her to Opal's room.

Opal was sitting up. The bandages had been removed from her face. The bruises were gone. Opal would remain a beautiful woman. Harriet fought back a bit of envy. She closed the door. Harriet had rehearsed what she would say, but face to face with her rival, she lost her words. She stood staring at the perfect face.

Opal stretched out her arms. "Hat, Oh Hat. I've missed you so. How can I thank you? For everything. How can I say I'm sorry. I'm so sorry, Hat." Opal started to sob.

Harriet approached the bed tentatively. She pulled a Kleenex from the box on the bedside table and handed it to Opal, who continued to cry.

"You know, Opie, crying makes your nose red. It's really unattractive. You should stop before that handsome doctor comes in."

It worked. Opal's sobs turned into a rueful laugh, followed by a productive honk.

"So how are you doing? Are they gonna let you out of here any time soon? Are you going back there? To the Starlight?"

Harriet was secretly worried Opal would ask Sam for a job at the Silver Slipper. She would have to put her foot down.

"I can't, Hat." The crying continued. "I can never work again."

"You mean at the Starlight?"

"No, not anywhere. Ever again. I'm sick. I mean, really sick."

"What's the matter?"

"I have the...a...a social disease. You know what I mean?" It came out as a whisper. She looked down.

"What?" Opal jerked like she had been slapped. Harriet tried her best to soften her voice. "How? I mean, how did you get it?"

"I don't know. But they did all sorts of tests. I just wasn't getting better. They couldn't figure out why. So they finally discovered it. I begged Mike to give me some other job. I need to work Hat. I need money, I don't know how we're gonna live....." She started crying again.

"Have you thought of contacting your parents? I mean, they should take care of you. Isn't there room for you and Zeke to move back to Bakersfield? Stay with them? I know it might be an imposition, but you're their daughter after all....."

"They'll never take me back. They made that clear."

"Why? Just because you left? I mean, that's perfectly understandable, after losing your husband in the war, you'd need to get away...."

"I never had a husband. I made that up. I was never married, Hat. Ezekiel's a bastard. Don't you dare say anything about this."

"Of course I wouldn't, Opie. But what happened?"

"His daddy was a traveling preacher. Ran a revival meeting. He said I was such a pretty little girl, he asked my ma if I could help with the meetings, taking up the collection. I helped, all right." She sniffed.

"Then he left and I missed my monthly. Of course, he was long gone. Ma and Pa couldn't believe it was him. They thought I'd been sleeping around. I tried to tell them. They threw me out. I can never go back there. I don't know what'll become of me. Or Zeke."

Now she was crying full out. Harriet couldn't help putting her arms around Opal. She held her, trying to think of something to say.

"Do you think you got it at the Starlight? I mean, after you left the Shoe?"

Opal pushed out of the hug. She looked at Harriet carefully. She must have known what Harriet was thinking.

"Oh don't worry, Hat. I didn't give it to your Sam. I'm sure it was one of Mike's customers."

"Then you need to talk to Mike. He needs to make it better. Give you some sort of allowance. You own your house after all. How much will you need to live on? The Starlight should pick up the tab."

"The house? I'll have to sell that. I'll need money, Hat. Money for medicine. Just to stay alive. You have no idea how expensive it is. And my savings, all the money I put away to send Ezekiel off to a good college. I'll need that to live on. I don't even know how to tell him. Poor little boy. We've lost everything."

Harriet got up. She didn't know what to say. Was Opal expecting Sam to come to her aid? Would he? Would Harriet let him? She and Sam had so many challenges. Taking on the bank loan, building the Silver Slipper. She had been happy to face those challenges. They were building a life together. She had always done what Opal asked, what Sam asked. But this…this was unfair. This was too much. She didn't know how to tell the woman in the bed, but she was not going to help.

"Look, Opal. I've got to run. I've got to meet with the bankers this afternoon…" Harriet tried to think up excuses.

"I understand, Hat. I'm not your problem. I'm so grateful for everything you've done for Ezekiel. Don't worry about us. We'll make it. Somehow." Opal managed a teary smile.

"I know. I'm sure you will. And don't worry about Ezekiel. We'll take care of him till you get out. He's a very smart, grown up little boy, Opie. Don't underestimate him. He'll understand."

"He loves you, Hat. Do you know when we got our house he asked about you every day. 'When can we visit Aunt Hat?' He tried to get me to read him all the stories you shared. He compares me to you all the time. I always come up short."

"I'm sure he loves you too, Opal. You're his mom, after all. Listen, I really have to run." She ducked through the door with a final wave. She almost ran into a young doctor. He was a good looking man. But there was no way Opal could attract him. Not now. Not ever.

Chapter 23: Shadows

Hattie walked to her car, finally able to take a deep breath. Opal would never again come between her and Sam. And she had been punished far worse than Harriet ever wanted.

She enjoyed the air, pine-scented, crisp with the promise of spring. She could look down on the lights from the Strip, less than an hour's drive away. The area would be spared the coming summer's searing heat. There were no homes, but there were flags marking the construction of utilities and roads. Who owned it? What plans did they have? She would have to check.

◄ ►◘◄⚹►◘◄ ►

The following months were so frantic Harriet didn't have time to investigate the area. Their general contractor, Meeks, was supposed to oversee construction, but neither she nor Sam was willing to leave their baby in his hands. They visited the site twice a day, met with Meeks and some of the key sub contractors. They interviewed interior designers, landscape architects, chefs, potential businesses that would rent space in the casino, entertainment directors, promoters, advertising executives, slot machine salesmen. They had what seemed like endless meetings with the Gaming Commission investigators. They watched in horror as another new casino left angry crowds standing outside its doors on opening night – the Gaming

Commission hadn't yet completed its opening count. Without the opening count the casino couldn't open for business.

"They probably lost hundreds of thousands of dollars," Sam said, shaking his head. "We need to be sure that doesn't happen to us."

Then there was the mob, the various "gangs" vying for control of all the casinos. They had already taken over the Desert Inn. And they owned the Starlight, the casino where Opal met with disaster. They were circling around the Slipper, waiting for a chance to move in for the kill. Harriet was amazed at their creativity. They had missed out on the financing – thanks to the Mormons. So they made a run through the general contractor and his subcontractors. Sam and Harriet poured through every invoice checking for kickbacks, overcharges, suspicious add-ons. It seemed there was a confrontation with the contractor's accountant every week. Sam left the accounting battles to Harriet.

"They'll be nicer to a lady," he said defensively. "Besides, you're better with numbers."

Harriet tried to get her husband involved, but he was still too busy with the Horseshoe to pay much attention to their own casino. Sam was wrong – the mob had no compulsions about being rude to a woman. Her only advantage was that they underestimated her. Their attempts to divert funds were so clumsy they often made her smile. But he was still busy with the Horseshoe.

"And we need that extra money, Hat," he reminded her.

"No," she explained patiently to the electrician. "I will not pay for five men to install the conduits when only one did the work. I was there. I know."

The confrontations were unpleasant at best and frequently turned into shouting matches. She found herself resorting to the crude language of her opponents. She had to. Phrases like "son of a bitch" and "shit a brick" coming from the mouth of the little lady had a certain shock value. And somehow they seemed to demonstrate that she was not a little lady. Which was not exactly what she wanted. But it worked.

She used the same words to Junior, who was a bit taken aback at first but later admitted he found it funny. And to Sam, who just raised his eyebrows and held up his hands as if to ward off the devil.

The only person to suggest, gently, that she needed to "wash out her mouth" was Jack. She still saw him occasionally, though the casino consumed most of her days and he was busy with his new job as editor in chief of the Las Vegas Review Journal.

She looked forward to his calls.

"Let's have lunch." Jack didn't have to say who was calling.

"I don't know, Jack. I've got meetings at nine and eleven and three and ..."

"Great – that leaves the noon hour free. We need to catch up. Meet me at the DI."

"Okay." She smiled into the phone.

"Who was that?" On that particular morning, Sam sat at the kitchen table, finishing his breakfast.

"Jack Hartman. He wants to have lunch."

"What's he want?" Sam's voice still had a defensive edge when he talked about Jack. God knows, Harriet thought, there was no reason for it. Sam knew she had no time for anything but their casino.

She had finally delivered Ezekiel back to his mother. The two were in the process of selling their house and moving into a small bungalow downtown-a "gift" from the Starlight. Mike had finally come through. She knew she should make time to visit them but she never seemed to get around to it. And Opal hadn't called since the day she came to get her son.

Harriet felt the tiniest tickle of guilt that she always had time when Jack called. "I told you. Lunch."

Sam frowned before returning to his breakfast. Harriet ignored him. It seemed to Harriet that she was entitled to have lunch with her friend. She was doing more than her share of the work. So many days lately, Sam begged off their morning site check, saying he was too tired, or that he had work to do at the Horseshoe. She wasn't sure what work that would be, Jake Baxter had gotten his gaming license a month earlier, but Sam did look tired. He had lost weight. He had developed a nagging cough that woke them both up in the middle of the night. She was able to go back to sleep but Sam often said he had stayed up. He was up that morning when she entered the kitchen, drinking a cup of coffee with his morning cigarette.

"I see your cooking skills have improved," she joked as he poured her a cup and handed her a slice of toast.

"What's up?" Junior joined them, still in his pajamas, rubbing sleep from his eyes.

"I've got the morning meeting with Meeks, then an interview with another landscape guy, then..."

"What's happening with the boxing ring," Junior interrupted. "Kearns says he knows of a good promoter, a guy named Don Elbaum, who can hook us up with a designer."

"I really don't have time for this right now." Harriet's reply was sharper than she intended. She was punished by the look on Junior's face.

"Let's discuss it this weekend, okay, Sweetheart?" She tried to ruffle his hair. He jerked back.

"It's not time yet, that's all, Junior. But I'll discuss it with the landscape designer I'm meeting today. I'll make sure he includes it in his plans."

Junior took a bite of toast, apparently mollified.

"Can you talk to Harris today, Sam?" Their relationship with Percy Harris was a constant source of worry. Each draw on their line of credit was a reminder. They had so many weeks to complete the casino. They only had so much money left in their account. With Jake Baxter taking over the Horseshoe Sam's supplemental income was about to end.

"Sure. I'll call him after breakfast."

Harriet was relieved that Sam was able to handle their dealings with the bank. At least that was one less thing to worry about.

She discussed her situation with Jack over lunch. "Seems there's always too damn much to do and too damn little time." She saw his frown and quickly corrected the sentence, though it seemed the swearing was more than justified. "I mean, there's just too much."

He laughed.

"So do you have time to talk about that property up by the clinic?" He smiled at her. Of course he knew she could make time for discussing real estate. It was their favorite topic. She had told him about the property and he had followed up without even being asked.

"What did you learn?" She leaned forward, elbows on the table.

"It's owned by the same folks who own the clinic-some of the folks who own the Starlight. They live in Chicago, but they have a contact here – the floor boss at the Starlight. They're willing to talk. The plot is eighty acres, zoned for residential and commercial. It's surrounded by federal land. Not sure who they got at the federal level to convince the government to pry those acres loose. It's prime real estate. Rumor is the Starlight wanted to build a resort/casino there but they decided it's too far out of town. They've lost interest. Now it's just sitting there….." He paused waiting for what he knew would happen next.

"How much?"

His smile broadened.

"Figured you'd ask. I made some discreet inquiries. A grand an acre and they'd want to keep the clinic. They need it. Since you went to visit Opal, you know why."

"No problem. But I don't have a lot of spare cash just now. Think they'd come down?"

"Probably but it'll set you back at least fifty."

"Damn."

"I have an idea."

"What?"

"Talk to Harris."

"You mean Percy?"

"Yep. He thinks a lot of you. And your instincts about the property are right on. It's a great parcel. He may be able to finance the purchase, or hook you up with some developers who'd go in with you."

"I don't want to take on any more debt. I can't imagine anyone else is interested in that land right now, no matter how beautiful it is. It's too far away from everything. How about an option? Could I tie it up for a year for five or ten grand?"

He smiled again. "Hat, you're somethin' else. I love the way you think. I'll see what I can do."

She left the lunch in a good mood. Her meeting with their third candidate for landscape designer went well. She had remembered to discuss the boxing ring idea and he was excited about it.

"You could build a dual purpose space," he proposed. "Tennis courts with portable grandstands. Tennis is all the rage right now. Even in this desert heat. Put up night lighting set up a little snack shop close by. Then you can convert it to a boxing ring when you need it."

She thought it was brilliant. She shared the plan with Junior over dinner. He loved it.

"Where's Dad?"

Sam had turned in early, saying he wasn't hungry.

Chapter 24: Finished

Two months later, Harriet and Sam and Junior stood in the middle of the space that would become their casino, necks craned, looking at the steel beams overhead. Junior was excited. He was already planning his opening night party.

Hatch still worked at the Horseshoe, but Bingo and Sam had already agreed he would come to work at the Silver Slipper as soon as it was finished. They still talked often. Hatch told them Junior was a real man about town, bragging to his buddies about his casino.

"What can I do, Hatch," Harriet complained. "He's too big for you to turn him over your knee."

Hatch shook his head. "He needs to work."

"I know. I don't know how to make him. There's plenty to do around here."

Harriet was worried. They were two months behind schedule and almost a hundred thousand over budget. She ticked off ways they could cut corners, save money. The landscape designer would have to scale back his plans for exotic palm trees. The boxing ring would have to wait. They would leave a space, perhaps covered with some inexpensive tennis courts, but the boxing ring, the grandstands, the snack bar were cancelled for now. She hadn't told Junior yet.

Sam didn't seem to share Harriet's concerns. But he rarely got excited about anything these. Once his job at the Horseshoe finished he spent most days at home sitting on the couch watching

TV. Harriet had no idea why he kept losing weight. He seemed to be tired all the time, and almost every sentence ended in a terrible cough. The coughing was sometimes accompanied by bloody spittle that stained his handkerchiefs. She tried to get him to see a doctor but he told her to stop nagging. Her first thought was that he had caught Opal's social disease. She wondered if Opal's symptoms included the horrible coughs. She was relieved that Sam was not interested in sex. Just in case. She couldn't afford to get sick; she needed all her energy to save the casino.

She talked to Junior about doing more to help, but their son was terrible at numbers, so he couldn't work on the accounting. His few attempts to work with subcontractors had turned into shouting matches. He had never developed a knack of getting along with people. And in the end he was more interested in hanging out with friends, talking boxing with Kearns, getting drunk and trying to snag girls. He didn't act like Harriet's impression of a twenty-three-year-old. He still lived at home. His "work" consisted of "helping" with the plans for the boxing ring. Harriet still hadn't told him about the fate of his prize project. She was amazed that he knew so little about the construction that he hadn't figured it out for himself.

Her only comfort was talking to Jack Hartman. He was always supportive. She always felt she was unloading her burdens on him, but she had no one else to talk to. That day they discussed the problems with bringing the casino in on time. Jack suggested she meet with Percy Harris.

"He's a reasonable man, Hat. He has no interest in owning an unfinished casino. He'll work with you. You should talk to him now. Keep him informed about the construction delays. Don't spring a problem on him at the last minute."

Harriet nodded. She hoped Sam would talk to Harris about the unexpected delays. She suspected the mob was behind many of them – critical building supplies that failed to show up on time, building inspectors that seemed to impose unreasonable, time-consuming conditions on the wiring, the plumbing, the windows. The Slipper would compete with the DI and other strip establishments the mob owned or controlled, so the mob clearly had an interest in stalling its progress or even causing it to fail. But of course she couldn't prove anything. She tried her best to cope with each day's problems and fell into bed past midnight most nights exhausted.

The third time Sam confessed that he had not kept his promise to meet with Harris, Harriet took matters into her own hands. She took Jack's advice and arranged a meeting herself. Harris was surprised when she walked into his office alone. He nodded non-committedly as she explained her problems. She had worked with the contractor to prepare for the meeting. She presented an amended construction schedule and budget. They needed six more months and another half-million dollars. She swallowed hard as she pushed the folder, including the contractor's estimates, across his desk.

"I see. I see. Hmmm." He studied the pages carefully. Finally he looked up.

"It seems you've done everything you can to meet the loan requirements, Harriet. And I can see you have some problems. I agree with Meeks. Looks like your competition from Cleveland is behind this somehow." He smiled. "We can't let them get their hands on the Slipper now, can we?"

Harriet ventured a smile in return. "It would be terrible, Percy. The Slipper's going to be the best place on the Strip. And I've tried to cut the budget every way I know how. I even had to cut Junior's boxing ring. I've worked with Meeks on this. We think it's a very reasonable estimate."

"I wouldn't want you to underestimate, Harriet. I'm gonna have to take this to my board in Salt Lake. I have a feeling they'll approve your request. But I don't want to have to go back to them again. Casino financing is a new area for them. I talked them into coming to

Vegas. This is their biggest loan by far. One delay they'll understand. But more....more will make them very nervous."

Harriet nodded gratefully. She hardly heard what he said after "approve".

"So why don't we make this request for a nine-month extension," he suggested. "Just to give you even more wiggle room. That's less than a year, which is always a red line for them. And the half-million sounds like it'll work."

She agreed gratefully.

"Do you have any alternatives yet for long-term financing, just in case the bank won't help you out?"

Harriet froze. She hadn't expected the question. All the while she had assumed Percy would work with them. She had trusted him, and relied on Sam to find a backup lender in case one was needed. He hadn't said anything about it. Both had let her down.

"You're a damn idiot," she said to herself. To Percy she replied, "I think Sam has some leads but I hope you're still interested."

"Well, it's still early," he mused. "Assuming you can bring this in on time, maybe a little under budget, there's still a good possibility our bank will do the long-term financing. How's Sam, by the way?"

"Oh, fine." She tried to sound confident. He frowned.

"I confess I was surprised when you showed up alone today. But relieved. Sam's been cancelling our meetings lately. Usually at the last minute."

Harriet was shocked. "He seems to have picked up a bad cold, can't shake it. It makes him tired. I didn't know he had missed your meetings."

"Well, no harm done. I drive by the construction all the time, so I have a good idea how it's going. But I'm glad you came to see me. We should talk more often."

Harriet added one more job to her list. She would have to tell Meeks he needed to stay at the site more, exercise more control over the time and materials, take over the meetings with the interior designer. At least she had bought him nine more months.

On the way home she decided she wouldn't tell Meeks they had a nine-month extension. She would say the bank would probably agree to five or six months. Harris had recommended a backup construction company, Mormons from Salt Lake, who would complete the job if Meeks got behind schedule. She would tell Harris about her little deception so he would play along. She was worried that if word got out about a nine-month extension it would reach the mob.

And she would have it out with Sam. She couldn't do everything. No matter how tired Sam was he had to get his butt out of the chair and help. She shook her head. She had begun to talk to herself like she talked to the construction workers. Well, that was the least of her problems.

⊷⊶✳⊷⊶

"Sam, I met with Percy Harris today."

"What?" At least he looked worried.

"We're behind schedule and over budget and you've been missing your meetings with him. Thank God I paid him a call. He's gonna ask his board for more money and more time. We need it, and he says you haven't tied down any takeout financing yet."

Sam looked down.

"Sam, what the hell's going on?"

His head jerked up again, on puppet strings.

"I'm sick, Hat. I'm sorry."

"Did you get it from Opal?"

"From Opal? Hell, no! Is that what you think?"

"Then what the hell is wrong with you?"

"I don't know."

"Then go see a doctor. Or get up and get to work."

He launched out of the chair, stalked into the living room and turned on the TV full blast. She thought about following him, but she was so tired suddenly. She went into the bedroom to lay down for a minute. When she opened her eyes it was early morning. Sam had fallen asleep on the couch in his clothes.

Harriet was blessed with good health. She had always been grateful, except now she realized she had no idea how to find a doctor. She called Jack.

"Are you sick, Hat?"

"No, it's Sam. He's tired all the time, and he has this cold that won't go away."

"If it were me I'd take him to LA. I wouldn't trust the docs around here to treat a broken arm. It sounds like TB or maybe a lung infection. I'll ask around and get back to you."

Harriet thanked the Gods that Jack was still her friend. He called a few days later. "I wanted to be sure I got the right man. This guy's the best."

She gave Sam the name of the doctor and drafted Junior to drive his father to Los Angeles. "And you make sure he gets to the doctor," she said, handing him the address. "No damn excuses. You won't screw this up. Understood? And call me when it's over."

Both men nodded solemnly. Harriet left to attend yet another meeting with Meeks. At least the loan modification had been approved. She had nine months. And Percy agreed they should keep the new arrangement quiet. He was happy to play the bad cop, agreeing to threaten to bring in a Mormon contractor at every opportunity. She circled their new completion date – November 1, 1963, on her calendar. It was more than fifteen months away but she knew it would come too soon. The August heat seemed to foreshadow the hot times ahead.

With Sam and Junior off in LA, Harriet decided to visit Opal. They had talked by phone once in a while but she had put off a personal visit. She invited Opal to have lunch at the new restaurant at the Desert Inn.

"I can't make it to the DI, Hat. Too far. How about downtown at the Golden Nugget?"

Harriet didn't like the downtown casinos. They were losing ground to the ritzy new buildings going up on the Strip – the elegant little La Concha with its ultra-modern design had opened the previous year. The Klondike, a fake western mining town featuring cheap food was set to open that month at the far end of the Strip. The downtown places couldn't compete with the new developments. The frayed carpets, the smell of too many bodies, carelessly-maintained bathrooms and stale smoke that clung to everything, the warm drinks and wilted lettuce all screamed of trouble. But she agreed to meet at the Nugget for Opal's sake.

Harriet arrived first. She ordered a coke. She couldn't afford to drink liquor during the day. She needed a clear head. She finished her coke and checked her watch. Opal was late. Same old Opal. The woman had no concern for Harriet's schedule. She had nothing to do but sit around her house and she couldn't even make a lunch engagement on time.

When Harriet looked up Opal was walking slowly towards her, a timid smile on her face. She was still beautiful, but she had aged years. Her gait was slow and unsteady. Seeing her former rival try to make her way towards their table sent a thrill of fear up Harriet's spine. Opal reminded her of Sam, haggard and tired. She even coughed.

"Sorry I'm late, Hat. I know you're busy. It seems I just can't get myself together these days." She coughed again.

"Are you coughing a lot," Harriet ventured cautiously.

"No, it's the damn smoke in this place. Makes me choke up. I gave up ciggies. Doctor said it'd be hard, but probably for the best. Liquor, too. I've turned over a new leaf, Hat. Living healthy. I have to. Otherwise I won't live to see Ezekiel graduate from college."

"Where's he going?" Harriet was happy to change the subject. She stubbed out her cigarette.

"Don't know right now. It'll probably be the community college here in Vegas. It may be all we can afford. The Starlight's gonna help. Ezekiel'll have a part time job here. In the count room. Just till he graduates. Then we're getting' the hell outta here." Opal waved her hand to include all of her surroundings.

"I'm really sorry, Opie. I mean, everything that's happened. How are you making out?"

"It could be worse. I was able to sell the house for a decent price. It should cover my medicine for a good while. The bungalow's not great like our house, but it'll do. Ezekiel's taking it pretty well. He hates the summer, but at least he can hang out at the Starlight pool. And he's really focused on his last year in high school. He's Senior Class President. I'm so proud of him."

The waitress came and took their orders.

"How's Junior?"

It was an afterthought.

"He's fine. He's helping with the Slipper. Except this week he's in LA with his dad."

"What for?"

Harriet focused on her lap, carefully refolding the napkin. "Sam's developed a bad cough. And he's losing weight. He's seeing a specialist. I finally put my foot down, otherwise he would have just suffered through it. I sent Junior along to make sure he follows orders."

Opal's smile froze. "You're worried. I can tell. You think he caught something from me?"

"I don't know. Did he?" Harriet looked into Opal's eyes.

"Well, let me tell you, Hat. If he had what I have you'd know it. First, there's no cough. It's all about sores. You know, down there. " She glanced at her lap. "And itching, and pain in your stomach." She stopped short and glanced at Harriet. "But of course we only did it, you know, once. And that was before I had my problem. So I'm sure I didn't give him anything."

Harriet nodded.

"You should come by my place sometime," Opal continued hurriedly. "Maybe have dinner? Believe it or not I can cook now. Ezekiel would love to see you. He told me, when he was elected class president, to be sure to tell you. He wants to make you proud of him. I can never thank you enough for taking care of him. He still doesn't know what happened to me. I just hope he doesn't find out, you know, working at the Starlight."

"He won't hear it from me. Don't worry." Harriet wondered if Opal was fishing for her to offer Ezekiel a job at the Slipper. She knew it would never work. Junior would have a fit.

Harriet went from lunch to the construction site. She made a quick inspection then left for home. She wanted to be sure not to miss Sam's call.

It was Junior who called.

"We have to stay here for a couple more days. They're taking some tests."

"Did they tell you anything?"

"Nah, just they need to take more tests."

"How's your dad?"

"He's okay. He's sleeping right now."

"Sleeping? But it's only six."

"Yeah, the docs gave him something to make him sleep and he took it and he went to sleep almost right away."

The next day Harriet had an important decision to make – to exercise the option Jack helped her get on the property by the clinic or let it go. She had hoped for some news about Sam that would help her decide, but it was not to be. She drove up to the property. One breath of the clear mountain air convinced her. She called Percy Harris. Her first idea was to take the balance of the purchase price from the construction loan. He said that wasn't possible. "But I could loan you the money."

"On what terms? I'd really have no way to repay it."

"Then why do you want to buy the property?"

"It's beautiful."

Harris laughed. "I never thought I'd hear you talk about buying something beautiful, Harriet. You are always so business-like."

"It's going to be a resort getaway someday. Just not right now."

"Well, then see if you can get an extension on your option. In another year the casino will be up and running and you'll know your financial situation a lot better."

Harriet called Jack to discuss strategy. He thought she might be able to get another option. He hadn't heard of anyone else interested in the property. He volunteered to see if the owners would be willing to extend the option.

Harriet went home, but she couldn't sit still. There was too much going on. She waited for the phone to ring. Who would call first? Sam? Junior? Jack? She decided to clean the kitchen. She scrubbed the floor. Then she took everything out of the refrigerator and cleaned every shelf. She defrosted the freezer. Then she cleaned the oven. Still no call. She cleaned the bathroom. Then the master bedroom. She took everything out of the closets and cleaned the floors and shelves. Still no call.

It was getting dark. She turned on the television. She sat in the chair and looked at the screen without focusing. She thought about going out for dinner but then she would miss the call. She decided to make something, but there was nothing in the refrigerator except milk and butter. She made herself some breakfast cereal and coffee.

She was just sitting down to eat when the phone rang. It was Sam.

"They haven't finished all the tests yet."

"Jesus, how many tests do they have to take?"

"Dammit Hat, you're the one who wanted me to go through this.

So don't complain."

Harriet took a deep breath. "So how do you feel, Sweetheart?"

"Lousy."

"I'm really sorry. I miss you."

"I'll call you tomorrow."

"Will you be coming home tomorrow?"

"How should I know?"

"Okay. We'll talk tomorrow."

Harriet finished her cereal and went out to the back yard. She sat in a lounge chair and lit a cigarette. She wished she were sitting on the mountain property.

Jack didn't call.

She called Jack the next morning. His contact hadn't been able to reach the owners. He would call as soon as he heard something.

She went to the construction site. The electrical inspection was just completed. They had passed. She took it as a good sign. She met with Meeks. They were on schedule and still within the new budget. Another good sign. She went to her favorite new restaurant at the La Concha and treated herself to a big lunch. She bought groceries —enough for dinner for all three of them. She would make meatloaf and mashed potatoes.

It was a hot day. She thought about driving up to the property (she already thought of the mountain retreat as hers) but decided to go home instead. Once she got home and unloaded the groceries she realized she had nothing to do. It was only two o'clock. She cleaned the living room and mowed the lawn. That was Junior's job but it gave her something to do. She went back in. It was only three o'clock.

She decided to take a shower. She had just lathered her hair when the phone rang. She ran to the living room soaking wet, trailing soap suds on the clean floor. It was Jack.

"They're interested in extending the option but they want more money."

"How much?"

"Fifteen grand. And the purchase price will be ninety grand."

"Shit."

"I don't think they have other offers, Hat. They know you're interested and they're testing you. I wouldn't bite if I were you."

Harriet decided she would hold off for a week or so. Jack agreed.

"Don't let 'em see you're anxious."

She had just hung up when the phone rang again. It was Junior.

"Mom, we have to stay." His voice was shaking.

"What do you mean?"

"They're checking Dad into the hospital here. He's real sick, Mom."

"What's wrong with him."

"He has cancer."

Harriet sat down. The remnants of the shower ran off her body onto the floor, a cascade of fear.

"How long will he have to stay?"

"They didn't say, Ma. You need to come."

"I'll be there tomorrow."

Chapter 25: Family Emergency

Harriet didn't know anything about cancer except that it was bad. Real bad. She thought about calling Jack but decided not to bother him. It was too personal somehow. Too painful to talk about. He would offer to help, demand to drive her to LA. She remembered the look on Sam's face when she and Jack had walked into Junior's hospital room. There was no way. She called the Greyhound bus station. There was a bus leaving for LA at eight the next morning. She made a reservation. Finally she got up, almost slipping in the pool of water around her. She dried herself off, made another bowl of cereal, ate it and went to bed.

She was at the bus station when she realized she hadn't let anyone know where she was going. She called Percy Harris. It was too early. The bank was closed. She called Meeks, thank goodness the construction office opened early. She told him she had a family emergency. She would be in LA for a few days. She decided it was best not to tell him what was wrong.

⦿

For the rest of her life the memory of the Greyhound bus trip would sicken Harriet. An hour out of Las Vegas she began to grow nauseated. Half an hour later she was in the tiny toilet room throwing up as the bus launched over the road. She stopped heaving when there was nothing left in her stomach. She finally fell asleep in her seat, exhausted. She woke up on the outskirts of Los Angeles.

When she got to the LA terminal she realized she had no idea how to reach Sam or Junior. She hadn't even asked them what hospital Sam was in. She took a taxi to the hotel where they were staying. She called the doctor's office but no one there was able to help her. She reserved another room for herself, then sat in the lobby waiting for Junior.

He finally showed up at five. She took one look at his face and put her arms around him, rocking him like a baby.

"He's real sick, Ma. Real sick."

"Let's go get dinner, Sweetheart. I'm starving."

They drove around looking for a place to eat and finally settled on a small local restaurant. Junior told her what he knew, but he didn't really know much. The doctors didn't want to talk to him and neither did Sam. Harriet's heart went out to her son.

"I'm here now, Junior. We'll take care of this together, right?" She tried to smile confidently.

The next morning Junior drove them to the hospital. Sam's room was in a special ward with signs on the doors that said "Radioactive".

"What's radioactive mean?" Junior asked. "Is it like the atom bombs?"

Harriet didn't know.

She and Junior spent the morning in Sam's room waiting for the doctor. He finally came at eleven. He was obviously in a hurry. He talked about radiation therapy and x-rays and possible surgery. Harriet didn't understand anything he said and he said he really didn't have time to explain. As he was about to rush out the door Harriet asked "How much will this cost?"

"The radiation treatments will run ten to fifteen thousand. Depending on how he responds. He's going to be very sick, you understand. He'll lose his hair. He'll probably be unable to keep food down. It's best he stay here for a few weeks. That'll cost another four or five hundred. And if we have to remove a lung there'll be an extra two or three thousand. After that, then we'll have to see."

"See what?"

"See how he does."

"How long before he gets well?"

"Well? I can't really say if he's going to get well. He has cancer." The doctor looked at her like she was an idiot, like she should understand what cancer meant. "We'll probably have to remove the right lung. He should have come to see us sooner." Now the look was accusing. He was out the door before she had a chance to ask more questions.

She turned to Sam. Had he been listening? They had discussed him like he was already gone. He was lying on the pillow with his eyes closed. He looked dead.

Harriet and Junior had lunch in the hospital dining room. When they returned to Sam's room he was awake and eating. Harriet decided that was a good sign. She tried to keep calm. She had to make some plans. At least Sam was awake to discuss them with her. She couldn't be in two places at once. She had to go back home. Junior would have to come with her. They couldn't afford for him to stay. Harriet didn't want to say anything, but she knew they had never planned on something like this. She had no idea what to do.

"I wanna go home." Sam suddenly sat up and tried to get out of the bed. Harriet ran over to keep him from disconnecting a tube in his arm.

"Either you stay or I go."

Harriet almost laughed. Her husband sounded just like her son. "Sam, that's not possible. You have to stay and I have to go home and oversee the construction."

"That's bullshit. They don't need you. Meeks can handle everything."

"No, Sam. You know Meeks doesn't pay attention to the subs'

invoices. He relies on me to do that." Harriet spoke to him like he was a child, slowly and softly.

"I'm not really sick, you know," Sam's hollow eyes searched hers, looking for affirmation. "It's all a scam. Doctors trying to milk us."

"Sam, if you like I can ask another doctor to take a look at you and decide if these doctors are right. But these doctors are supposed to be the best in the country. So do you really want me to spend the money to do that?"

Sam threw himself back against his pillow and closed his eyes, ending the conversation.

"Good bye, Sam. I'll call you when I get home."

"Don't bother."

"I love you, Sam."

There was no response.

When visiting hours were over Harriet and Junior went back to the hotel. Harriet went to her room and cried herself to sleep.

The next day she and Junior left before visiting hours began. They called Sam's room but no one answered.

For the next six weeks Harriet commuted to LA every weekend. The trips took three or four days out of every week. She made up excuses. A personal emergency. A sick relative. She didn't tell anyone about Sam. She was afraid if Harris found out he would stop making advances on the loan. And if Meeks found out? And word got to the mob? How could she handle everything all by herself? She said a silent prayer to the gods that construction was on schedule. The exterior and load bearing walls were complete. They only had to finish out the interior and the landscaping. They had passed all the inspections. She was hopeful they would be able to handle any small problems that remained.

At the end of six weeks the doctors sent Sam home. A week later Harriet wished he had stayed in LA. They had removed his right lung. He had no hair. His eyes were black sockets. He walked like an old man. And when he coughed it sounded like his insides were coming out. The doctors said they weren't sure they had "gotten everything". Harriet had no idea what that meant.

Sam wanted to see the casino. Harriet drove him to the site the morning after his return. When Meeks saw Sam his face went beet red. She ignored his attempts to get her alone. She escorted Sam around the casino and tried to act like nothing was wrong. She prayed silently that Sam wouldn't start coughing. Men were laying carpet. The elevators were in. The ground floor finally looked like the casino it would become, though they hadn't started on the upper floors yet. They had a little more than a year left on their loan. Harriet hoped Sam was pleased. He didn't say anything; he just nodded as Meeks took them through the various areas – the shops, the theatre, the guest rooms, the restaurants, the restrooms.

Harriet asked if he wanted to see the landscaping. He said he was tired. She helped him to the car, avoiding Meeks' stare.

Sam went to bed when they got home. It was one o'clock in the afternoon. She sat in the kitchen listening to him cough. He would never be the Sam she knew ever again. He would never be her lover, her companion again. He would be an old man. Or he would die. She didn't know what was worse.

Junior left early the following morning. He got home late that night, after she had brought Sam his dinner in bed and settled in beside him. During the night his coughs woke her up. In the morning his pillow was covered with rusty red stains.

Chapter 26: How Things Get Worse

During her worst moments, Harriet made herself feel better by telling herself things couldn't get worse. She was wrong. Suddenly, just when she stopped worrying about the casino, the construction workers went on strike. They had unionized. They were demanding higher pay, overtime bonuses. Meeks said he couldn't afford it. Harriet said it should come out of his contractor fee. Meeks refused. Construction came to a halt. The front of the casino was filled with angry men carrying picket signs.

Harriet had spent the last two months avoiding Percy Harris. While the casino was on track she had no need to visit his office at the bank. So she had no need to tell him about Sam's health. Now her time had run out. If the strike continued they would be behind schedule. She called to make an appointment. He told her he was glad she called. He was about to call her. She dressed in her best suit, hoping it would boost her courage.

"So what's up with Sam?" The question, his first comment to her as she entered his office, caught her off guard. She had planned to bring up the subject later, after she presented the latest figures and discussed how to handle the strike. She sat down slowly.

"He's sick, Percy. Very sick."

"I wondered. He's usually a man about town. Nobody has seen him for months. And of course he's never called me. I tried to reach him at your house but nobody picks up the phone. Except you, of course."

"He's been in a hospital in LA. He has lung cancer. But I've picked up the slack. And everything is on track, Percy, except for the damn strike."

"It's the mob."

"I thought we'd scared them off with the threat of bringing in a Salt Lake construction company."

"Looks like they're calling our bluff. Of course, they still think the completion date is less than a year away. So we have a little wiggle room. But I'm not sure what that'll get us. And with Sam out of the picture..."

"Sam's not out of the picture, Percy. He's just sick. He'll get better."

The banker looked at her, then looked down. He fiddled with the papers on his desk. She realized suddenly that bankers didn't really look like other people. Percy had never looked like a friend.

"I think we need a contingency plan, Harriet. My people in Salt Lake don't like surprises. I told you that. What if Sam....doesn't make it?"

"Then I'll handle it myself, just like I've handled everything up till now. Sam's been sick for months, Percy. Everything's been just fine till the strike."

"But now it's not fine. And even if we handle the strike somehow, how are you gonna open the casino without Sam's gaming license?"

She hadn't thought of that.

"Can Junior get a license?" She thought of Bingo's son Jake taking over the casino when his dad went to jail.

"He's an unknown, Hat. And things have changed lately. Nevada's under a lot more scrutiny from the feds and this new Gaming Commission's responding, getting tougher about who they hand out licenses to. I bet Junior doesn't have a clue about gaming regulations and he sure doesn't have the experience with gaming operations that his dad has."

Harriet knew he was right. "I'll have to find someone."

"How? This is not like posting an employment application in the newspaper, Hat. A gaming license is a special thing. The people who hold them are rare, and they don't just come to work for a start-up casino owned by a woman."

There. It was out. She was a woman. She saw from the look on Percy's face that he regretted his words, but it was just the truth. She decided to ignore it.

"Is there anything you can do to help end the strike," she asked. "You talked about calling their bluff. Is there a construction company in Salt Lake I can start to hire? To scare Meeks and his connections? After all, what's left is the finish work and the hotel floors. How different can it be from any other hotel building?"

"I don't know, Hat. But it's a good idea. I'll ask around. Even bringing someone to the site to discuss taking over might get 'em back to work. Of course, you're talking about bussing crews from Utah, crossing picket lines, pissing off the locals. Added costs. But maybe it's worth it. But what are you going to do about Sam and the license?"

"I'm gonna worry about that when the casino is ready to open. At least we'll have a casino, Percy. If worst comes to worst we can sell it. Maybe you've got some suggestions."

"You mean other than the mob?"

"I mean anyone who'll pay you off and give me a little money to take care of Sam."

Harris saw Harriet out. He took Harriet's two hands between his own and gave them a little squeeze. "I'm so sorry, Harriet. You don't deserve this."

"You can say that again. But it's not over yet, Percy. And it's almost Christmas. Maybe Sandy Claws will come."

"I'm praying for you."

Chapter 27: Merry Christmas

Christmas was coming. Harriet watched crowds of happy holiday shoppers braving winter winds that tried to snatch the packages from their arms. Winters in Las Vegas made up in wind what they lacked in snow.

Harriet didn't care. For her, Christmas meant eleven months to complete the casino. She thought back to the good old days when eleven months was a lifetime. More than enough time for her to conceive and give birth to Junior. Yet it might not be enough for the Slipper to be born. She thought of the casino as her baby. She couldn't help it. She had sweated, prayed, worried over the structure on the Strip more than she had ever thought about the baby in her belly. And now her child might be born dead. Her living child was no help at all. He was running away... in his mind and heart and his body, too.

Harriet didn't blame Junior. She had to steel herself every time she went into the master bedroom that had become Sam's sole domain. She had moved into the spare bedroom.

The coughing had grown worse. Sam had lost more weight. She had to help him to the bathroom. Sometimes he didn't make it, leaving a mess on the floor. He absolutely refused to go back to LA for more tests and treatment.

"I want to die here," he said weakly. And Harriet knew it was true. He was going to die. And her dream of their casino might very well die with him.

She dragged herself to the shops to buy Christmas presents for Sam and Junior. She had to pretend. She even bought a new fake Christmas tree. It was all pre-strung with lights. She asked Junior if he wanted to help decorate it. He said he was busy.

She bought little presents for Percy Harris and even one for Meeks. A sort of peace offering, she hoped. He was in the midst of battling the new Utah contractor. She had managed to stay out of the fight. Percy led everyone to believe the new contractor was a requirement of the bank. Every day fights broke out in front of the casino, union men against "Damn Mormon scabs". Only the political clout of the Mormon church and politicians in Las Vegas prevented an all-out war.

The battles brought home to Harriet how firmly the Mormons, the "LDS" as they called themselves, had entrenched themselves in her city. They were on the Gaming Commission. The sheriff was Mormon. There were LDS in the state legislature. And of course, they controlled the local banks.

"You'd think they could control the mob," she said to Jack over lunch. He had invited her to a new restaurant for a Christmas treat. She had long ago told him about Sam. It seemed the whole town had found out. She had hoped he might offer some suggestions about getting a gaming license, but he was no help.

"I can't believe the Gaming Commission can't recommend someone, Hat. It's in their best interest to keep the Slipper out of the hands of the mob."

But the Gaming Commission was unhelpful. At least for now. She hoped they were just waiting to see how the construction battle played out.

Meanwhile, waiting for her at home, there was Sam with his incessant demands, his horrible cough. And his eyes. She had nightmares about his dead eyes.

"You look awful, Hat." Jack's comment brought her back to the present. "Is Junior helping?"

"Junior's not up to helping, Jack. His idea of solving a problem is threatening to punch somebody's lights out."

"What are you doing about money?"

She wished he hadn't asked. He was the only person who could have posed such a question without getting a slap in return.

"We're managing so far. But Sam's treatment is so expensive, you have no idea. We're okay but the money won't last 'til next Christmas."

"Junior should get himself a job. It's the least he can do. I see him driving around town with a bunch of his friends. It's like he doesn't have a care."

"He's running away, Jack. Hell, I'd run away if I could."

Jack reached over and took her hand. "No, Hat. You'd never run away. It's not in your nature. You're a fighter. And you'll fight this thing to the end. And, heck, you'll probably win."

He had never held her hand before. She wondered why he had done that. Was she so pathetic? Later that evening, sitting on her back patio enjoying a smoke, she considered whether he might be right. She walked over to their safe, under the long-deserted doghouse. She peered into the dark hole. For so many years, they had put cash in there—so much cash they had never even bothered to count it. They used to joke about having to build a bigger safe. These days she counted the bills at the bottom of the hole every week just to make sure she had the numbers right.

Would it help to count the money again? She already knew how much was there. To the penny. It was not enough. It was so far from enough she couldn't even think about it.

She stayed on her knees. Suddenly she had lost the strength to get back up. There she was on her knees in the dirt, looking into the empty safe where she and Sam had stored all their dreams. And she was alone. All alone. And the sun was setting. And it was almost Christmas.

Chapter 28: Gingerbread Men

Harriet turned off all the lights except the ones on the Christmas tree. She sat in the living room looking at the repetition of red, green, blue, yellow blue shining on the tinsel. She had hung the expensive china ornaments she and Sam bought their first Christmas in Las Vegas, but she had also made little woven baskets of colored paper and filled them with peppermint candy. She and Ma used to make the baskets, she remembered Ma showing her how to cut the halves, each half carefully cut into even loops, and weave them together. She was so proud when she was able to complete a perfect little heart-shaped basket.

Now Ma was dead. She had opened the envelope from home joyfully, Christmas was still the only time she expected a card from her family. But instead of a card, the envelope contained a letter from her sister.

"Ma took sick a few months ago. She died last week. It was peaceful. A lot of folks came to the funeral. Pa's taking it hard. He's moving in with me and Harry. Here's our address. Keep in touch. Love, Nellie."

She held the letter close to her heart. Another piece of her life gone. And she had no chance to say goodbye. She hadn't thought about her parents dying. They were always supposed to be there, even though they were far away.

She had been thinking of her family a lot lately. They never had a lot of money, even after Pa took up moonshining. They had clothes and food but not much else – a doll for her and her sisters to share;

a toy gun for her brothers; apples and raisins in their stockings. But Christmas was always magical back then. She searched her memory for clues. What had produced their happiness? What could she reach back and take from those early years on the farm and weave into her house in the desert?

She remembered the church service Christmas Eve. They plodded into Selma in the wagon pulled by Old Tom, his harness decorated with pinecones and "sleigh bells" that her Pa tied on. The children laughed as they piled into the back of the wagon under a load of blankets. The bells jingled merrily in the winter night, the sound carried on Old Tom's breath to the dark forest all around them.

They sang all the way to church. They gathered with the townspeople in front of the chapel, where the children always built a nativity. Then pastor rang the bells and the congregation filed in singing "O Come All Ye Faithful."

The pastor was a righteous old man. She both loved and feared him. On Christmas Eve he told the story of the Christ child, the wise men, the angels, the shepherd in a booming voice. "Behold! I bring you tidings of great joy!" And everyone nodded. The tidings had been delivered.

They sang on the way home, too. Then Ma tucked them into bed and told them to close their eyes and go to sleep "So Sandy Claws can come." Harriet didn't remember whether she believed in Sandy Claws back then. She remembered curling up next to her brothers and sisters in the big bed, closing her eyes and drifting off, hoping to hear the sound of reindeer hooves on the roof. On Christmas morning she was always the first to get up and tiptoe into the living room to see what was under the tree, what was in their stockings. She remembered the excitement but she couldn't recall any particular present.

Ma always made ginger snap cookies. The ones she put on a plate for Sandy Claws were gone Christmas morning but they still had some tucked in their stockings. She loved the way the crunchy, cinnamon-dusted ginger cookies melted on her tongue. She resisted chewing as long as possible, knowing if she swallowed the taste would begin to disappear.

She breathed in the smell of the spruce Pa and the kids had cut from the forest. It mingled with the cinnamon and baking cookie dough and apples and damp mittens and….

She opened her eyes. The family farm faded like Old Tom's breath in the night air. There was no smell of spruce. No smell of cookies. No Christmas carols ringing in her ears. No brothers or sisters or Ma or Pa. Ma would never celebrate Christmas again. In the bedroom, Sam began to cough. Soon it would become a chest-racking fit that tore at his remaining lung. She knew she should get up and go to him but she was so tired. She couldn't get out of her chair.

The doorbell rang. Junior had probably forgotten his keys. She willed herself to stand and walk to the door.

"Merry Christmas!" It was Opal and Ezekiel. Ezekiel was holding a present. "Can we come in?" Ezekiel was through the door before she could say yes or no, wrapping her in a big hug. She extracted herself, embarrassed by the unbidden thrill of being held in the arms of a teenage boy. But what a boy! "Tall, dark and handsome," her ma would have said. And the violet blue eyes, like a male Elizabeth Taylor.

"I wasn't expecting company," Harriet muttered.

"Aren't you happy to see us, Aunt Hat?" Ezekiel's bright eyes clouded with concern.

"Of course. Of course I am, Zeke. It's just that I haven't cleaned lately and Sam's sick, of course, and…"

"We came to pay you a visit, Hat. Not to check on your housecleaning. But I do want to see Sam. Is he awake?" Opal's question was answered by a cough from the bedroom.

"I'll just go say hi." She was off down the hall before Harriet could stop her. Harriet led Ezekiel into the kitchen where she could keep a closer eye on the bedroom.

"We should have stopped by earlier, Aunt Hat. I've just been so busy with school and Mom's still trying to get used to staying home. But we baked you some cookies, see?" He unwrapped the present, a paper plate piled with gingerbread men. Each one had raisin eyes. Harriet sat down.

"Are you okay, Aunt Hat?" Ezekiel wrapped her in another distracting embrace.

"I'm fine, Zeke. Just fine."

Opal came back to the kitchen and sat at the table. Ezekiel sat between the two women.

"He was real glad to see me, Hat. He said he hadn't had company since he took sick."

"Truth is, Opie, I wouldn't have had time for company if they had come."

"That's what I wanted to talk to you about," Opal took a cookie from the plate. "Are you gonna have one?"

"I have some milk. How about milk and cookies?"

Harriet poured three glasses. She picked up a cookie and lifted it gently to her nose. It smelled of ginger and cinnamon. She took a bite and held it in her mouth, rolling the flavor around with her tongue till it filled every corner.

"Don't you like it?" Ezekiel looked at her with concern.

"I love it, why?"

"You got a strange look on your face, like you wanted to spit it out."

"No, not at all, Zeke. I was enjoying it. That's all." Harriet took a swallow of milk. "My ma used to make ginger cookies for Christmas. It's been a long time. That was real nice of you,"

"So I wanted to talk to you about an idea I had," Opal continued. "I'm just sittin' at home doin' nothing and you're busier than God knows. So I thought maybe I could come over and stay with Sam during the day...keep him company, cook dinner, help out."

Harriet almost choked on her cookie. "You don't have to do that, Opie. I mean, it's a wonderful offer but Sam's real sick. I wouldn't put that burden on anybody."

"It's not a burden, Hat. Sam and I go way back. And I owe you. How long did you take care of Ezekiel here? And I know Bingo never paid you a penny. And it'd be better than sittin' around our little hole on Fourth Street feelin' sorry for myself. And it'd free you up. You must have a million things to do and Sam's no help."

Harriet took another bite of cookie. It was the sweetest, most wondrous cookie she had ever tasted.

"Let's take Sam some milk and cookies." Opal rose slowly and grabbed another glass, filled it with milk and took a cookie from the plate. The three of them headed to Sam's room. Sam had stopped coughing, Harriet noticed. He smiled when they came in.

"Look what we have for you, Sam. But you have to promise to be a good boy," Opal teased. Sam chuckled, which produced a small cough. "Can you come to the kitchen so we can all eat together? Otherwise Harriet here is gonna clean out the cookies before you can get another."

The two women helped Sam out of bed and escorted him to the kitchen.

"Opal's gonna be staying with you, Sam, so I can get some more work done."

"You mean tonight?"

"No, I mean during the days from here on…for a while. Till the casino's finished. I guess. Is that right, Opie?"

"Sure. I don't have anything to do with myself, so I thought we could hang out together. How 'bout it, handsome?" She turned her dazzling smile on Harriet's husband and he blushed like a little boy.

Harriet could only watch in wonder. Even with her disease, Opal still had the power. But Harriet was not complaining. She hadn't seen Sam look so good for months. And she had just received the best Christmas gift ever. She helped herself to another cookie.

Chapter 29: No Parking

Harriet was at the construction site at eight sharp the morning after Christmas. She told Joe Douglas, the new Mormon construction chief, she wanted an office space finished out as soon as possible, with a telephone hook-up and a desk.

"I'll be spending my days here from now on," she announced. It made a huge difference. She was able to patrol the site all day, keeping an eye on the workers and materials.

"You don't wanna slack off with old Hat around," the crew muttered. But they worked. And Harriet complemented a job well done. After the first two weeks she was sure the construction was moving more quickly.

She toured the grounds at least twice a day. The landscaping was also progressing, though the cold, windy January weather made planting difficult.

"Folks think Las Vegas is hot just because it's a desert. They don't realize it's three thousand feet high. And farther north than the ski slopes at Flagstaff. Only reason we don't get much snow is 'cause it's so dry." Harriet was encouraging a group of Mexican workers trying to manhandle a palm tree into a garden spot by the pool. The men nodded, intent on their work. She decided to check out the new garage. It was the first structure finished. She saw it was filled with cars.

"Who's collecting rent for the parking garage," she asked Douglas.

"Rent?"

"You're kidding me. No one's collecting rent?

"Nobody told me about it, Ma'am. I'm just a construction guy."

Of course he was right. She apologized. A few inquiries revealed that the Desert Inn valets used her parking garage to stash their cars. For free.

"The Desert Inn's supposed to pay for parking," she instructed Douglas. "I thought I told you. This is the only available parking on the Strip. They can't just use it for free."

Douglas scratched his head. "How're you gonna collect it, Hat?"

"You mean Moe Dalitz isn't just gonna come over here every month and pay?"

They both laughed.

"You need to set somebody up to get the money when the cars come in.

"How would we do that?"

She decided she would charge five dollars per car. She told Junior he had a new job – parking attendant.

"Ma…I can't believe you're gonna make me sit out there in the cold freezing my butt for a few bucks."

"We need the money, Junior. I'm afraid this is your responsibility."

Junior was installed in a small tent at the entrance to the parking garage. After a month, Harriet realized he was shirking his job. A few confrontations with her son failed to produce results. And she discovered something worse – most of the cars were being parked after five, when the shows started and the high rollers cruised in. Junior was only supposed to collect fees from nine to five. The Desert Inn was getting away with their takeover of her garage. She marched over to the Desert Inn to see Moe Dalitz, the mobster responsible for the trespassers.

She was always nonplussed by Dalitz. He was small and wiry with thinning hair and eyes framed by thick horn rim glasses.

Nobody would believe he was a mob boss. He looked like a college professor or accountant, and he was invariably polite to everyone. He listened to her complaints without looking up from a pile of paper on his desk, which only made her angrier. When she finished her tirade, he entertained her with a world-weary smile and a sigh. "I can't control my valets, Mrs. Wilson. You need to post a guard at the entrance."

Harriet was sure he laughed his head off as soon as she left his office. She and Douglas had to come up with a solution.

"We need to order some sort of gate that will close off the garage. And we need a guard who can scare those jerks off...Hatch." The solution was obvious. She had been looking for some way to hire the big man. This was it. Douglas had no idea what she was talking about.

"What?"

"You don't know him, he's been a family friend since we came to Las Vegas. He's at the Horseshoe right now but he wants to work for us. This is perfect. He'll pay for himself."

Harriet talked to Hatch. The big man's face broke into a huge grin. "I'll give my notice today."

"You still have a gun, Hatch?"

"You kidding, Missus?" He pointed to the bulge under his jacket.

Douglas ordered a heavy wire mesh closure that rolled down from the ceiling. It clanked into place slowly at the push of a remote button. Douglas installed it early one Friday morning.

"Don't you think we need to let people know about this?" Douglas asked.

"I don't really think so."

Douglas took one look at Hatch and the gate and started to laugh.

By ten that Friday evening the garage was full of cars. None of them had paid admission. Harriet watched Hatch close the gate. He settled himself in a small tent at the entrance. Harriet asked if he needed a heater. "I have a heater," Hatch said, patting the bulge. They toasted the event with champagne. Then Harriet went home.

Sam was still up when she walked in. He called to her and she answered from the doorway, keeping one eye on the phone in the living room.

"Where did you go so late?"

"To the casino. I had to check on something."

The phone rang.

"Who the hell would be calling at this hour? Aren't you gonna answer," Sam asked.

" I don't think so."

Sam looked at her suspiciously. "What if it's an emergency?"

"Oh, I'm sure it is."

Sam stayed up while Harriet finished her dinner.

The phone rang every five minutes. Harriet ignored it.

"Okay, Hat. I give up. What's happening?"

She told him.

"You're taking on Moe Dalitz? Are you nuts?"

"He's parking in our garage. For free."

"So now he's gonna blow up OUR garage."

"I don't think so. 'Cause where'd he park all the damn cars?"

"Hat, I swear. You're a wonder."

The phone rang again.

"So when do you plan to answer?"

Harriet walked over to the phone. She lifted the receiver off the hook and put it under a sofa pillow.

"What if they jimmie the gate?"

"They won't. Hatch is guarding it."

"Hatch?"

"Yep. He's working for us now. I think he's more than a match for Moe's valets. Besides, I have a feeling Mr. Dalitz and his valets are gonna have a lot bigger problem on their hands when their guests can't get their cars."

She returned to her casino late Saturday morning. The work crew was off but Hatch was still sitting by the gate. She brought him a cup of coffee and a roll.

"I think your shift is over, Hatch."

"Yep."

"Anything happen?"

Hatch munched the roll slowly and took a big gulp of the steaming hot coffee.

"Not much."

He stood up, cracked his knuckles and headed for the casino. Harriet accompanied him. They walked out the front entrance. Harriet showed Hatch the new light display. A crowd of people had gathered, inspecting the waves of sparkling lights lining the front and admiring the giant silver slipper that revolved slowly over the door. It had been installed the previous week. The picketers had thinned out, discouraged by the winter weather. Some people tried to follow her through the door, thinking she was open for business.

"Not yet, folks. Come back for our grand opening." Some people asked Harriet when that would be.

"We'll let you know, don't worry," she replied.

Harriet asked some of the onlookers if they were from out of town. Many were from Las Vegas. Harriet had an idea. "We may have a special pre-opening for locals," she said. She would tell Douglas to put all the men to work finishing the casino floor and the restaurants and leave the hotel floors for last. That way they could open early and start bringing in money. Jack would help with publicity. And the locals would be a good test crowd for the games and restaurants before they went national.

She was surprised to see Douglas come to meet her at the entrance. "Since when did you work weekends, Joe?"

"Hat, do you have any idea how many calls I had this morning?

Dalitz found out where I was staying somehow."

"Really?" She flashed him her most innocent look.

"Don't screw with me, Harriet. I've been threatened twice today already. I swore I didn't have the garage door opener. I just thank God I can finish this job and go back to Utah. Hopefully he can't reach me there. Anyway, he wants you to come to his office right away."

Hatch was standing at a distance, inspecting the entrance.

"Hatch, can you stay around a while?

"Sure."

She turned to Douglas. "I have a few things to take care of around here. Call him and tell him if he wants to talk he can come see me in my office."

"Harriet Wilson. Do you have a death wish?"

"No, Joe. I just have nothing to lose. That's all."

Dalitz burst through her door fifteen minutes later. He saw Hatch and stopped mid-stride.

"You fucking bitch." The change in his demeanor was quite satisfying. He was shaking. Harriet stayed in her seat, leafing through papers on her temporary desk.

"That's really no way to start a conversation with a lady, Mr. Dalitz. Especially if you want something from me. And I assume that's why you're here?"

"I'll sue you. You won't have a penny left when I'm finished."

"For what? Protecting my garage? But of course you can do what you want. I'll just keep the gate closed till the court finishes with you."

"You bitch. You fucking bitch."

"As I said, Mr. Dalitz. That's not the way to have a business discussion. So you'd best be on your way. I have work to do."

He finally stopped. Harriet motioned to a plastic chair. He sat down. "What do you want?"

"I want to rent you my garage, of course. That's what I always wanted. For six months, till we open. At twenty thousand dollars a month. Unlimited access."

"That's robbery. Highway robbery."

"That's the deal if you want it. And you owe me for the last two months, since the garage was finished. Otherwise, the garage stays locked up until our grand opening. Now, I don't have much time to talk. So yes or no."

"Yes, damn you."

"So as soon as you bring me the money—one hundred sixty grand—in cash, in advance—I'll open the gate."

"Fuck you."

"And one more thing. The pickets, the union, they go away. Permanently."

"I have no control over the union."

"Oh, dear. That's too bad. Because unless they go away we don't have a deal."

"Fuck you."

"I have other things to do, Mr. Dalitz. So you decide. You don't have to tell me now. Just whenever."

Hatch walked to the door and gestured for Dalitz to leave.

"Okay, okay. It's a deal. But one condition. This stays between us." Dalitz looked at Hatch nervously.

"Agreed. Hatch agrees, too. Right, Hatch?"

"Right."

At noon a messenger showed up with a check for a hundred and sixty thousand dollars. Hatch sent him away.

At twelve-thirty a messenger showed up with a briefcase filled with cash and a note from Dalitz indicating that he had heard that the pickets were gone and would not return. Harriet counted the money out on her desk. It was a hundred sixty thousand dollars. She told Hatch to open the garage.

"So am I out of a job, Missus?"

"Hell no, Hatch. You have a permanent job with me, for as long as you want."

Hatch smiled.

She left Hatch at the office and went home early that afternoon. She heard talking from the bedroom. Opal was sitting on Sam's bed. They were chatting. It occurred to Harriet that she never sat on Sam's bed chatting like that. She pushed a surge of jealousy out of her mind and walked into the bedroom.

"Hi."

Opal turned, startled. Harriet wondered what they had been talking about. But again she pushed down the thought. After all, one of them was dying of cancer and one of them was dying of the clap. How much trouble could they get into? And Opal's help had allowed her to turn her life around. As far as Harriet was concerned, giving the woman access to her dying husband was a small price to pay.

"Why don't you take the rest of the day off, Opie? Thanks a lot." Harriet shooed Opal out the door and returned to Sam. Did he look disappointed?

"I have something to show you. This is just between us, okay?"

"What is it?"

She returned to the car and retrieved the briefcase. Sam looked at her quizzically. She opened it and dumped the money on Sam's bed.

"Holy shit."

"You can say that again, Sweetheart."

"What is this?"

"It's eight months rent for use of our parking garage, forty grand for the past two months and six months paid in advance."

"I bet Percy Harris is gonna be happy to see this."

"I don't intend to give this to Percy Harris."

"What?"

"Percy doesn't need to know about this, Sam."

"But why? Why wouldn't you use it to pay down the loan?"

"Because a hundred twenty thousand won't pay off the loan and I don't wanna give a big chunk of this to the IRS. So until we have enough to be sure we can keep the casino, we don't pay anybody any more than we have to."

Sam looked down. "Okay. Whatever."

"Don't you care, Sam? It was your idea to finish the parking garage and rent it to the DI."

"It's your show now, Hat. You do what you need to."

"I thought you'd be more excited about…about this."

"I'm happy for you, Hat. You know that."

Harriet put the money in the back yard safe. She gave the lock an extra twist for good measure. She already knew what she would do with the money. At least part of it. She would buy her parcel in the mountains.

Chapter 30: Juice

February was almost over and Harriet still hadn't heard from the Clark County Commissioners about her plan to open the casino before the hotel was completed. It had come as a shock that she even needed their permission.

"It sounds good, Hat," Jack had commented on the plan as the two walked around Harriet's new acquisition, the mountain parcel, on a chilly, windy March day. "But you need to get clearance from the County."

"Why? It's my property, my money. Why would they interfere?"

"Because they control all the development in the county and you applied for permission to build a hotel-casino, not a casino with hotel to follow. They're afraid you'll open the casino and then forget about the hotel."

"Why would I do such a thing?"

"That's not the point, Hat. You just need to ask their permission, that's all. Hopefully they won't have a problem with it."

Harriet hated government officials. It was a leftover from the days she and Sam had to get permission from the sheriffs to put up their tent. The secretary at the commissioners' office took her name and the letter she had carefully prepared describing what she wanted to do and told her they would "get back" to her. That was almost a month ago and she had not heard a thing, despite several trips to the office and assurance that they were "considering" her application. She began to worry whether Dalitz had a hand in the problem, but she had learned that the commissioners were mostly Mormons who, being very practical people, had no love for the mobsters.

"You know, if I don't hear back soon I may have to sell out to Moe Dalitz," she told one of the commissioners. He just nodded and expressed his hope that she could find away around her problems. But he said nothing about the application. Meanwhile the casino was almost finished. She walked through the entrance each morning, into the beautiful space with its high ceilings and custom lighting, her feet sinking into the wall to wall carpet, past the shiny new slot machines and the gleaming gaming tables with their untouched green surfaces, past the restaurant entrances—three colorful eating establishments, casual dining, high roller restaurant and buffet, all standing empty with doors open like the mouths of hungry children—and wrung her hands in despair. In a week or two the crew would have to start completing the hotel floors.

There was another problem as well—Sam. He held the gaming license. And he was getting worse every day. He improved temporarily after Opal started her visits, but the Opal effect was starting to wear off. Lately his coughing had gotten worse and he was gasping for breath. The doctors ordered an oxygen tent and the local hospital sent a medical technician to install it and show her how to regulate it. They gave her morphine for him. "In case the pain gets too bad." The tent helped him breathe but he had to give up smoking. They said a cigarette was too dangerous in the oxygenated air. Without the cigarettes he was in a foul mood. She gave him morphine to keep him calm, but the pills made him sleepy and dizzy.

He was losing weight again, faster than before. He seemed to be shrinking in front of her eyes. Opal refused to notice. She greeted Harriet with a smile every morning and every evening. Sometimes Harriet came home to find Opal sitting on Sam's bed, the tent pushed back, Opal chatting merrily as she tried to get him to eat. Harriet was too worried to join them. She sat in the kitchen picking at her dinner.

"How's Sam?" Harriet would ask each evening."

"Oh, great. He's much better," Opal always called over her shoulder as she rushed out the door.

Usually Harriet finished her dinner and watched the television for a while before heading for her bedroom. Junior was rarely home. The day he learned there would be no boxing ring he told her he never wanted to speak to her again. He was at the construction site so rarely he didn't figure out that his boxing ring had been eliminated until after Christmas. She made the mistake of telling him that if he helped more around the site he would have learned earlier. He stomped off.

She bit her lip. She apologized, told him there might be a way to build the ring later, after the casino opened. But he was too angry to listen. Hatch tried to talk to him but he ignored him.

Hatch told her Junior was staying with friends. He and his buddies dropped by the casino once in a while but he always avoided her.

She looked at the TV until the last show finished. Then she got up and walked down the dark hallway to the guest bedroom, past Junior's abandoned room and Sam's room. She looked in on Sam, who was usually asleep. Sometimes, though, a coughing fit kept him up and she had to give him morphine. The doctors warned her about the dangers of becoming addicted. She laughed. "How long do you think the addiction will last in his case?"

Then she went into her room, closed the door and climbed into bed to sleep with her problems.

<hr/>

A week later, as she passed his door, he called out.

"Hat, come in for a minute."

He seemed lucid. She went in and stood by the bed next to the oxygen bottles.

"We need to talk."

She sat down on the chair by the bed.

"You need to get ready."

"Ready for what, Sam?"

"You know what. When I'm, you know, gone. How are you gonna manage the casino?" The question was followed by a coughing fit that caused the oxygen tent to pulse in and out.

"Don't worry, Sam. I'll manage. I've managed so far."

"No. No, you got by. That's all. You're gonna need help. You need a juice guy."

She started to protest. Winning the battle of the parking garage, defeating the unions and the mob, that was more than getting by in her book. But she listened, happy to be having a conversation with her husband.

"What's a juice guy?"

"I'm surprised you don't know. Probably 'cause you're a woman. People don't talk to you about these things. It's how you get things done in this town." He started coughing again. "I need some water."

She brought him a glass from the kitchen and pulled back the tent. He took a few swallows. The coughs stopped. "You're a smart woman, Hat. For sure. But you don't have juice. We need help from the county, the good ole boys. Without that all your smarts won't count for nothin'."

Harriet thought about the stalled application. "So how do I get it?"

"Get ahold of that lawyer, Wildcat McDonald."

Harriet had heard the name but she had never paid much attention. "What can he do for me and how much will it cost? I ...we don't have a lot of money just now, Sam."

"I can't say, Hat. Just talk to the man. Promise me." The sunken eyes stared at her. Perhaps he was delirious, but Harriet decided to follow up. If anything, it would show Sam she still respected him.

Harriet talked to Jack to get his impression of the man.

"I can't believe I didn't think of him, Hat. Wildcat's a local hero." According to Hartman, Wildcat's size belied his accomplishments. He had led his high school football team to a State championship, playing the last two games on a sprained ankle. He graduated the spring after Pearl Harbor and enlisted in the Army the next day. He learned to fly and became a decorated Army Air Corps pilot. He was almost court-martialed for sinking a Russian freighter in the last days of the war. He and his buddies later testified it was flying a "Jap" flag. They were acquitted. He remained friends with all his army buddies, despite political differences. The friendships remained after many of the buddies left the army and got elected to various offices all over the country.

McDonald's family was already important in Nevada politics. His father was a former editor of the Nevada State Journal and a close friend of Senator Pat McCarran, a fellow descendant of Irish immigrants. The son stepped into his father's shoes. By 1960 he was a force in Nevada politics. He was powerful, opinionated and quick-tempered and not always discreet in making his views known.

"I've known Wildcat for years," Jack assured her. "You won't find a better ally, if he likes you. Do you want me to make the introduction?"

Two days later Harriet was admitted to a large, comfortable office filled with photos of famous people shaking hands with the man she was about to meet.

"Mighty pleased you came to see me, Darlin'." Wildcat's voice was surprisingly charming–like the voice of a prince coming from the little frog of a man who had greeted her at the door. He let go of her hand and sat down – whereupon most of him disappeared behind a huge desk that took up most of the room. Harriet thought about the Wizard of Oz behind his curtain and had to resist the urge to giggle.

"I've heard about you. You're a helluvawoman. Word is you brought Moe Dalitz to his knees." The sentence was punctuated by a throaty chuckle. "Is he still giving you problems?"

"No, actually, it's Clark County." Harriet had no idea why she felt completely comfortable confiding in this man. But she did. He motioned her to a chair, she sat down and told him her story.

Wildcat listened as she described the stalled application, the pending threat to the gaming license and her problems with Moe Dalitz. Harriet tried to describe all the facts as unemotionally as possible. She didn't want him to think she was a helpless female. When she finished the room was quiet. She bowed her head and took a deep breath. When she looked up he was standing by her chair. His head was just a bit taller than hers, though she was sitting down.

"Don't you worry about a thing, Darlin'. My brother-in-law is the Chairman of the County Commission. I'll get this set right in no time."

Harriet was so relieved she almost burst into tears. She grasped his hand and shook it. "Thank you so much. How much will it cost?"

He stepped back, insulted. "It's not about money, Hattie. It's about helpin' this city. After all you did for us, getting' the Convention Center, I should pay you. We need more people like you. If your casino fails Mister Dalitz will step in and pick up the pieces. That's the last thing we need. I'm surprised the Commission hasn't acted quicker on this. By the way, what do you plan to do about the gaming license?"

"I haven't even had time to think about that. And my husband, Sam, is still alive. I guess at some point I'll have to find a partner."

"Have you thought about getting a license for yourself?"

"I've never known a woman to have one. I guess I just thought that wasn't possible."

"It is for sure, Darlin'. There's been several women licensed in the downtown joints. I just helped Jessie Beck up in Reno get one. She bought the Riverside casino a few months ago. She's doin' fine. There's no reason you can't be the first woman to get a license for a place on the Strip. And it'd be my pleasure to make it happen."

He returned to his desk and sat down, studying her.

"What would I have to do to get licensed?"

"Not much. There'll be a background investigation. You haven't been in any trouble have you, Darlin'?"

"Well…I killed a couple of men in Arkansas back in 1940. But there were no charges. They were tryin' to rob us. And they shot my husband. And I was about to have a baby. So I didn't have much choice. Would that count?"

Wildcat's head bounced up and down behind his desk, his laughs exploding to the corners of the room. "Jesus Christ, Darlin'! You kill a couple of scumbags. Then you screw Moe Dalitz. You're my kinda woman!"

"So you'll help me?"

"Hell yes! You just go take care of your casino and your husband and I'll fix everything else. I should have your county permit in a week. The gaming license'll take a little longer, maybe four or five months. But don't you worry. Just keep your Sam alive 'til it comes through."

He stood up again and Harriet got up, her knees shaking with relief.

"How can I ever thank you?" She grabbed his extended hand again, pressing it between both of hers.

"Don't worry, Darlin'. There'll be ways."

◄•►▷•◈•◁•►

She stopped at the grocery store for some milk and cookies. They didn't have gingerbread but Sam liked chocolate chip, so she got a dozen of those. She paid a brief visit to the casino to let Hatch know she would be out for the rest of the day.

"You look happy, Missus. What's goin' on?"

"Don't I always look happy?"

"Hell no. You usually come in here lookin' like the sky is fallin'." That was the longest sentence she had ever heard from Hatch.

"Well, maybe I've got some help to keep the sky up. At least for a while."

He patted her arm. "Go home."

She was so excited she forgot that Opal would be there until she saw her car out front. She would give her the afternoon off. The kitchen was empty. She called out "I'm home." Opal hurried out of the bedroom door, looking disheveled.

"Is everything alright? We didn't expect you." She looked down. "I mean, I haven't done any shopping for dinner."

"Don't worry about it, Opie. You can go ahead and leave. I'll handle things here. I have something to discuss with Sam."

Harriet tried to read the look on Opal's face. Was it concern? Relief? Jealousy?

Sam was upset.

"Why'd you send Opal away? And what're we gonna do for dinner? You should have gotten something at the store."

Nothing could spoil her mood. She smiled down at her husband. "Maybe we'll just have milk and cookies. Who knows?"

Sam looked at her curiously. She returned to the kitchen.

"I'll be back in a minute. What were you talking about?"

"Oh, just things. She was telling me Zeke will be the valedictorian, And he has about a hundred girls hanging around."

"That's nice, dear." Harriet poured two glasses of milk and carried one and the plate of cookies into Sam's room.

"What's this?"

"Dinner."

He rewarded her with a wry smile. "Doesn't look all that healthy, Hat."

"I won't tell if you won't." She returned to the bedroom with the milk. Sam had parted the curtains. She turned off the oxygen.

"Don't suppose I could have a cigarette with those cookies? For dessert, sort of?"

She thought for a second. "What the hell. I'll join you." She retrieved her pack from her purse, lighted one and gave it to Sam. He took a deep, satisfied puff. She lit her own and blew a lazy smoke ring towards the ceiling.

"You're better today, Sweetheart."

"It comes and goes."

"Is Opal helping?" She watched his reaction. He blew his own smoke ring at her.

"Sure. It's great to have someone to visit with. And she's a pretty good cook." He looked at her face. "Of course, she's kind of a Nazi when it comes to smoking and such. Keeps on at me about staying healthy. That's a joke." He coughed. Harriet handed him the milk and he took a long swallow.

"I talked to Wildcat today. I really like him. And he said he'd help. That was a great idea, Sam. Thanks."

"I figured he'd take a likin' to you. He's a good person to know, though you wouldn't think it from the looks of him."

"Looks aren't everything, Sam." They exchanged looks over their glasses of milk.

"That's for sure." He looked down. "How about a cookie?"

She exchanged his cigarette for a cookie. They munched in silence.

"Good cookies." He took another swallow of milk.

"Wildcat says he thinks he can get me a gaming license. You know.... just in case..."

"It's not in case, Hat. It's when." A cough followed, along with a sigh.

"Oh, Sam. I'm so sorry. I'd do anything to save you...to help you. This wasn't how I dreamed we would turn out. And now we're about to have our dream casino. I want you to share it with me."

He handed her the milk. She put it on the side table next to the morphine pills. He took her hand.

"Believe me, Hat. I would give anything to do that. But life deals us a hand and we just have to let it play out, you know."

"I'm so happy life dealt me you, Sam."

"I'm not sure why, Hat. I ain't been nothing but trouble."

"How can you say that? You got me away from the farm."

She realized, suddenly, that she had not even told him about Ma's death. He had removed himself so far from her life. She swallowed hard. Fortunately, Sam was busy munching another cookie.

"You introduced me to this world," she continued, finally. She waved her hand towards the window. Outside they could see the desert, the distant downtown casinos and, far beyond, the mountains where Harriet's new acquisition lay, waiting to be developed. At eight thousand feet, Mt. Charleston was still capped with snow, starting to turn neon pink in the sunset.

"I used part of Dalitz's money to buy a piece of property. It's up there." She pointed towards Mt. Charleston.

"Jesus, Hat. Don't we need the money just to keep things steady around here? I mean, my expenses, the casino, everything."

She took hold of his hand. "It's beautiful. Sam. And it'll be very valuable one day. And I got it for next to nothing. How about we go for a drive up there? We can watch the lights come up on the Strip. I'll even let you smoke another cigarette."

She helped him into the car.

"It feels good to get out, Hat."

"Doesn't Opal ever take you for a drive?"

"Nah. I guess we never thought about it. I've been so sick during the day. And the morphine and all. I'm not very good company."

She asked if he wanted to try to drive. He smiled grimly.

"You better do that. I'm sure glad I taught you."

She laughed. "And I'm glad for automatic shifts."

"And paved roads," he added.

"And road signs," she contributed as they pulled out of their subdivision.

"How's Junior doing?"

Harriet was surprised he asked. She assumed Junior came home when she was out during the day. "I hardly ever see him. He was so upset when I couldn't fit in the boxing ring. But the trouble is, he never wanted to help around the casino. Never even showed up most of the time. He didn't even realize the boxing ring wasn't going in 'til the outside landscape was almost done. I'll never understand that boy."

"I know he's been a disappointment to you Hat. To both of us, I guess."

She glanced over at him. He was looking out the window.

"I love him, Sam. I wish he could be different but he is what he is. He'll always be my baby. And who knows? Maybe he'll grow up one day. He's been through a lot lately. He just doesn't handle problems well."

Sam didn't say anything.

"I love you too, Sam. You've never disappointed me."

Sam continued to look out the window. What did he see?

"You need to stay friends with Opie, Hat."

"Why would you say such a thing?"

"'Cause it's true. She wants to be your friend. She looks up to you. You have no idea."

"So what? What does that have to do with you and me?"

"She's part of us, Hat. She has been for so many years. I don't know how to explain it. You're the smart one. You put words to it. Please. Promise me."

"Of course, Sam. I'll do whatever you want. Opal's been a great help to me, taking care of you. I won't forget."

"That's true. But that's not what I'm talking about."

"It's getting dark, Sam. Maybe we'll just take a drive down the Strip instead? You can check out the Slipper."

"Sure. Whatever you want." He finally looked at her. And half-smiled "But I still get my cigarette."

Chapter 31: Strip

They drove down the length of the Strip, past the Slipper. She pointed out the lights around the entrance, the silver slipper turning slowly over the door. She asked if he wanted to go in. He said no. She didn't even try to argue.

They stopped when the casinos stopped; pulling over by the Welcome to Fabulous Las Vegas sign, now completed and lit up. They looked down at the road stretching south across the desert towards California. Harriet saw potential. She didn't ask Sam what he saw.

"The Strip, that's so ugly," he said suddenly. Bingo told me the owner of some whorehouse from Los Angeles started calling the street the Sunset Strip, and the name got shortened. Maybe somebody will come up with something nicer, something that's real Vegas." He began coughing. "I won't be around to see it, though."

They turned the car around and by that time the Strip was all-alight. The Silver Slipper was turning proudly above the entrance, shining. The mountains were disappearing into the night. They caught that magical moment between dusk and dark, when God and man fought for their attention. They pulled over again. Harriet handed another cigarette to Sam and they sat together passing it back and forth. Harriet remembered the first time Sam had lit a cigarette for her. Afterward he had kissed her, enjoying the taste of tobacco on her lips. She realized with a shock that she had not kissed him for years. Did she want him to kiss her now? In this beautiful moment?

As if in reply, Sam began to cough. This time he could not control it. A trickle of blood formed at the edge of his lips.

"We need to get back home," Harriet said.

✦ ❧ ✶ ❧ ✦

The drive haunted her dreams for the rest of her life. The setting always remained the same.... the neon snow, the lights shining down the Strip, the smell of the shared cigarette, the sky growing dark. She could never quite fix in her mind the meaning of the occasion, though. Was it their last chance? A moment wasted? Or was it some coming to terms? Some silent accord that settled matters between them forever? Or was it just an unspoken goodbye?

Sometimes in her dream they didn't turn back. They drove south through the desert towards the neon snow and it started to fall all around them. Sam stopped coughing and turned to her and suddenly they were outside in the snow and it was cleansing them and they were kissing and Sam was telling her he loved her and they were lying in their sleeping bags and he was making love to her, fast and furious and desperate before the snow melted.

Sometimes after he said he hated the name "The Strip" he turned on her. His eyes were opaque. His mouth was twisted and smoke was coming out and he said, "Please don't strip, Harriet. It wouldn't be pretty." And the smoke became blood and soon blood was everywhere.

Sam's cough grew worse as they approached the house. She had to half-carry him to his room. She was surprised how light he was. He was too weak to help himself. She wiped the sputum off his face, wrestled off his clothes and settled him into his bed with a dose of morphine. She fixed the oxygen tent around him. The sound of the zipper closing made her shudder. She turned on the oxygen. She went into the kitchen. She had forgotten to turn the calendar to March. It was March. The Ides of March.

Chapter 32: Paper

Harriet preserved two pieces of paper in gold frames and hung them on her bedroom wall, where they remained for the rest of her life. The first was the approval from the Clark County Building Department. She finished the casino and held a "locals only" grand opening. Of course, nobody checked to see if the thousands who walked through the door were locals. They spent money at the restaurants, lost money at the gaming tables and the one-arm bandits and left happy. The pre-opening gave Harriet a chance to preview the restaurant menus, the service, the staff and the arrangement of the gaming tables. She was grateful for the opportunity. She saw room for improvement everywhere. She fired some of the original staff and promoted others. She had to remove the manager of the buffet. He was skimming money. She replaced him with someone Percy Harris recommended – a Mormon. She was shocked a member of the Church of the Latter Day Saints would work in a casino.

"It's something the Church is struggling with," Harris replied thoughtfully. "It's clear we're in Las Vegas to stay, but how do we make a place here without compromising our beliefs? Anyway, that's not your problem. Keele is a terrific guy. Honest as the day is long. And hard working. He's interested in the food business. He'll make a great manager."

And Harris was right.

The second piece of paper was her gaming license. Wildcat got it for her, pretty much by explaining to the Gaming Commission that Mrs. Wilson was a heroine. "I told 'em you only shot those two bastards to save your own life, your husband's life and the life of your unborn child," Wildcat said, wiping tears from his eyes.

The license arrived in the mail in May, three days before she had to check Sam into the Vegas hospital. Opal tried to stop her, pulling at the stretcher as they loaded Sam into the ambulance.

"He has to go. It's too much for you to cope with," she told Opal. "You've done more than your share. I can't thank you enough."

'No, Harriet, you don't understand," Opal sobbed. "I want to do it. I want to be near Sam. He…he's meant so much to me. He helped me get started. I had nothing. You remember. He…both of you… took me in. He's my only friend. And you, of course."

"I understand, Opie. We'll always be friends. You and me. And Sam's responsible for that. So we both have him to thank, don't we?"

Opal looked away.

Junior showed up as they were loading his father into the ambulance. He stood, hands in pockets, back turned on his mother, watching it pull away, sirens wailing.

"Are you coming to the hospital, Junior," Harriet asked.

"Nah. I hate hospitals. Besides, I already did that with Dad, remember? Once is enough." He walked away towards his car.

"Junior!" Harriet hurried after her son. He stopped.

"He loves you, son," Harriet said. "He's not good at showing it. I love you, too. There's just you and me now. I'll have to start calling you Sam." She tried to put her arms around him. He pulled away.

"Just leave me alone," he said. He was crying.

"It's okay, Sam. It's okay to cry," she said softly. "Come on. Let's go to the hospital. We can get a bite of dinner after. We can talk about the casino. You know, with the early opening I have money to redo the tennis court and make that boxing ring."

"Really?" He smiled.

"Really. I've been meaning to tell you but you're never home.

She and Junior got into her car and drove away. In her rear view mirror she saw Opal, still standing in front of the house, looking down the street where the ambulance had gone.

<hr />

She signed all the admittance papers. The orderlies wheeled Sam into his room. There was another patient in the room. The two beds were separated by a curtain. The other man had an oxygen tent, just like Sam's. He breathed like Sam, she could hear the rasping sound through the curtain. Sam paid no attention. His eyes were closed. The nurse hung a bag by Sam's bed and stuck a needle in his arm. She hung another bag and put another needle in his other arm. She taped the needles down, adjusted the bags and left without a word.

Junior stayed at the entrance, looking down the hall, down at the floor, anywhere but at the bed where his father lay. There was nothing for her to do but put her arm around his shoulder and walk away together.

"Want to go see some property I bought, Junior? I mean, Sam?"

"Where is it?"

"It's up in the mountains. It's really beautiful. And cool, too."

"What're you gonna do with it?"

"I'm not sure yet. What do you think we should do?"

"How should I know?"

"So, want to go see it?"

"Nah. I wanna go home."

She dropped him at the house and headed for the mountains. She needed to sit there, on her land, and look down at the city and think. In the end she was glad her son had stayed home. She needed to be alone.

She picked up a handful of the mountain soil. It was different from the sand on the Strip. It wasn't full of the potential for new life like her father's farmland, but it wasn't dead either. It clung to her. Like Sam. She was surrounded by pine trees and scrubs and weeds with clusters of mustard yellow blossoms. She wished she knew the name of the plants. Her plants. She would learn the names.

She walked the boundaries of her land. North to west to south to east. She watched the sun set behind the mountains. Mount Charleston, looming above her, was already a dark outline. The shadows crept across her land and finally caught up to her, just as Las Vegas lit up three thousand feet below. She shivered. Evenings were cold in the mountains. She started for her car, but stopped. The shiver was her connection to her land. She was communicating with the cold clear air. She invited it into her body, taking deep breaths. The shivering increased. Could she become accustomed to the cold? Would it eventually feel natural? Even warm? Was the mountain asking her to test herself?

She shook herself out of the trance. "Last thing I need is to catch pneumonia," she said out loud. In response a bird called from one of the nearby trees. She got into her car and headed back home.

She parked outside the house and unlocked the door. Junior was gone. She reminded herself she had to stop calling him Junior. He had to be Sam now. He had to grow up. It was quiet inside. No sounds of coughing. There would never be those sounds in the house again. She decided she didn't want to stay home. She drove to the Slipper. The lights were so bright, flashing silver and blue across the front, a shimmering wave cresting at the big revolving silver shoe. Those lights would never go out. Casinos never closed, never went dark. Not unless there was some terrible catastrophe. They didn't even have locks on their doors. For some reason the thought gave her comfort.

Inside, the floor was just beginning to get busy. A few blackjack tables were going. She was glad she had opted to feature the big two card games–blackjack and poker–front and center. She had put the craps tables in a separate area to protect serious card players from the loud outbursts. Other casinos had large areas devoted to bingo and keno, where players could stay for hours without losing their shirts. But that meant the players took up space without making big money for the house. She wanted people to come, play and win or lose big, not hang around taking up space.

People were crowding around the Wheel of Fortune. It was spinning, the steel-tipped leather flapper clicking as it rubbed against the spokes. Eventually the wheel would come to a stop on some number and people would lose or win. She had seen people lose thousands of dollars at the Wheel of Fortune, but they kept on playing, convinced that one day the big wheel would turn their way. Just like other humans, she thought. They all believed things would go their way eventually. But so often things never turned out the way people planned.

As if to challenge her, the Wheel stopped on a number that somebody had marked with a thousand dollars. The crowd erupted in cheers. Harriet smiled to herself: "Next time, sucker."

The slots had been her one concession to cheap gambling, but only because their return was so good. She had two rows of the "one arm bandits" installed towards the back of the casino where there was no room for tables. Everyone seemed to love the slots. Ladies would come in, sit down and pump nickels, dimes and quarters into the machines for hours. Some wore white gloves, though the palms and fingers of the gloves soon turned black from the coins and handles. They watched, mesmerized, as the cherries, lemons and bananas spun around. The slot machines were busy around the clock. It was a game people could play all by themselves, Harriet thought, watching the ladies at their task.

She moved to the craps table. A ceiling fixture designed to look like a canopy hung over the table. Beneath it, an excited crowd watched every throw of the dice. She checked out the bets. Nothing much. And not very sophisticated. These people were tourists, just learning how to gamble. The big players hadn't shown up yet. In three or four hours the place would be full and both tables would be humming.

Her plan had worked. The casino was open and making money, though not enough yet to pay for construction of the boxing ring. Junior seemed to have lost interest in boxing, anyway.

The unions had backed off. She wondered if Wildcat had a hand in that. After her parking agreement with Dalitz expired he had no reason to be nice to her. And he had every reason to want to see her fail so he could get her Slipper and its coveted garage on the cheap. But he had kept his distance.

Douglas was completing the hotel floors on schedule, despite having to work above the casino. It wasn't the best way to finish construction, having to make accommodations for an operating business under their feet, but they managed. She managed. She managed everything. Now she would have to. Alone. She looked back at the ladies at the slots playing in the shadows, alone, and felt a sudden kinship.

People came up to say hello and ask about Sam. Many of them knew her. Others knew who she was. She told them he was doing fine in the hospital. They mumbled something and walked away. She noticed, for the first time, how so many of them were couples. They made her feel even more alone. She looked around for Hatch. He had a new title, head of security. He had his own office now. It had a desk and a chair and a phone. Nothing else. The desk was regular size but it looked too small for him. He was seldom there, anyway. He stalked the floor watching for trouble like a lion looking for prey. She would be standing by some gaming table watching the action and suddenly have a feeling she was being watched. There Hatch would be, standing in the shadows.

She let herself into her office next to the cage. She had decided to have the office built out even though when the building was finished the offices would be on the second floor. She had a beautiful walnut desk with a leather chair and shiny black phone. She would have an even nicer space when they moved. She looked forward to going to LA to pick out some artwork. Maybe she would ask Jack if he wanted to come along. She would tell him she needed his help. They could spend the weekend. Somehow the thought didn't give her as much pleasure as she expected.

She shuffled through the papers on her desk, trying without much success to focus. She glanced over the bank statement and smiled. It would make Percy happy. She was "on target" as he liked to say. There was money for the quarterly interest payment and even a small reduction in principal, and she was paying for the balance of the completion costs out of cash flow. She would not need to borrow the full amount the bank had committed. And the bank had already agreed to close into a ten-year term loan that would get them well on the road to success. They were set to close in November when the construction loan came due.

She still didn't think of the numbers on the bank statement as real money. Her real money, the green bills wrapped in bundles tied with string, was buried in the safe in the back yard. That money she could hold in her hands and count and smell and plan with.

She had her eye on more real estate. She had managed to save enough to take out options on some interesting parcels in the mountains and some on the outskirts of downtown. She loved to drive around and look at potential acquisitions. When she was sure about a parcel she tried to get an option. It was her favorite form of shopping. She wasn't sure why she was attracted to a particular plot. Most were vacant—she enjoyed thinking about the potential of an empty piece of land. If something appealed to her she would get out of her car and walk around it, looking at the view from the ground. She always knelt down and took a handful of dirt and let it run through her fingers, testing it for some undefined quality.

She decided on the spot, yes or no.

She kept a black notebook listing each of the lots she had taken an option on and the due date and exercise price. She listed other lots she wanted to buy. She wrote down the lot description, the broker or seller and a price she would be willing to pay. In cash. Always. She promised herself she would never borrow money again. Under the lot information she wrote her impressions and whether it was a "must have" (number 1) a "like if the price is right" (number 2) and a "possible bargain buy" (number 3).

She was pretty sure she could take her time...nobody else was buying where she was looking. She wouldn't make her move until after November, when she closed on the new loan and didn't have Percy looking over her shoulder every minute.

She took one last look at her notebook, examining each of her potential purchases, adding some new ideas about a parcel she had listed a week ago. Her notes were in pencil so she could erase and rewrite as things changed.

She tucked the book in her purse, arranged the papers on her desk into piles according to priority, turned off the lights and closed and locked the door to her office.

"On your way home, Miss Harriet?" That was Edward, one of the security guards. Hatch had hired him. She loved all of them. She was learning all of their names and all about their families. Edward's wife was expecting their first. She invested a good deal of money in their uniforms. The guards took pride in their job and they were all very protective of her. Hatch made sure they all called her "Miss Harriet". She wasn't sure why he had come up with that name. She smiled up at the big man.

"Yep. I'll see you tomorrow, Edward."

He escorted her to her car.

Chapter 33: Home

She had nowhere else to go. She started the car and headed home. She was grateful for the long days of late spring, the house didn't seem quite so lonely in the evening light. She reminded herself she should turn the entry light on when she left for the day.

The house was still quiet. Junior was gone, as usual. Well, she would get a good night's sleep at least. She turned on the TV and sat for a while, but she wasn't able to focus on what she was watching. She decided the TV was old. She had heard color TV sets were becoming much more reliable. She would have liked to watch the Walt Disney's show, "The Wonderful World of Color" on a color TV, but they cost almost a thousand dollars. And there weren't that many programs in color anyway. Maybe she would splurge after November. To celebrate.

She walked slowly down the hall into her room, past the master bedroom. Out of habit, she went to check on Sam. He wasn't there, of course. He would never be there again.

"I'll be able to move back in," she told herself out loud. "I'll redo the master bedroom. I can start tomorrow. I'll get rid of Sam's bed and all his stuff and have it painted. Maybe I'll put in new carpet. Wall to wall."

She opened the closet door. It was full of Sam's stuff. She had moved her clothes to the back bedroom so she wouldn't disturb Sam in the mornings. "I need to call the Mesquite Club and ask if I can donate Sam's clothes. There must be plenty of folks who would want these things. They're all in good condition," she told herself, picking through the suits and shirts. She realized Sam hadn't worn any of the clothes for months. When was the last time he had gotten dressed? She tried to remember the day. The last day.

She hadn't thought of it before, that there was a last day for everything. The last day she had seen her ma and pa. The last day she had held Junior. The last day she had made love with Sam. The last days would happen to Sam and her and everyone. Just like the Wheel of Fortune stopped spinning.

"I'll call the Mesquite Club tomorrow," she told herself. The club was the local charity organization, started by the wives of the city's original settlers, the "pioneer families". They had come to Las Vegas in 1905, before the casinos, back when the railroad had started the town and auctioned off lots for as low as a hundred dollars. Seven-fifty for a corner lot. The ladies of the club were proud of their heritage. They didn't let newcomers in unless they were descendants of the "founders." But they would accept donations from anybody. And they were friendly enough. She had met two of the original members at the opening of the convention center – Mrs. Clark and Mrs. Stewart. They were charming and gracious, complementing her on her contributions to their city. She enjoyed talking to them about the "early days" when Fremont Street was just a dusty road with a few stores. Like Selma. They remembered the thirties when Nevada had legalized gambling, and how Fremont Street began filling up with saloons. The ladies had tried to fight it, but it was a losing battle. They had watched with dismay as grifters and drunks replaced hard-working railroad men and construction workers who had built the dam.

"Fremont isn't what it used to be," they said in unison, shaking their heads sadly. Maybe your convention center will help change things for the better."

They described with horror the first neon sign on the street—the "Boulder Club", how it "disturbed the neighborhood" because it stayed on all night. Now the neighborhood was Glitter Gulch and the ladies of the Mesquite Club had moved away from downtown.

Harriet was interested in where they had moved. Had they thought of moving up to the mountains where it was cooler? No, they had never thought of that. They looked at her like she had suggested they move to the moon. They just moved farther out, to the new suburbs that were springing up around the valley. She had options on several parcels between Glitter Gulch and the suburbs, expecting them to fill in with stores and businesses.

The ladies were in their eighties now, their husbands long gone. Just like hers would be.

She shifted her focus back to the master bedroom. She decided she would stay in the back room for a while. She would move into the master bedroom after it was redone. She liked the back room. It was the coolest room in the house and she could see the city lights from the window. She brushed her teeth, scrubbed her face, slipped on her nightgown and lay down, looking out the window. She realized she had never thought of the lights as disturbing the neighborhood. She loved to lie in bed and watch the neon tubes creating letters and fountains and runways of light, twirling, spinning, turning the sky pink, then blue, then white. Until she fell asleep.

Chapter 34: Something Else

Harriet's life took on a new rhythm. She got up in the morning and fixed herself breakfast. She dressed and went to the hospital to visit Sam. He was usually clear-headed in the mornings right after he woke up. She sat with him while he ate his breakfast. Then she went to the casino. She treated herself to lunch at one of her favorite restaurants. Sometimes Jack joined her, but she got the impression he felt uncomfortable around her. So many people were, they didn't know how to treat her. Jack seemed reluctant to talk about Sam's situation and what would happen after he died. Their talk got more and more impersonal—the weather, the business, the city.

Once in a while she lunched with Wildcat. She loved talking to him, but he was rarely available. "I'm doin' the Lord's work," he would say. Which meant he was strong-arming somebody for something. And when they did have lunch it was like being with a celebrity. They could hardly get a bite to themselves. Sometimes a man would just pull up a chair at their table, offer to buy them drinks, and start talking to Wildcat without waiting for an answer like she wasn't even there. Harriet got upset but Wildcat just smiled.

"You might need that guy one day, Hat. And folks have long memories around here. Remind him of the time the two of you had lunch with me. And be nice." In time she realized that being seen in his company was important—it singled her out as a mover and shaker in the town. And being in the middle of the beehive that was

Wildcat's world took her mind off Sam. The little man was the only person who wasn't bothered by Sam's situation.

"How's he doin'?" he would ask, taking her hand and looking into her face like he cared about the answer.

And she would tell him, honestly, because she knew she could.

"You need to get ready," he told her one day.

"For what?"

"For when he passes. Have you thought about a service? Where to hold the burial? Sam has lots of friends, you know. They don't want to come around now – too uncomfortable. Nobody likes to look at death. Afraid it'll look right back at 'em. But once he goes—well—they'll all show up in their finest to pay their respects. You'll see. And it'll be a big occasion for you, too." He gave her hand a squeeze. "It'll be hard but it'll also be the beginning of a new life for you, Hat. You won't be Sam's wife any more. Hell, you haven't been Sam's wife for quite a while." He saw the shock on her face and squeezed her hand harder. "I mean, you're your own person, Darlin'. You've made a way for yourself without him. But folks don't know how to treat you, 'cause of him. He's been holding you back." His grip tightened, preventing her from pulling away. "Once he passes they won't have to worry about that. Hell, the casino folks already call you Miss Harriet. And that's what you'll be. So you need to get ready, is all I'm saying."

"And how would I do that, exactly?"

"Plan a big shindig. I'll make sure everybody who's anybody in this city shows up. We'll line up some speakers to talk about Sam, what a great guy he was, how much he did for the city."

'What did he do for the city?"

"Hell, Hattie, that's not the point. People get paid to say these things. I'll get Mayor Gragson. He'll love to speak. He can talk about how Sam and you were a team. Equals. The two of you contributed so much to the city, with helping start the visitor's bureau and the convention center and all. He's big on equal rights and stuff. It'll be a great promotion for you. He'll let everybody know he considers you one of our civic leaders. I can hear him now— 'It was Sam Wilson's dying wish. His wife will carry on his vision….'"

Wildcat was getting all teary-eyed.

Harriet giggled. "You are something else, Wildcat. I never thought of Sam's dying as a promotional event."

"That's my point, Sweetheart. Leave it to me."

She saw Opal more than she wanted. Why had she assumed the two would part company once Sam was in the hospital? It turned out the opposite. She saw Opal almost every day, sitting in Sam's room. Opal was there in the morning before her and in the evening when she came for a visit.

"Don't you have anything else to do, Opie," she asked every few days, trying to keep the irritation out of her voice.

"Not really," Opal would say. Her answer was always the same. She would get up, vacating the chair beside Sam's bed and leave a few minutes after Harriet came in.

Opal invited her to Ezekiel's high school graduation, and she was happy to attend. Neither woman mentioned Sam. They sat together and cheered as their protégé marched down the aisle at the head of the class. Harriet was as proud as if he had been her own son.

Ezekiel gave the commencement address. He talked about Las Vegas and the class's obligation to contribute to their city.

"This is a young city," he said. "Kinda like us. Just starting out. It needs our help. And it will reward us for everything we do. We give and it gives back."

Harriet smiled. Opal was angry. "I don't know why he's talking about staying here. He promised me we would leave as soon as he's able to get a good job somewhere else."

"He's young, Opie. Maybe he's torn between what you want and what he sees. You need to let him be his own man. I'm sure he'll succeed in whatever he does. And I'm sure he loves you and will take care of you whatever happens."

Opal shrugged. Ezekiel joined then, looking devastatingly handsome as usual in his gown.

"I want to take you to lunch to celebrate," Harriet told them. "But I have a feeling Zeke would like to be with his friends today." She could see a crowd of good-looking youngsters who were obviously waiting for their friend.

"Thanks, Aunt Hat." He wrapped her in a big hug. "And thanks for the graduation present. You're the greatest!"

She had given him a thousand dollars cash in an envelope.

"Don't tell the IRS," she joked.

Ezekiel never took her up on her lunch offer, but in August she had lunch with Opal. She seemed to suffer more than Harriet when Sam had a bad day, which happened more and more often.

"He didn't eat anything," Opal said as she walked in one morning in late August. "They say they're gonna start him on intravenous." She started crying. Thank heavens Sam was asleep. Harriet pulled her out of the room.

"Opal, get a hold of yourself. Sam is going to die. There's nothing we can do about that except to keep him company and make him comfortable." For some reason she thought of what Wildcat had said about Sam's funeral and felt a flood of guilt. Before she knew it she had invited Opal to lunch.

"He's all I have," Opal sobbed over their soup. "Him and Ezekiel. And you, of course." She looked at Harriet, like a child caught stealing.

"Opal," Harriet whispered. People were staring at them, "Why do you say those things? Why are you so wrapped up in Sam? Sam is my husband. He's all I have. I don't have a son like Zeke. I hardly ever see Junior. Sometimes I think he could care less about me. All he wants is money. Sam doesn't belong to you. He belongs to me. I know you're his friend and all, and he means a lot to you, but that's it. He's just a friend. Maybe you should stop coming to the hospital."

"No!" The restaurant suddenly got quiet. "He needs me," Opal hissed. "He loves you, Hat. But he loves me, too."

"That's enough!" Harriet pushed back her chair and grabbed her purse. Opal grabbed her arm. The whole restaurant was watching.

"Please, Hat. Please sit down. I have to say this and you have to listen. You're the smartest, brightest woman we've ever known, Sam and me. Even Zeke says you're a genius. We could never be like you. Well, maybe Zeke one day but not me and Sam. It's…it's intimidating. Even before Sam got sick he couldn't keep up with you. And every time he dropped the ball you picked it up and ran with it. Better'n he ever could. He tried, at least. He really needed to prove he was the man around the house. But he couldn't. When he was with me he felt good. I made him feel strong and smart. A man needs that, Hat."

"This lunch is over." Harriet tried to tear her arm away.

"Please don't be angry, Hat. Please. I can't help being what I am. And you can't fight against your nature. And if you think you want to get back at me for that, for what Sam and I have…had… remember; when he's gone you still have your life…all your friends and the casino and your property. And I'll have nothing. No one but Zeke and even he will leave after a while. And I'll be alone. God is punishing me for everything I've ever done wrong."

Opal was crying quietly. Somehow that touched Harriet more than the loud sobbing. It sounded helpless. Lost.

Harriet sat back down, ignoring the curious stares. "Did he tell you he loved you?" Harriet had to know.

"No. You know he's not good about saying things like that. But he told me he loved you."

"He said that? He used those words?"

"Sure. Lots of times. He said he loved you so much but he was always letting you down no matter how he tried. He can't tell his feelings to your face. I don't know why. He just can't. And something else, Hat. I think he needs to tell you he's afraid right now. Really afraid. But he can't. Even after all this, he has to be strong for you." Opal said quietly. "I don't think he ever will tell you, even at the end. He'll never tell any of us to our faces. Not you or me. He'll never say how much love is in him. Not even to Junior, his own son."

"He told me I had to take care of you," Harriet said, finally, softly.

"He did? Really?"

"Yep. He said we should be friends. He told me you wanted to be my friend."

"Oh, I do, Hat. More than anything. And Zeke, too. We've known each other for so long. And you've done so much for Zeke and me I know I haven't been much of a friend to you. But I want to be."

Harriet thought about Christmas Eve and the gingerbread cookies. And how Opal had taken care of Sam so she could tend to her business. And how she had let her do that, even suspecting there was something between them. Just so she could do her work. She had fought so hard for the convention center. For the casino. Even for her property in the mountains. But she had never fought for Sam. She looked across at the beautiful face watching her with hope and concern. How was it that beauty counted for so much? Opal had powers that Harriet would never have no matter how hard she fought. Without lifting a finger, just by smiling, Opal could make magic. She could make Sam feel better. Even now at the end.

She reached across and patted Opal on the knee. "I think it's gonna be alright with us, Opie. I just need some time. And we need to see Sam out. Both of us. Together."

Opal said something in return but Harriet didn't hear it. She was looking at her future and thinking about getting home, and getting on. And maybe being something else from what she was.

Chapter 35: Things Happen in Threes

Things happen in threes. So Harriet's mother always said.

"What things?" Harriet would ask.

"Just things," Ma would reply knowingly.

The first thing happened on November 1. She got her completion certificate from the County Building Department right on time, with Wildcat's help. He wanted to arrange a grand opening with all the city notables present. Jack featured the casino, and her role as the developer and manager in an article on the front page of the Review Journal. He wanted to put her picture in the article but she absolutely refused. "Put a picture of the Slipper. We need the publicity."

Percy came to her office to close on the financing. She signed and initialed each page. Beside her name was another blank.

"We need Sam's signature," Percy said.

"How do we do that? He's in a coma."

"Oh, dear. I didn't realize."

"I didn't even think about telling you. I'm sorry. He's been in the hospital for so long, sometimes I forget he was part of all this."

"I'm not quite sure what to do. The bank requires both of you to sign all of the loan documents. I've never had a situation where the co-signor is alive but unable to sign. And he was the principal borrower, you realize."

"So what do we do," Harriet asked.

"I'll have to go back to the head office and explain."

"But the construction loan is due. I don't want to go into default and have some sort of problem. Not with everything else I have to face right now."

'I understand, Hattie. I'm sorry I didn't think of this. Things have been going so well with the construction and all. It just slipped my mind. But I'm sure it won't be a problem to get a brief extension while we sort this thing out. I'll be in touch."

Percy gathered the precious papers and put them in his briefcase.

"Wait." Harriet motioned to his chair and he sat back down.

"Sam's not going to get any better. That means I'll have to be the borrower. Will the bank have a problem with that?"

"To tell you the truth, Harriet, I don't know. I'll talk to them and get back to you."

Harriet watched his retreating back, trying to read his posture. Did he look confident, worried, defeated? She had come so far, fought so many battles. How could this trip her up at the last minute? She would have to postpone the grand opening. That was never a good thing. It shook people's confidence.

"What the hell kind of banker is he?" Wildcat harrumphed. "Maybe I need to get their banking license pulled, the SOBs."

"Please don't do that, Wildcat. I have enough problems as it is. I need them to work with me, at least until I can find some solution. And I need you to postpone the grand opening. Find some excuse."

"No problem, Darlin'. I've got another big event planned for Governor Sawyer. I was tryin' to work that one around the opening, but now I don't have to."

At least she could honor the hotel reservations. All the rooms were full, despite the fact that November was typically a slow month. She had managed to book Shecky Greene for the showroom. He was one of the most popular comedians in the country. On a whim, she decided to have a young singer who had made a big hit on the Jackie Gleason show recently for Greene's warm up act. The kid,

Wayne Newton, had just released his first song, *Danke Schoen*. Everybody loved it. Wildcat worked his magic and the grand opening would be moved forward to December 1. She would have to find some more great entertainment for that weekend. But that was the least of her problems. She prayed that by then everything would be settled.

She had developed a new routine, going to the casino early in the morning and returning home late at night. She decided to put off redecorating her house for a while so she could devote all her time to the casino and Sam.

The second week in November Sam's doctor asked if she planned to be out of town before year-end.

"No, I've got a ton of work here. We're having the grand opening December 1 and I'm sure there will be lots of loose ends to take care of between then and New Years. We're having a big New Years Eve celebration. I hope you can make it, Doc."

"The reason I ask is because I'm not sure Sam's going to make it to next year. He could go very quickly, Harriet." He put his hand on her shoulder. "I just want to be sure you're around. And prepared."

Harriet tried to avoid his eyes. So much was happening very quickly. The bank loan could go wrong, Sam could die. What else could happen? She lay in bed nights, eyes fixed on her window, worrying.

Thanksgiving was coming. The weather was turning colder. The holidays made Harriet think of home. She wondered how Pa was doing without Ma. He always managed to shoot a turkey for their feast. She would help her ma pluck it and make cornbread stuffing. The family hunted together for mushrooms and walnuts that grew wild in the woods. Her last Thanksgiving at home, Pa brought a keg of whisky. "To celebrate," he said. Their lives had gotten better that year, she remembered. He poured five glasses, a few swallows in each, and all the older children had joined their parents in a toast.

Harriet still remembered how the stuff burned all the way down her throat but she was too grown up to cough.

Where would she be this Thanksgiving? She decided she would spend the day with Sam even if he was hardly ever conscious these days. They had increased the morphine so he was out of his mind most of the time, and when he was awake he was in so much pain she wished he were back asleep. It hurt to be around him. But she would be there.

Junior never came to see his dad, or her either, except at the casino, where he dropped by with a bunch of unsavory types and bummed meals off her. She heard him bragging that the place was his. She never heard him talk about her, or the work she had done. She was worried about him and about herself. The casino had been such a wonderful idea–something their family was going to build and share together. Instead it had turned into a nightmare. It was probably contributing to Junior's spoiled attitude and without Sam the financing had become tangled in the bank bureaucracy. Harriet's life seemed to be a series of problems. Thinking about Thanksgiving made her wonder if the casino was worth it. Was she thankful for the Silver Slipper? It gave her something to do but that was a small return on all the effort and time she put in, all the sleepless nights she had sacrificed.

She knew Opal would be at the hospital. Maybe they would just have the Thanksgiving special at the casino buffet and then she could head up the mountain to her property. It might be snowing up there. She loved the smell of snow in the woods.

◆◆◆✳◆◆

She was sitting at her desk Friday morning the week before Thanksgiving, preparing for a busy weekend, when the phone rang.

"Mrs. Wilson?" Her stomach flopped against her ribs.

"Speaking."

"This is the hospital. The doctor said you should come as soon as possible. It's your husband."

She ran out the door, dropping papers as she went, her heart pounding. Then she remembered Junior. And Opal. She had to let them know.

"Miss Harriet? Are you alright?" It was Hatch. He always seemed to appear out of nowhere when she needed him.

"I've got to get to the hospital. It's Sam. Please find Junior and call Opal Cullen and let them know this might be the end. They should come right away." Then she was out the door running for her car.

She had no idea how fast she was going, whether there were lights or stop signs. She remembered passing cars and thinking how strange it was that other people were going places. She ran through the lobby up the stairs to Sam's room.

She noticed that the other bed, the one beside Sam, was empty. Nurses and the doctor surrounded Sam's bed. They turned to look at her. The scene had a strange unreal quality; she thought she might wake up at any minute.

"He went into cardiac arrest a few minutes ago. We tried to revive him. We're so sorry, Mrs. Wilson."

Opal came through the door behind her and stood, looking wide-eyed at the crowd around Sam. Harriet's first thought was to tease Opal about how she had managed to get to the hospital so fast. But then she saw the look on Opal's face change slowly to horror. Her voice came out in a whisper, as if the sight had taken the breath from her. "Oh my God. Oh, no. Please no."

Harriet turned and took Opal in her arms. Opal wrapped her arms around Harriet and they cried on each other's shoulders.

The nurses and doctor left quietly. She heard the door close. She let go of Opal and the two women walked to Sam's bed. His eyes and mouth were closed. They had taken all the needles out of his arms and they were hanging limply from the bags. The sheets were rumpled, as if Sam had been having a bad dream. But Sam was perfectly still.

Harriet sat on one side of the bed and Opal on the other. Each took one of his hands. Harriet could feel the hand growing cold in her own. She rubbed it, trying to keep it warm. She wished she could have been there in the end to say goodbye. But she knew that Sam hadn't been up to saying anything for a while. She tried to remember the last time they spoke to each other. She couldn't. At first, when Sam was checked in and she knew it was close to the end, she had taken each of their conversations home with her and treasured it, knowing it might be the last. But one day followed on the next and the next and there were so many goodbyes and she stopped keeping track of what was said. And now she couldn't remember. And she felt like she had let her husband down somehow.

"Goodbye Sam. I love you," she said, kissing his hand. This time she would wait for an answer forever. She thought she was ready for this, but she would never be ready. She told herself that he was at peace, that his suffering was over, but it didn't help. Absolutely nothing helped the pains that were shooting through her. She lowered her head slowly to his chest and cried. And there was no one in the world except Sam and her.

She wasn't aware of time passing until she heard Opal calling her name. She looked up. Opal was standing by the bed.

"Are you okay?"

Harriet smiled to herself. It was strange that Opal was playing the comforter now. They would take turns. "Yes, I'm alright, Opie. Did you want to spend a few minutes with him?"

"No, thanks. It wouldn't help." Opal wasn't crying any more. Her voice was lifeless, resigned.

"I guess we need to take care of things."

She wondered where Junior was. She called the casino. The

operator told her Hatch wasn't there. She suspected he might be out looking for her son.

"Mrs. Wilson....do you know what's happened?" The operator sounded frightened.

"Yes. I'll handle it. Don't worry." She hung up.

She pulled the sheet over Sam's head. She didn't know if that was what she should do but it felt right to her. Then she and Opal walked out of the room.

Harriet was surprised when they reached the lobby. There was a large crowd, doctors and nurses and others, standing at the reception desk. Some people were crying. Sam's doctor walked up to her, obviously upset.

"Don't worry, Doc. You did all you could."

"No. That's not it. You haven't heard. President Kennedy's been shot. He's dead."

Chapter 36: Thanksgiving

Was it a good thing or a bad thing that Sam had died on the same day as President Kennedy? Harriet could never decide. In a way it was bad. Her grief was swallowed whole by the grieving nation. Even Junior seemed more upset about the President than about his father. Hatch had finally found him and brought him to the hospital but it was an hour later and she had already left. Hatch brought him home. The three of them stayed home together, the first time in months they had been in the same house. Junior didn't say a word. He turned on the television to watch the news coverage. Hatch just stood by the door, like a guard at attention.

"Are you all right, missus?"

"I'll be alright Hatch. Thanks."

"I'm sorry." He turned and left without another word.

There was no Thanksgiving. No grand opening. The casinos that were never supposed to close all closed. They stood, lights turned off in mute tribute, doors tied shut with black bands, black-banded guards in front. Harriet brought each of her guards, standing straight and blowing on their hands to keep them warm, a hot turkey sandwich from the restaurant. The hotel had a few guests but they all huddled around television sets watching the drama unfold. The funeral, the shooting of Oswald, the new president. The widow with her two small children.

Sam's big funeral celebration never happened. Things were so chaotic that Wildcat was unable to arrange any memorial service. She heard he had gone to Washington to meet with the new President. She had no idea his contacts reached that high.

In another way the timing was good. She decided that she didn't want to make a public display of herself. She didn't want to see Opal for a while. She and Junior sat in front of the TV and watched. Junior finally reached for her hand. He was crying. They could both cry now without being specific about the cause of their grief.

When their tears stopped Harriet told Junior stories of how she had met Sam, of running away from the farm; of the night he was born, of their trip across the west with Bingo and Hatch and Weasel. Junior told stories about Sam in the Elks Lodge in San Antonio, trying to keep him from emptying the customer's drinks, taking him to the bathroom when he had to throw up, teaching him how to hold a deck of cards, how to cut the deck, how to deal. Harriet was amazed that all the spankings, all the nasty names Sam had called Junior, had been wiped from her son's mind. He remembered the good times. She was grateful for that.

Harriet took her cue from Junior. She remembered the good times. Their travels, together, the fun with Mike and Lucy, getting run out of town by the sheriff, eating fresh-caught fish from the mighty Mississippi. The day Sam proposed. Their first Christmas in Las Vegas. The fun they had planning the casino, all sitting around the kitchen table with the milk and cookies. People pictured Death as coming with a scythe. For her it came with an eraser. It wiped out all the bad memories and left only the happiness.

In the end she decided to have Sam cremated. There was hardly anything left of him to bury, and she didn't like the thought of him alone in the ground. She got his ashes in a little urn, which she kept in her bedroom. One day she would go back to the Mississippi and spread his ashes on the water. They would float down to New Orleans. The mob there might get upset—one of Bingo's guys sneaking into their territory. The thought made her smile.

The assassination stalled the bank's decision as well. Finally, on December fifth, Percy Harris called.

"Can you come by the office?"

She could tell by his voice that it was not good news.

"How are you holding up, Harriet?" He was polite. She had to decide whether to play on his sympathy or show her strength.

"I'm doing well, Percy. How are you?" Her voice was calm.

"I'm okay, Harriet but I have some bad news." He shuffled the papers on his desk. "The folks in Salt Lake are nervous. I tried to explain that you've been the backbone of this operation for a year, even longer. But you're a woman. They've never dealt with a woman borrower before at least not in the gambling business. The LDS is a pretty male-dominated group, you know."

"I see. So what does that mean for me?"

"They suggest you sell the casino. Or look for another lender. They'll give you plenty of time to do it. We don't want to scare off potential buyers or lenders. Say, a year?"

"So they'll extend the loan for a year?"

"Yes. I might be able to get a bit more time but right now that's where they are."

She took a deep breath. She realized she hadn't done that in quite a while. She let it out, smiling. Harris looked up, surprised.

"You don't seem very unhappy about this, Hat."

"At least I know where I stand."

"I tried my best. I swear to you. This is so unfair, after you've worked so hard – miracles, really."

"I still have some miracles left in me, Percy. But next time they'll be for my own pleasure."

Chapter 37: No Problem

"You have to do what???" Jack almost fell backwards in his chair.

"Sell the Slipper or find a new lender. Harris won't close the loan now Sam's gone."

"How much time do you have?"

"A year. Maybe a little more. So do you have any ideas?"

He looked at her carefully. "Moe Dalitz would dance a jig to buy it from you, but I assume you don't want to give him the satisfaction."

"On the other hand, if I sold to Dalitz it'd be a black eye for Harris. At this point I don't see much difference between the two."

"There might not be much difference, Hat. The Mormons and the mob are closer than you might think, at least when it comes to money."

"Jesus. Anyway, you're right. I don't want to sell to Dalitz unless he's my last resort."

"Hopefully he won't learn about your predicament."

"Harris wouldn't tell him, would he?"

Her question was answered a week later. Dalitz called and asked if they could meet.

"I can't believe Percy told Dalitz about the loan," she said to Wildcat over drinks. "Why the hell would he do such a thing? He knows how much trouble that man has caused me."

"Bankers are sons of bitches, Hat. Harris might be all sympathy to your face, but his bosses want this loan off their books and the mob is ready and willing to buy. If it makes any difference, I'll do what I can to make that Mormon bastard regret his big mouth."

Harriet rode the elevator to the Desert Inn executive offices, her stomach knots tightening with each ding. The guard who accompanied her showed her to a lobby and spoke briefly to a well-dressed receptionist, who looked at her and pressed a button on an intercom.

"He'll just be a minute," the woman told her. But it was more than a minute. It was almost half an hour before another woman appeared and motioned for her to follow.

Dalitz was in a jovial mood. "I hear you're havin' to sell the Slipper," he said, shaking her hand. "I wanted to let you know I'm interested. But you already knew that, right?" He laughed.

"Where did you get that idea, Mr. Dalitz?" She took some small satisfaction in his reaction. Maybe he would tell her the source of his information.

"Vegas is a small town, Mrs. Wilson. Word gets around. And a widow like yourself, well, a casino's a lot to handle."

"Well, I'm sorry to disappoint you. I'm not interested in selling right now."

His eyes widened then narrowed behind the coke bottle lenses of his glasses. "I see. Well perhaps I was misled. If you do decide to sell I hope you'll give me a chance. I can make you a very attractive offer. Right now, that is. Things could change later of course."

"Of course," she replied. "But I'm not interested right now."

❖

"So you didn't even hear what he had to say," the newspaperman shook his head.

"I just couldn't do it. I thought I could but I just couldn't, Jack. There has to be some other way."

"Maybe Wildcat has some suggestions."

"I'm workin' behind the scenes to put pressure on Harris's head office," Wildcat said. "It's one thing to turn a woman down for a loan. It's another to tell the mob about a customer's predicament. That's pretty low, even for a banker. Maybe I can get them to change their minds. But in the meantime, you need to look for other lenders."

"Like who?"

"Like the banks the Teamsters control. Continental Illinois Bank in Chicago, for example. They're the major source of money in this town."

"But isn't that just Dalitz in another suit?"

"Not necessarily, Hat. First, they're lenders. Dalitz wants to buy. Second, Continental Illinois is a federally chartered bank so they have to hide their brass knuckles. They're not as bad as they were in the old days. Meaning they have to act on the up and up."

"Sounds to me like just two heads of the same monster, but I'm happy to talk to them. Can you get me a contact?"

"I'll do two things, Hat. I'll get you a contact and I'll get you a good lawyer. 'Cause you don't want to go to those guys alone."

Chapter 38: Who's To Say?

Harriet had never been to Chicago. She was impressed by the city sprawling along the shores of Lake Michigan. Wildcat had arranged a suite for her at the Palmer House, his favorite Chicago hotel. She almost tripped over a suitcase as she entered the huge lobby with its painted ceiling and gilded crown moldings. She stared, transfixed.

The bellman laughed. "It happens to a lot of people, Ma'am. Looks more like the Sistine Chapel than a hotel, don't it. Mr. Potter Palmer, he had some grand ideas. And his wife, well, she was even grander."

"And they were worth it," she said, admiring the Chinese ceramic vases holding potted plants that accented the spacious lobby seating. She decided she would redecorate the Slipper hotel to make it look more like the Palmer House. "If I can keep it," she reminded herself.

Her new lawyer, Matt Butler, joined her for dinner.

"I've spoken to their lawyer and sent him all our information. I have to say, you've done a wonderful job with the Slipper, Mrs. Wilson. I'd be amazed if the Teamsters wouldn't be interested in this loan." He smiled at her. "Of course, you have to realize that the Teamsters' ultimate goal will be to get control of the Slipper. So today we just listen to what they have to say and tell them we'll get back to them. You should think of them as a last resort."

"I guess they'll be my next to last resort. I already have a last." She told him about Dalitz.

"You are a lady in distress if I ever saw one," he said, patting her shoulder. "This casino business is tough even for a man. How'd you come to get involved?"

She told him her story. He seemed to listen with genuine interest. Wildcat had said he was a good man. When she had finished, Butler shook his head in amazement. "Wildcat said you'd surprise me. He was sure right. I'm gonna do whatever I can to make this work for you, Mrs. Wilson."

"Call me Hat." She shook his hand warmly. He paid the bill and she escorted him through the magnificent lobby to the entrance.

"Get a good night's sleep," he ordered. "You'll need it."

A hot breath of air blasted through the door, accompanying his departure. Chicago heat. It was different from Las Vegas—more humid but equally unpleasant. And it reminded her that six months of her year had already been used up and she was nowhere. She and Jack and Wildcat had followed every lead, explored every opportunity with no success. No lenders. No buyers. Not even any partners willing to take a piece of the Slipper in exchange for help with financing.

"I'm stickin' to Fremont Street, Hat," Bingo had told her in response to her invitation to invest. "The Strip's gotten too dangerous, even for a man. And you're a woman. Now don't take offense." He pushed her gently back into her seat. "I know you're a hell of a woman. But today the casino business is high finance and high risk. I'm happy to stick downtown with my place and the locals and the small fish. The dollar a night folks, as they say. It's a lot less stressful. And safer." He looked at her carefully. "You got a bodyguard, Hat?"

She laughed. "Of course not, Bingo. They wouldn't hurt a woman, would they?"

"Who's to say?"

<hr />

She had thought seriously about resisting Wildcat's offer to find a good lawyer. It would be another expense and she was quickly running out of money. But as she and Butler approached the Continental Illinois' offices on State Street she was glad she had agreed. Even the building was intimidating. The front door was a solid steel structure that looked like it was intended to ward off gunfire. Butler announced their presence into a speaker and the door opened a crack to reveal a pudding-faced man in uniform who looked like he was having a bad day. Harriet was reminded of Hatch but quickly learned the two men were very different. There was no softness to this man. She could almost smell the bad temper-it followed him like the odor of garlic on his clothes.

"We're here to see Mr. DiFigueroa. Mr. Butler and Mrs. Wilson. We're expected." Butler announced calmly.

Pudding Face opened the door to admit them. Harriet found herself in a small well-lit entry guarded by yet another steel door. Their escort pushed a button and the door opened. Harriet caught her breath. They were admitted to a mahogany and steel masterpiece.

"It's beautiful." She couldn't help herself. "But it doesn't look like a bank. Not the banks I know."

"That's 'cause it's a different kind of bank. Not the kind you make deposits in, the kind that lends money and makes deals. And some of the deals might cause these bankers a bit of trouble. Borrowers can get very unhappy when things go bad."

"Who designed it?"

"What?"

She laughed. "The bank. Not the trouble."

"Oh, Louis Sullivan," Butler told her. She had no idea who that was.

"Does he design casinos?"

Butler laughed, upsetting Pudding Face. "He's out of the picture,

I'm afraid. Maybe you've heard of his student Frank Lloyd Wright?"
Harriet was vaguely familiar with the name.

"Chicago was their home, at least till Wright got chased out.
You'll see a lot of their work around here. Damned impressive. But
they're both dead now. Wright just died a few years ago." Butler
talked about the two geniuses as they entered an elevator with yet
another steel door and rose to a special floor that was accessible only
with a key. The upper floor was even more impressive than the lobby.

"They have great taste, I must say," Harriet smiled.

"I heard that." A tall, slender silver-haired man approached from
behind an etched glass divider, smiling.

"How are you, Ed," Butler and the man greeted each other warmly. "This is Mrs. Wilson."

The man shook her hand. She felt a blush creeping up the back
of her neck. He looked like Cary Grant.

"Harriet, this is Mr. DiFigueroa."

The two men exchanged small talk as they were escorted to
a conference room behind more etched glass. Finally DiFigueroa
turned his attention to her.

"So what do you think of our city, Mrs. Wilson?"

"It's magnificent!" She wanted to add "And so are you." Instead
she added, "And so are your offices. I was asking Matt if your designer ever worked on casinos."

DiFigueroa smiled charmingly. "You have wonderful taste. I can
already see we're going to get along famously."

A pile of papers was scattered across the mahogany conference
table. DiFigueroa ignored them. "Would you care for coffee or tea?"

"We'd love to, Ed, but we need to get down to business. We have
some other appointments today."

She was about to correct him when she felt a sharp kick under
the table. DiFigueroa grinned.

"Well then, I won't waste your time. Mrs. Wilson," he turned his smile directly on her, "you have an exceptional property here. We're impressed with the numbers, quite remarkable for a casino owned by a woman. You're very skilled at what you do, for a woman."

"I have a lot of help."

"Yes, well, the Strip's a tough place."

"I've done alright, as you've said."

"Yes. So I did. Well, we're interested in taking out the bank loan. We would offer a five-year loan with options to renew for another ten years. For a fee of course. Interest only with a balloon."

"That sounds ..." another kick under the table,

"We're really looking for ten years, Ed," Matt intervened.

"We would maybe go seven but there would be some significant conditions."

"Such as what?" Matt was doing the talking now. Harriet tried unsuccessfully to reach down to massage her leg without attracting attention.

"We'd want to put our own managers in. Nothing against you, Mrs. Wilson." He smiled at her warmly. "It's just that this would be a significant investment and you're in a high risk business. We would need a great amount of protection. Your name would stay on the casino of course. And you would as well. As senior manager or some such title. But we would need to control the revenue."

Two more kicks from Matt guaranteed her silence. "Why don't you send me some revised documents, show me what you're thinking in the way of supervision and control and I'll discuss it with my client."

"Of course," DiFigueroa rose, signaling the end of the meeting. "A real pleasure to meet you, Mrs. Wilson. I did some investigation into your background before the meeting. I like to know who I'm talking to. I have to say I found it hard to believe what I heard about you. But it was true. And more. You've managed to exceed my expectations." He folded her hand in a warm grip. She could have melted into the Persian rug under her feet. She looked up at him and beamed.

"And you have certainly exceeded mine, Mr. DiFigueroa."

He leaned over and touched her lightly on the elbow; his breath warmed her neck as he came closer. Her heart raced as she realized he was about to whisper something in her ear. Something he didn't want Butler to hear. Her whole body tingled.

"And don't worry about the bruises on your legs, Harriet. I'm told they disappear in a few days." He released her, still smiling.

She stumbled backwards.

"Thanks again, Ed." Matt grabbed her arm and steered her towards the elevator. "We'll be in touch."

She didn't breathe again until they were out on the street, Pudding Face closing the door behind them. Then she laughed. Matt joined her as he put her into a cab. The merriment lasted all the way back to their hotel.

"I'm glad you took it in good spirits. Now you see why Wildcat wanted me along. He would have had you eating out of his hand in there. Of course, you'd be dining on pure poison. The guard is his alter ego."

"You mean Pudding Face?"

Matt laughed harder. "What a great name. Anyway, I'll look at his papers and get back to you with recommendations. We haven't seen their best offer yet."

"I hope I don't have to deal with them, Matt. But they may be our only hope."

"That's why I'll keep the negotiations going. Let me know if there's a change from your end."

"Why don't you talk to the guys at the Starlight?" Junior's question came out of nowhere. Harriet didn't know whether to laugh or cry. It was September first; she had two months left to find a solution. She hadn't seen Junior for weeks and suddenly he showed up out of nowhere with a suggestion. Maybe it wasn't the best suggestion but it showed that he was thinking about their problems.

"What gave you that idea, Dear?" She tried to sound enthusiastic. "Nadeen."

"And who is Nadeen?"

She was fairly sure her son was blushing. "She's Mike Williams' daughter. You know, the Starlight Managing Partner."

She knew Mike as the man who had taken care of Opal after the rape. She had met him but never spent much time with him. Opal didn't like him.

"I'm terrified of him, Hat," she confided over lunch the next day. "He's all smooth and friendly on the outside but on the inside…he has no heart."

Hattie was reminded of Ed DiFigueroa.

"Well, Junior is dating his daughter, Nadeen."

"Nadeen! Tell him to watch himself. She's Mike's little girl, a real tramp, though you wouldn't know it from her looks. She goes to a private school in Switzerland to give her some polish. But when she's home she screws anybody Mike tells her to. Can you imagine? His own daughter? Which means Mike has put her up to dating Junior for some reason."

"Which means Mike thinks my son is a way to get to me…to the Slipper," Harriet finished.

The two women looked at each other. "Damn." They both said the word, then laughed.

"Well, it won't hurt to hear what he has to say. He can't be any worse than Dalitz or DiFigueroa." Harriet had entertained Opal with stories of her Chicago trip.

"Sounds like they have a better class of mobsters up there," she had commented.

"I haven't told you about Pudding Face," Harriet replied. "But now I'm worried as much for Junior as for the Slipper. He's obviously taken with Nadeen. And who could blame him? He's not that good looking or smart or smooth. She's probably the best thing he's ever dated. If I say no to Williams she'll dump him for sure. Then he'll blame me. I can hear him now. First I killed his boxing ring, then his chance at happiness with Nadeen. Jesus."

"Isn't it amazing the ways they find to get to you? Money, threats, sex, you name it. Why do you want to do this, Hat?"

"I don't know, Opie. I'm beginning to think it's pure stubbornness. I can't remember the last time I felt happy. It seems like every day there's a new problem."

◆━◆━✦━◆━◆

The meeting with Williams went as expected. Harriet didn't know whether to be proud or sad that she had become so cynical. First the comments on her "wonderful son." Then the invitation to get together for dinner, "the four of us". Then the discussion about the Slipper. The news of her distress was all over town now. She couldn't even get up to being upset about it any more. She just looked at Williams and smiled sweetly.

"It sounds wonderful, Mike. And Junior's so happy. But isn't Nadeen going to school in Switzerland? I heard she was just back for a few weeks."

Williams' smile cracked for just an instant.

"Well, she's going to school right now but she's almost finished. Then she'll be coming back here permanently. I'm sure the two lovebirds can wait for a year or so."

"Maybe we can get together then. I wouldn't want Junior to get his hopes up. But you didn't invite me here to talk about Junior, did you?"

"No. As a matter of fact I heard you were thinking of selling the Slipper. I wanted to let you know we'd be interested in buyin'."

"And who is 'we'? Not you and Nadeen, I suppose."

Mike's smile was a bit uncertain now.

"Well, no. The owners of the Starlight is who I meant."

"And who would those be? Because Opal Cullen, my friend, had a really bad experience here and I don't want to deal with the same people who turned her out after she was raped."

"We didn't turn her out!" Mike's voice rose. "We took care of her. We still are taking care of her. We provided her a nice place to live and a good allowance and her son is gonna come to work for us. If we buy the Slipper he can work there if he …if you want."

"So you want me involved? After the purchase I mean?"

"Oh, sure. We don't even have to buy the whole thing. We could invest enough to take the bank out of the picture. We'd be your partners."

Harriet suppressed a shudder. "I see. Very interesting. So could you maybe put in a little more so we can build the boxing ring?"

"The boxing ring?" He looked like he was trying to decide if she was kidding again.

"Surely my son has told you about his interest in boxing?" She let the silence make her point. "I mean, that's been his dream since I started the Slipper. I had to take the ring off the construction plan when Sam got sick. We just ran out of money. But you would build out the ring so he could promote fights there? Boxing's the next big thing in Vegas, I hear."

"Well…that's certainly something to think about." Mike smiled noncommittally.

"Why don't you put your proposal down on paper and send it to me. Be sure to include the boxing ring. Junior will be thrilled. Of course, I have several other offers right now. So it will take some time to get back to you."

She laughed to herself as he closed the door behind her. She really had Williams jumping to her tune. But the laughter died. Now she had something else to worry about. Junior. Perhaps she could stretch out her response until the last minute. Maybe he'd grow tired

of Nadeen or she would dump him for some other reason. Anyway, it wouldn't last long. Her year was almost up with no good solution in sight. As she waited for her car she heard the sound of a fire engine. Strange, they usually stayed off the Strip. It was so congested it was hard for fire engines to make their way to the fire unless.....
She looked down the street to see where they were going. Could it be? No, please no. It looked like the fire was at the Slipper. The whole block was consumed in smoke.

"Please God, no." She thought briefly about the last time she had uttered that prayer as she jumped into her car and headed for her casino.

She cried with relief when she realized the fire was next door at a new construction site. The firemen were hosing down the Slipper to make sure it didn't catch the blaze.

She pulled into the valet area in front of her casino, choking from the smoke. The fire would put a dent in her business for sure. Nobody liked coming to a place next to a burnt-out ruin. The smell was awful. It was depressing. Maybe bad luck. She almost ran directly into Moe Dalitz who was standing at the entrance.

"Bad fire." He looked at her through his thick glasses.

"What are you doing here?"

"Just checking. On the Slipper. That fire will affect your business, you know. I'll have to reduce my offer."

She looked at him silently.

"Lots of bad things happen around here, Mrs. Wilson. You never know when one might happen to you. You think some more about selling, you hear?" He walked away.

"Everything alright, Missus?" Hatch was suddenly standing at her side, watching Dalitz.

"Oh, Hatch. I don't know. I just don't know."

"Bad fire."

"Yes. I'm afraid it was started on purpose, just to frighten me."

"Are you frightened, Missus?"
She looked up at his face, crinkled with concern.
"Not while I have you around to protect me, Hatch."
"I will protect you, Missus. Don't be frightened."

Chapter 39: Friends

The phone in her office was ringing when she walked in. She hesitated before picking it up. Finally she lifted the receiver. "Come see me." It was Wildcat. He never bothered to introduce himself. He didn't have to.

"I'm on my way," she replied. She was still shaking.

"I've got you another year."

She looked at him dully. She couldn't really focus on what he was saying.

"Well, ain't you pleased? You look like you've seen a ghost."

She told him about the fire and her run in with Dalitz.

"Jesus Christ, Darlin'. Why the hell you want to stay with the Slipper is beyond me. It'll be the death of you." Then he saw the look on her face. He jumped up and came to her. "I'm sorry, Hat. I didn't mean that. That was really stupid of me. Nobody's gonna do nothin' to you. Not while I'm around."

She realized she was crying. He patted her shoulder, reached into his pocket for a hanky and held it out to her. It was soiled. She made a face. He looked at it remorsefully and quickly tucked it back into his pocket. "Sorry, Darlin'."

At least she had one more laugh inside her. "It's alright, Wildcat. It's the first time I've smiled all week."

———◆❖◆———

"You have to stop thinking about it, Hat. Focus on the good things in your life. Like tonight." Opal was helping her get ready for a big event—dinner with Jack Hartman. Sam had been dead for almost a year. She told herself it was all right to look forward to her first real date. She needed something to take her mind off her business.

At first Opal didn't understand why her friend was going into a tizzy. "Hartman? But what do you need my help for? He's like your brother. You've seen him a million times."

"Right. But not like this." Harriet realized her face was hot. Opal looked at her carefully.

"Harriet Wilson, are you interested in Jack Hartman?"

"The answer's yes, if you must know. This is a real date. The first time we've had dinner since Sam died. And I want it to be special. So will you help or not?

"Oh, Hattie. Of course I'll help. I'm so happy for you."

"Don't be happy yet, Opie. First I need to get him. But he's always been interested in me. That I know. And he's been keeping his distance since Sam died. I think he wants to give me some time. Then out of the blue he called me and asked me to dinner. Said he had something important he wanted to discuss with me."

"That's wonderful. I'm sure you're right. He's been waiting for you for years. So it's my job to make you absolutely glamorous! Where do we start?"

They drove to LA for a day to shop for a dress. Harriet's personal shopper at I. Magnin was delighted to help. They picked a yellow brocade empire style cut just below the knee. Harriet got shoes and a delicate brocade handbag to match. Opal pronounced her "marriage bait."

Opal was at her place at five. Jack was picking her up at eight.

"We'll do your hair, then your nails then your make-up," she announced. She laid out her dishes and jars on the kitchen table. Harriet was intimidated.

"You'll look great!" Opal assured her. "Don't look in the mirror till we're finished."

At seven-thirty Opal had finished and proudly turned her towards the mirror.

"Don't you like it?" Opal was elated.

Harriet stared at the mascaraed, ruby-lipped, rouged and powdered face surrounded by teased hair. It was amazing. But it wasn't her. It wasn't even who she wanted to be.

"I think we need to take a little off," she suggested timidly. "Jack won't recognize me."

She went to work with a washcloth, over Opal's loud protests. At quarter to eight most of the face was gone. Harriet was pleased. The eyeliner had left a soft brown lining around her eyes. She kept the mascara, it made her lashes stand out. Her cheeks had a natural blush from being scrubbed. Her lips were reasonably red with most of the lipstick wiped off. She left her hair as Opal had arranged it. She liked the way it curled softly around her face. She put on the special dress and a pair of diamond earrings. She looked at her manicured nails.

"Don't you dare take the polish off, Hattie."

"Harriet held out her left hand and slowly slipped off her wedding ring. She smiled sadly at Opal. There was a knock at the door.

"Good luck." Opal gave her a big hug and kissed her cheek. "Oh my God. I've left a lipstick stain on your cheek." She grabbed a Kleenex and rubbed it off, laughing.

Harriet was pleased with the look on Jack's face when he saw her. It was a smile, then a questioning sort of look, then a larger smile. She held out her hand and he took it and kissed her on the cheek.

"You look amazing. Is this the new Harriet?"

"Do you like her?"

"You bet."

She slipped her arm through his. He helped her into his car.

"This is new," she commented, feeling the leather seats.

"It's a Ford Fairlane Thunderbolt," he announced. "It has tremendous power, but it's comfy too."

"Just like you," she joked. "Powerful and comfy."

He didn't say anything. Maybe she had embarrassed him? He turned on the radio. "It has a great sound system," he said. They drove down the Strip listening to Frank Sinatra.

"I love Vegas," she said. "Especially at night."

"I'm glad, Hattie. I love it, too. And I have something special I want to ask you."

They pulled up to Piero's, Jack's favorite restaurant.

"I'm so glad you picked this. It's been ages since I've been here," she said. She took his arm as they entered. Piero's was the usual crowded, noisy place. She had forgotten how noisy. Not quite the atmosphere for a romantic proposal. But it would have to do. They were shown to a table in a back corner. At least it was more quiet there.

Jack ordered wine. "Here's to the future." He lifted his glass.

"To the future," she replied.

"So how are you doing, Hat?"

"It's been pretty rough the last few months. I'm really wondering if I should start fresh."

"That's what I wanted to talk to you about, Hat. Starting fresh."

Her heart performed an acrobatic trick in her chest. "Yes, Jack."

"You know this is Nevada's centennial?"

"What?"

"Yep. Nevada joined the union in 1864. One hundred years ago next month. I'm on the centennial committee."

This wasn't going as she expected. Was he too shy to ask directly?

"That's wonderful, Jack. A fresh start, a new Nevada. A new us."

"Us? Well, I guess, sort of. What I wanted to ask you was if you'd like to contribute to the celebration fund."

"The what?"

"The centennial celebration fund. We're having special events all over the state, but especially here in Vegas. I know you've been too busy to notice and I haven't wanted to bother you with everything else you've had to cope with, but I thought you might want to part with a little donation for the big dinner at the Convention Center on October 24. I would be your escort, of course. But I'm also master of ceremonies. I know things are a little up in the air with you right now so don't think you have to contribute. But it'd be great if you could."

"And that's why you asked me to dinner?"

He looked blank. "Yes, why?"

"Jack Hartman, you scumbag. You're no different than any other damn man. I thought you were, but I was wrong. You ask me out all sweet and take me to a great restaurant and talk about the future, and it's all to hit me up for money." She realized she was attracting attention, but she didn't care.

Hartman's mouth was open but nothing was coming out. She bolted from her chair and stormed through the restaurant, bumping into diners on her way. He followed her, throwing money at the stunned waiter who had shown up to take their order.

"Harriet. Please. Please stop."

She was too angry to stop. She hailed a cab.

"Please let's discuss this." He took her arm. "I didn't mean to upset you. I had no idea…"

The cabbie pulled up, she yanked free and got in, slamming the door behind her, leaving him standing at the curb.

◆•⋉⋊•✳•⋉⋊•◆

"You're a stupid ugly cow." The face in the mirror agreed with her completely, looking back with clown eyes that dripped mascara. She threw the new dress on the floor and kicked it for good measure. The shoes followed. She tried to open the window and throw them out but she was crying so hard she couldn't see the latch. "Damn". She soaped up a washcloth and scrubbed her fact till it burned.

The phone rang. She ignored it. It was obviously Jack wanting to say something nice and soothing so she might change her mind and give him some money. "Go to Hell!" she yelled at the phone. It stopped ringing.

That was the last straw. She had been humiliated. She would leave Las Vegas forever. She didn't need to stay in this two bit town. She would sell the Slipper to Dalitz and go to Europe. She would travel around the world. Tomorrow she would call a travel agency and they would make all the arrangements. Then she would pick the most beautiful city she visited and get a house there and live happily ever after. Alone. Screw everybody. She scrubbed at the dripping mascara. For some reason it wouldn't come completely off. She still had brown splotches under her eyes.

She decided she needed a drink. There was a beer in the fridge. She drank it down and searched through the cabinets for something with more alcohol.

There was a knock at the door.

"Hattie? Can I talk to you?"

"Get away from my house. I'll call the police."

"Please, Hattie."

"To hell with you. Go away. All you want is my money. Well, guess what? You're not getting any. Not one dime. You rat."

"I hurt you. Please let me apologize. I was an idiot. I didn't mean it. I would never hurt you, Harriet. I love you."

"Jesus Christ. Some guys will do anything for a buck."

"I mean it. I love you. Just not in the way you want. I'm not that kind of guy. I guess you could say I'm a confirmed bachelor. Now can you let me in before I get in trouble out here?"

She slipped on a robe and opened the door a crack.

"What do you mean? A confirmed bachelor? You can't get married? You have Opal's disease?"

"Are you gonna let me in?"

She opened the door. He grabbed her and held her close to him, rocking her like a child.

"Oh, Harriet, Harriet. I'm so sorry. So sorry. I'd give anything to be your man. The kind of man you want and need. I've watched Sam running around with Opal. I hated him for that. But I could never take his place."

"Why?" She said into his shoulder.

"There are so many reasons. It would take a while to explain. Can we sit down?"

They sat. Her dress lay crumpled under the coffee table.

"That's a gorgeous dress. You should take care of it."

She got up, picked up the dress and put it on a hanger.

"You're the most special woman I've ever known. If I were ever to marry someone it'd be you. I love you. I have for years. But not …not the way a man loves a woman. It wouldn't be right to tie you down. You're much too good for me."

"No I'm not. That's just an excuse."

"It's not. Please believe me."

"If…if you don't like women, you know, in that way…or if you're sick or something…we could be married and just live together as friends. I'm not all that sexy. Hell, I haven't made out for years."

"Then let's just stay friends. You don't want to marry right now. And, frankly, I don't want to be Mister Harriet Wilson, or whatever. You're a powerful figure in this city, Harriet. Whatever you want to call yourself, you're a star. And men are going to be intimidated by you. Except for ones who want your money. Like me."

She swatted at him.

"I'm starving," Jack said. "Can we find somewhere to eat?"

They ended up at a McDonald's drive through. They each enjoyed a Big Mac, fries and a chocolate shake.

"I think I'm gonna pop," Jack said, holding his stomach. "So we're friends?" He wiped a dab of milk shake from his mouth.

"Friends."

"And you won't go off and try to bribe somebody into marrying you, right?"

"Right."

"And you'll contribute something to the centennial fund?"

Chapter 40: Centennial

October 24, 1964 was beautiful, cool and crisp. The city, her city, shone more brightly than usual. Elvis Presley's movie, *Viva Las Vegas*, had opened in May. It drew people to Vegas like Elvis's come-hither smile. She remembered her first ideas about publicity, reading about Palm Springs and its movie stars and wishing some star would take an interest in Las Vegas. All it took was one star; she only wished she could have designed an advertising campaign as good as Presley's movie.

The El Morocco opened. Las Vegas was filling up with more and more exotic casinos. The city was mobbed in August when the popular English group, The Beatles, came to town. The manager of the Sahara who had booked the show had a hard time convincing his owners there would be enough fans of gambling age to make a profit, but the owners finally gave in. The show sold out in minutes. They had to move it to the Convention Center. Her convention center. It only held seven thousand people, but they rearranged the stage so it was surrounded by seats, expanding the audience to over eight thousand. The Fab Four played two sold out shows.

Driving to the centennial celebration she saw her silver slipper, turning elegantly atop the casino.

She turned to her companion: "I think it's the loveliest sign on the strip, don't you?"

Opal looked out the window to check. "Absolutely".

The two women got out of the limo, lifting their ball gowns delicately. Opal was a vision in blue chiffon. Harriet was stunning in yellow –her favorite color.

"Thanks for the dress," Opal whispered as they entered. "I feel like Cinderella."

"You look like damn Cinderella," Harriet replied. "Just remember what happens at midnight."

The ballroom was filled with tables, each table with a blue linen tablecloth and a white flower arrangement. Lily and Opal were escorted to a table near the front. Jack was waiting for them.

"There you are. My two stars. You both look fabulous."

He planted a kiss on both their cheeks.

"So have you figured out what's wrong with him?" Opal whispered in her ear, nodding towards Hartman.

"Opal! We're not discussing this here. And the answer is no, I haven't. I can't find a way to ask."

"I think he had the disease," Opal said, pointing to her crotch.

The gesture made Harriet laugh.

"My two girls!" Bingo Baxter and his wife interrupted their tete a tete. Bingo had also contributed heavily towards the festivities.

"Old Las Vegas," he said sagely. "We're the backbone of this city."

"Who said anything about old?" Opal smiled her thousand-kilowatt smile at Bingo. Before he could think of a way to extricate himself Mayor Gragson joined them

"Damn right," he said. He had overheard them. He looked extremely dapper in his tux and spit-shined cowboy boots.

"You mean we're old, Harriet and me? That's a stupid thing for a politician to say."

"Hell, no. I was talking about the backbone of this city. Which you certainly are, Harriet."

"You ever gonna give up bein' mayor, Oran?" Bingo lit the mayor's cigar.

"Why? You up to runnin?"

"Me? Hell no. I just got my casino back. I have my hands full."

Harriet looked around. People were filling up the tables. She nodded to Mrs. Clark and her family. They had a table just behind hers. It seemed to signify the changing of the guard.

She saw Percy Harris. They exchanged nods. She wondered what Wildcat had done to him.

The Starlight Hotel had bought a table. Several of the people came over to say hi to Opal. Mike Williams came up to ask whether Harriet had come to a decision about the Slipper.

"To tell the truth, Mike, I've been so busy with other things, I haven't thought about it."

Opal watched him go back to his table and shivered. "It frightens the hell out of me that Ezekiel is gonna work there. But I don't see we have a choice. We need the money."

"Zeke's a bright boy," Harriet assured her. "He knows how to take care of himself. Hell, I wouldn't be surprised if he ended up owning the place one day."

"Never," Opal shot back. "He's gonna graduate college and get a job as far away from here as possible."

"What? And leave me? And all this?" Harriet gestured around the room, filling with ball gowns and tuxes. Opal managed a weak smile.

"How's Junior doing?" For some reason, Junior's moniker had stuck. Nobody thought of him as Sam, including himself.

"He's still dating Mike's daughter. I guess he will until I lower the boom on Mike's offer."

The lights dimmed. Jack left the table and walked to the stage draped with huge cobalt blue Nevada state flags. The crowd grew quiet. Jack cleared his throat.

"I want to welcome you all to our centennial celebration. As you all know, our flag," he nodded to the blue banners behind him, "says 'Battle Born'. And we know that's because Nevada became a state during the Civil War. But to most of us here tonight, it means something more. It means you have to be tough to make it here. Real tough."

A chorus of "You bet" and "Damn right" greeted the words.

"Nevada breeds tough people. Not just men. Women, too. I don't mean tough-looking," he nodded at Opal. The crowd laughed. "I mean tough in spirit. But at the same time, we Nevadans are generous. We help each other. We always have. It's the pioneer spirit that built this state."

More applause from the crowd.

"Now in a minute I'm gonna introduce Governor Grant Sawyer, who I'm sure will say a lot of wonderful things about this state and its people. After all, he's a politician and I'm just a humble newspaper man."

The crowd laughed and clapped. Jack was one of the best-known and loved newspapermen in the state. He had raised millions of dollars for charity and never asked for recognition. Tonight was his night. He was enjoying every minute of the spotlight.

"But before I surrender this here mike," he continued, "I want to thank some very special people who helped make this evening possible. You know them. You've known them for years. They're the movers and shakers in this city. One of them is responsible for our convention center. Some of you newcomers might not realize it, but without the convention center Las Vegas wouldn't be what it is today. Miss Harriet Wilson saw that, she realized that the center would bring people here from all over the world for all kinds of reasons. And once they came...well...you know what happens next.... We take their money, right?"

The crowd roared.

"Mister Bingo Baxter was one of the first to understand that people wanted to gamble in luxury, meaning wall-to-wall carpets and beautiful women and free drinks. And, oh yea, a million dollar horseshoe at the front door. Don't ask me why it makes sense 'cause I don't have a clue."

"And…." Jack looked out in the audience and Harriet turned to see a commotion at the entrance.

"Let me in, damn it!" She couldn't see who was yelling, but she recognized the voice. Wildcat.

"Gentlemen, please let the guy in. We need him up here," Jack called from the stage.

Wildcat trotted down the aisle to applause and catcalls. Harriet patted the empty chair next to her and he flopped down, exhausted.

"Sorry, Darlin' I had a meetin' run late."

"What could be more important than this?"

"Senator Cannon and Secretary Udall. He's secretary of the interior, you know."

Harriet kissed him gently on the cheek. "Name dropper."

"Pay attention down there in the pit you people," Jack continued. "That was Wildcat McDonald. He's small in size but great in stature. I promise you he's done more for this state than just about anybody. I can also promise he'll never talk about it. Now can the three of you stand up? Miss Harriet Wilson, Mister Bingo Baxter and Wildcat McDonald. They're the major sponsors of this event. Thanks to all of you."

The spotlight turned on them. They all stood up and waved, though the light blinded them and they couldn't see what they were waving at. The applause rained down on them. Finally Wildcat whispered, "I'm damn tired. Let's sit down. I need a drink!"

Chapter 41: Angel in Disguise

The Centennial celebrations and the holidays could only delay the inevitable. She had to deal with the Slipper. After months of indecision she feared she had no choice but to sell to Dalitz. She assumed he expected the bank to take over the place at the end of last year. Since they hadn't, and since Wildcat had somehow managed to threaten Percy into behaving decently, she assumed Dalitz didn't know about her extension. She prayed that he might suspect he had been misinformed about the bank's position. Maybe she had a small window to negotiate a decent price, but she had to close the deal quickly before he learned the truth.

"So what do you want to do?" Wildcat was looking at her carefully.

"I think I want to sell. And I never thought I'd say that, Wildcat, but I've had enough. I know if I stay in I'll have to deal with all those people. The Dalitz's and the Williams's and all the rest. And I'll probably die young. I guess the only people out there are Dalitz and the Starlight mob. I think I could work a better deal with Moe. The Slipper is a good fit for him and as bad as he is I somehow think he's better than Mike, despite what it'll do for Junior's romance with Nadeen."

"There might be somebody else."

"What? Who?"

"Well, there's this wild guy from LA. Howard Hughes. His family started Hughes Tool Company, they're in the oil business and he inherited the whole shebang. He's blown a lot in Hollywood, on starlets and movies. But he's just sold his stock in TWA Airlines for hundreds of millions dollars and he's out here looking at casinos. I don't know what he has in mind but it's worth talking to him."

"Can you get me a meeting?"

"Probably. One of my old Air Corps buddies is a top executive in his organization. I'll ask him to make an introduction. I'll get back to you."

Chapter 42: Toe Kick

Wildcat came through with the introduction. Two weeks later Howard Hughes met her and Wildcat for lunch at the Slipper. Hughes had the same dark good looks and twitchy mustache as Sam. But unlike Sam, his eyes moved nervously around him and he was constantly playing with his hands, as if he didn't know quite what to do with them. He stood up politely as Wildcat introduced them.

Harriet had prepared for the meeting. She had a pretty good sense of what casinos were selling for. The Slipper was new, well-built and well-run. The parking garage was a bonus. She had brought the casino in under budget and it was making good money. With a little luck she could sell for eight million and walk away with over three million dollars profit.

"I've heard a lot about you, Mrs. Wilson."

"And I've heard about you. You're buying up casinos, I hear."

"I would say I'm looking for opportunities." He was instantly serious. She tried to size him up. He had a reputation as an impulsive type, a playboy with money to burn. The reputation didn't quite fit the man looking intently at her from across the table.

She decided to change the subject. "You're from Texas."

"Yep. Houston."

"My husband and I spent the war in San Antone. I loved it."

"Really? I hate Texas. Flat and ugly. Couldn't wait to get away."

"I see. Where do you live now?"

He looked around, the nervousness reappeared. "Various places. Maybe here for a while. I'm about to buy the Desert Inn. I'm building an apartment on the top floor."

"You mean Dalitz won't own the Desert Inn anymore?" How could she have missed that? She tried to hide her disappointment. Now she wouldn't have someone to bid against Hughes. "Well, I can see why you're interested in the Slipper. It has a big parking garage. The only one around here. Dalitz rented it from me till the Slipper opened. The two properties complement each other."

"The Slipper looks into the Desert Inn," he said.

"What?"

"It looks at me when I'm in the Desert Inn. Into my space."

Harriet felt a warning nudge from Wildcat.

"I see."

"Why does it stop with the toe looking into my apartment?"

"You mean the slipper on top of my casino?"

"Yes."

"Well, that's just the way the designers built it, I guess. I never thought about it."

"Is there anything in the toe?"

"I never really checked. So what type of opportunities are you looking for?"

"Anything interesting." The eyes were focused again. On her. "I just bought the Spring Mountain Ranch from the Widow Krupp."

"Damn!" She realized she had cursed and glanced sideways at Wildcat. He grinned. Hughes was smiling. "I was looking at that property, too," she confessed.

The ranch was owned by Vera Krupp, a German actress and widow of the notorious German industrialist and arms dealer. She turned up mysteriously in Las Vegas after the war and moved to the secluded ranch south of the city. It was one of the parcels marked with a "1" in Harriet's notebook.

"I talked to her about selling right after the Krupp diamond was stolen. I thought she'd want to move out of the city. But she told me she loved the place. She said she'd never sell."

The story of the Krupp Diamond, its theft from Vera's ranch and its daring recovery had been front-page news for weeks. The diamond was supposedly the most valuable gem in the world.

"I can't believe she changed her mind so suddenly. You must have offered her a fortune." She looked at him speculatively.

"You buy real estate?" Hughes ignored the comment.

"I've bought a few parcels, including the one you're sittin' on. I'd love to buy some others. I think Las Vegas is a good investment."

"We agree on that Mrs. Wilson. So why are you selling this place?"

"It was our dream. My husband's and mine. Now he's gone, it's just not the same. I think the profits from a sale of the Slipper can jump start some of my other investments, ones I'm more interested in."

"I understand perfectly. I have to say it's a beautiful property. Very clean and well-run, from what I can see." He took a bite of steak. "If I bought it I'd want to rename it. Take the slipper down."

"That's fine with me, Mr. Hughes. I might want to use the slipper on some other casino someday."

"So perhaps we can discuss this over dinner one evening?"

She was taken aback.

"You are single now, right?"

She smiled at him. "Hell, yes."

"Then I'd love to take you to dinner. Perhaps at the Desert Inn? Friday night?"

"Thanks, it'll be a pleasure."

Chapter 43: New Life

Harriet sat on her patio and watched the sky grow dark. She lit a cigarette, inhaled slowly and thought about her life. It seemed like years since Sam died. She had hardly had time for anything except the next crisis. But now the crisis was about to pass. It was time for her to start fresh.

Her house was free and clear. It was in an older part of town, but the area was still nice. It had large old trees—a plus for a city that put a premium on shade. Bingo had finally built the promised golf course and clubhouse. They even had a community swimming pool. She talked to a real estate agent who thought the house could bring as much as a hundred thousand.

She opened the safe, took out all the cash and brought it into the kitchen where she stacked it on the kitchen table. With the additions from the past year it had grown to over four hundred and fifty thousand dollars. She looked through her little black notebook. Most of the parcels were still available. Hughes was interested. She would sell to him. She would sell the house, too. She made another decision, one she had been thinking about since Sam died.

"I'm changing my name," she announced to Junior.

"What? Why?"

"I hate Harriet. I've always hated it. It's an old-fashioned name. My middle name is Lillith. I'm gonna be Lily from now on. And take back my family name, Lane. I like the sound of it. Lily Lane."

"Ma???? What about me?"

"You can change your name too, Junior. I mean Sam. Who would you like to be?"

"That's dumb. I like being who I am."

"Then you can be, Sam. Don't you see? You can be whatever you want."

She could see the calculating look in her son's eyes.

"What if I want to be a boxing promoter?"

"Sure. How much will it cost?"

"I'll find out and let you know." He grinned happily.

"I'm selling the casino."

"What?"

"It was going to be a family thing, but with your dad gone and you not interested in running it…it's too much trouble. And I'm selling the house, too."

Junior sat down. "Where will we live?"

"I haven't decided where I'll live yet. You can move in with your friends or wherever. You're a grown man now Sam. You have to make your own way."

"But you'll help me. Right?"

"If I can. I'll help you get started in the boxing business. I know that's what you've always wanted to do. But you're going to have to make something of it. All by yourself."

"Sure. No problem."

◆•⊱◆✳◆⊰•◆

She was going out with a famous millionaire who had dated Jane Russell and Katherine Hepburn. She had read all about him.

Her friends reacted to the new name and the upcoming date in different ways. Opal was thrilled. "Let me help you get ready, please. At least I can get a vicarious thrill."

"But what do you think about my new name?"

"I love it. I never liked Harriet. Lily is perfect."

Jack called to warn her. "He's a weird duck, Hat. Be careful, there's a lot of rumors floating around about him."

"It's Lily," she informed him. "And I think I can handle him."

"It's what?"

"Lily. I've changed my name."

"Why would you do such a thing?"

"Cause I don't feel like a Harriet. I've never felt like a Harriet. I feel like Lily."

"Well, if that's what makes you happy, then I guess I can call you Lily. But Hughes is still a weird duck. You be careful, Lily."

She told Wildcat about the name change when he called to tell her to wear her best underwear. "Just in case he wants to make whoopee."

"I doubt that's what he's interested in, Wildcat."

"Well, now, if you were a Harriet I'd prob'ly agree with you. But Lily…that's a sexy name. Sort of invites that kind of thing, you know."

"You really know how to flatter a woman, Wildcat."

In the end, they had a great evening. Lily let Opal help her get ready. Hughes appeared to appreciate the effort. Or he ran a good bluff. He took her arm as they entered the Desert Inn and told her she looked marvelous. He didn't try to make whoopee. He told her he liked her new name.

"A woman changes her name when she gets married. She should change her name when she gets widowed," Lily informed him.

"It makes perfect sense," he agreed, grinning.

The weirdest thing about him was his eating habits. He ordered all his food broiled, with no sauces.

"And no runny vegetables," he told the waiter, who nodded. Apparently Hughes was a regular customer. Well, he owned the place now. She was still amazed she hadn't heard about the purchase.

She asked Hughes what had become of Dalitz. He shrugged noncommittally. She didn't pursue the issue; they had a lot to talk about. He was interested in Las Vegas and she was a great source of information. She asked what he planned to do with the Krupp estate. He said he was buying his casinos through his company, Summa Corporation. They were making acquisitions all over the valley. The ranch would be for the company executives to come and relax. He called it a "corporate retreat". She had never thought of something like that. She wondered whether that would be appropriate for her little parcel in the mountains.

They talked about the future of the Strip and the city. He said legitimate investors like him were getting interested. The mob was still scaring people off, but a few brave souls like himself, he said, saw the potential and wanted to get in early despite the risk.

"Like me," she reminded him.

"That's true. You were one of the first. How did you manage?"

She told him the story of Bingo and the parcels and Percy Harris and her fights with Moe Dalitz.

"That's amazing. I can't believe you want to walk away from all this."

"I'm not walking away from Las Vegas. Just from this project. I've done what I want. It's time to move on."

"I understand just how you feel," he said, offering her a cigarette. "I did TWA for a while. Got bored with it. Tried movie making. But Hollywood is a rat race. I walked away from both of them. There are lots of other things I want to do. "

"My son wants to be a boxing promoter," she interjected. She told him the story of Junior holding up the boxing ring.

"Sounds like a daredevil. Like myself," he mused. "I've never taken an interest in boxing. The fighters are all big dumb hulks. I like dealing with smart people. Like you," he added, leaning closer to her.

"So do you want to buy the Slipper or not?" She leaned away.

He laughed. "You're an interesting woman, Lily. The answer is yes. I'd like to buy the Slipper. I'll treat her with respect. I'll keep on your employees, just remove that damn slipper. I'll even pay to store it for you. The staff all love you, by the way. I've asked. So what's your price?"

"Ten million. And I keep the name. If you're taking down the slipper you won't need it."

"You can have the name, but ten million dollars is a lot."

"Not really. I know what casinos are going for and this one is just starting to show it can be a real money maker."

"Do you have other offers?"

"One. But I suspect there are lots of folks who would love to put me out of business. And take over the Slipper." She watched Hughes' face turn grey. "Probably a few of the mob boys," she continued. I don't care for them but their money is as green as yours. She noticed his right hand start twitching. "I haven't really put it on the market yet. And I don't want the mob to get my place. But I don't want to sell it cheap either."

"Eight million."

"Nine. And you build out the boxing ring and hire my son as your promoter."

He raised his glass to her. "Done. It's a pleasure doing business with you, Lily. You'll be getting a call from my associate Bob Mahieu about the closing."

Chapter 44: Hatch

"I've sold the casino, Hatch." She planned to speak to the heads of all her departments individually. Hatch was the first. He stood in front of her desk, refusing to take a seat, looking at her like he didn't understand.

"I think you'll like the new owner, Howard Hughes," she continued. "He reminds me a lot of Sam. I've told him about you. He says he looks forward to working with you. You'll stay on as head of security of course."

"I work for you, Missus." Hatch sat down.

At first she thought he hadn't heard her. Or perhaps he didn't want to work for Hughes.

"I'm sorry, Hatch. I'm not going to be in the casino business any more. At least not for a while."

"I am your friend."

The statement took her by surprise. She realized how many years she had known this man and how little she knew about him. Did he have a family, friends, a home? She had never asked. She had only learned his real name—Joseph Fields—when she saw it on the casino payroll. She had taken him for granted and he had always been there. She looked down, avoiding the grey eyes that were staring at her under bushy brows, expecting some response.

"I guess I always thought of you as a friend of someone in my life Hatch. First you worked for Bingo, then you became Junior's protector, then you came to work for Sam and me. I really don't know much about you. But I've always relied on you. That's for sure. I know you're a good man. I'm proud to call you my friend."

"I take care of you. You need protection. I protect you."

"I know that. And you protect Junior, too."

"You pissed off a lot of people in this town, Missus. Dalitz had to pay you a hundred sixty thousand. That's big money. You made him look like an idiot. His boys didn't like that. You need me. I take care of those people."

Harriet felt her hands turn cold. "What do you mean, Hatch?"

"People. The union guys, Dalitz's fucking boys, the Jew boys, they don't want you on the Strip. They don't like you. And when they don't like you bad things can happen."

Harriet tried to keep her voice calm. "I'm out of the casino business now, Hatch. But I know Junior still needs you."

"Moe's friends have long memories."

"So what do you want to do, Hatch?"

"I work for you."

The statement hung in the air between them. She realized suddenly that any further discussion could reveal much more than she wanted to or should know. Hatch stood up. He adjusted the bulge under his jacket.

"Junior needs money."

"What?" She hadn't seen much of Junior since they had the discussion about Hughes.

"He has markers all over town. Mostly at the Starlight, Mike Williams' place. He told Mike you'll cover'em."

She swallowed hard. "How much?"

"Forty, fifty thousand. People are gonna start collecting."

"My God."

"You need me. Junior can't help gettin' into trouble. He's just that way."

"What can I do?"

"You wanna pay the markers or you want the mob to teach Junior a lesson?"

"I'll pay, of course. I hope things will change when he starts working for Hughes."

"Hughes won't help. And Junior's never gonna be a boxing promoter."

He was right, of course. She had been deceiving herself.

"So what do we do from here?"

Hatch smiled at the word "we".

"Put the word out around town. Junior has a limit. Tell them what it is. You won't cover markers over the limit. I'll tell Junior."

Hatch was much smarter than she had ever thought. She had never even had to wonder or worry about him, she understood now. He meant it to be that way. It was best she didn't ever know the why of Hatch. He would just be there. She fought an image that was seeping into her brain—an image of Pudding Face guarding DiFigueroa.

"You know what I think, Hatch?"

He cocked his head.

"I think you need to come to work for me."

"Yes, Missus." He smiled.

"It's Lily now, Hatch. Lily Lane. That's my new name. I'm starting on a new life."

"Yes, Missus." He turned and left.

Chapter 45: Closing

Closing the sale of the Slipper took less time than she expected. Perhaps it was less time than she wanted. She was saying goodbyes again. To the other guards. To the casino staff, Brent Keele and the restaurant workers. She assured them they were in good hands. She had spent several days arguing herself out of believing what Hatch had said about Hughes. He was a bit eccentric, for sure, but he was certainly not crazy.

"Mr. Hughes has a lot more business expertise, time and money than I do. And he's gonna spend it on the Slipper. And he's not the mob, so you'll be safe. Hell, he might even bring some of his Hollywood friends to come and stay. How'd you like to meet Ann-Margret or Sophia Loren?"

But it didn't work. They all had tears in their eyes.

"It's a pleasure doing business with you," she told Hughes. They had become friendly. Hughes even talked about going into some deals with her, but she put him off.

She brought the check to Percy Harris and he gave her back the note marked "Paid."

"Thanks," she said.

"You're welcome. You were a great customer, Hattie. I'm sorry things ended like this."

"I'm not. And I'm Lily now. You've taught me something, Percy. Never trust a banker. By the way, I made four million dollars profit on the deal. I just thought I'd let you know, I'm not keepin' it in your bank." She turned and walked out.

She wasn't sure what to do with the money. She was afraid she would have to open a bank account, even if she disliked banks.

"I've made an honest woman of you," Hughes joked. "You'll have to file a tax return and report the sale and pay the taxes on the profit. I expect you made a killing. That means you'll have to put it in a place the Government can see it. And the IRS will keep track of you and your income for the rest of your life. That's the price you pay for being rich."

Wildcat affirmed what Hughes had said. "Oh hell, Hat, I mean Lily, everybody's opening bank accounts. Even Jackie Gaughan." He chuckled. Gaughan, the irascible owner of the El Cortez, bragged openly that he never opened a bank account or filed a tax return. Old timers knew things had changed for good when he finally gave in.

"This city's changing. It's becoming a real legitimate business center. The good old days of the first count are gone," Wildcat said wistfully. The Feds and the State are breathin' down the necks of all the casino owners. Hell, they watch 'em closer than their wives. And think of the money the banks are gonna make, with all those greenbacks flowin' through."

He and Lily looked at each other, each coming up with the same idea at the same instant. "Banks!"

"Why not put your money in your own bank. That way you can screw yourself!" He hooted.

"How easy is it to start a bank?"

Wildcat said he would look into it. "And I can tell you all my friends will put their money in your bank. Maybe we can go in as partners."

"That's a great idea. I'd love to be partners with you." Lily pecked him on the cheek. She thought of what Percy Harris would say and smiled.

Chapter 46: Rooster Tails

"Mornin', Partner."

The ringing woke her from a sound sleep. Eyes still closed, she reached for where the phone was supposed to be. Three rings later she remembered the phone had moved. Or rather, she had moved. She had sold her home. She was Hughes' guest at the former Slipper, now slipper-less and renamed the "Frontier West". She opened her eyes, found the phone and sat up.

"Mornin', Wildcat."

She had not heard from him since the casino sale closed two months earlier. He was off in Washington on some secret deal or other. She had gotten used to it. Being partners with Wildcat was a challenge, but unlike her former partner, Sam, he made it clear how much he cared about her. He praised her to his friends and to her face, never missed a meeting and kept every promise. Perhaps it was easier being friends than being married.

So far they had investigated the idea of starting a bank and decided against it. Banking was a regulated business and she had had her fill of bureaucracies. Besides, she wanted to spend her money on real estate. She had left most of the profits from the sale in Hughes' care until she could make some decisions. He signed a note payable to her. It was a way to defer the question of where to park her money.

"I'll pay you a good interest rate, Lily," he had called to assure her. "Can I have a suite at the Slipper hotel instead," she asked. "Until I find another place?"

"Of course. As long as you call it the Frontier West Hotel. Please stay as long as you wish as my guest."

"I trust him," she replied when Jack asked about the decision. "Or, at least, I trust him more than any damn banker."

She got a good price for her house. She examined all the old furniture and decided to get rid of everything. She asked Opal if she wanted any of it. Opal was delighted with the living room sofa and chairs, the television and the master bedroom set.

"You don't mind, me sleeping in Sam's bed?" she asked Lily, half in jest.

"He ain't there, Opie," Lily replied, practically. "And he ain't comin' back." The two women smiled at each other.

She gave the guest bedroom set and the dining room set to Junior, who was still smarting from her limits on his markers.

"To decorate your new place," she said.

"What new place?"

"The one you're gonna move into because the house has been sold."

"But I don't have a place to go," he whined. "And Nadeen dumped me."

Lily had no idea why the two things were connected. She assumed Nadeen had parted ways with Junior because he could no longer lose thousands of dollars at her father's casino. She shook her head. "Let's find you a place then, Junior. A place so nice Nadeen'll want to move in with you."

A month later she had installed Junior into a flashy bachelor pad on Tropicana. He complained that the old furniture wasn't "cool" but it fit perfectly. They drove to LA to pick out decorations to spruce the place up. Junior had a new car as well – a maroon Mustang. It was her attempt to pacify him for tightening the purse strings. He was always happiest when he had new things.

"How's the boxing ring coming?" Lily asked on the way back from LA. Junior hadn't mentioned it. She toured the swimming pool area each morning looking for signs of construction. Nothing was happening.

"I can't find any boxers or fights to promote," Junior complained. "There's no money in it."

"But Sugar Ray Robinson was just here at the Hacienda, wasn't he? Fighting that Hernandez kid, the local champ? That drew a lot of people, I hear."

"Only eleven hundred. That's not enough to pay the rent. And Hughes isn't really that interested in boxing. He only did it 'cause you asked."

"Well, that's an opportunity, Junior. You need to show him what you can do. Have you talked to Doc Kearns? Or how about that guy with the frizzy hair who hung around Kearns?"

"You mean Don King? He's in jail. People say he stomped somebody to death. And Kearns is dead."

"Looks like the field is wide open for you, Junior. You need to get to work, contact some of the good fighters, show Hughes you know what you're doing."

"Nobody ever sees Hughes, Ma. He has this weird guy, Mahieu, who handles everything. I can never speak to the man."

Lily changed the subject. Hatch was right. Her son would have to find his own way. At least, she sighed, he had a place to live, a car and some decent furniture. And he had Hatch looking after him, though he wasn't aware of it. She suggested to Hatch that he move into an apartment not far from Junior. He agreed. He said he didn't like the place he was living anyway. She offered him some of their old furniture. He looked offended.

"I take care of myself Missus." She had begun to notice things about her one and only employee. His dress, for instance. His suits were tailor made. She had no idea where he got the money, it certainly wasn't from her. She paid him a bodyguard salary. He bought a new car, a Cadillac Eldorado Biarritz.

"I'm hiring Hatch as my personal bodyguard," she told Wildcat. She watched his reaction carefully. She wasn't sure he even knew the man, but he seemed to know almost everyone in the city. His comments might give her a clue to Hatch's background.

"Good man," Wildcat said. That was all. She was tempted to ask if he thought she needed a bodyguard but decided against it.

On the last day in her old home, standing in the empty kitchen where so many plans had been made, so many crises averted, so many tears shed and hopes dashed, she asked herself if she was happy to leave. She had no idea what would happen next, but then her life had always been uncertain. She lived from surprise to surprise. She was a real gambler at heart, born and bred to make her way in the city she called home. And this was where the trail had led her.

She remembered Madame Zena, the old gypsy. Had the woman forseen this city in the desert? Lily had tried to find Mike and Lucy and their carny but they had disappeared. What would they think of the carny show sitting inside the multi-story steel-framed poker tent that people called a casino? What a turnabout!

And a turnabout for her as well. She was a guest in her old hotel. She would order breakfast from room service, spend the hot days on her mountain, look at properties in the evening. She would line up dinner dates with Jack, Bingo, Howard, Opie and other old friends. She would learn to play golf. She had made a list for herself. Then she tore it up.

"What the hell? I'm ready for anything." She was happy. And she knew she would eventually become accustomed to her new living quarters just as she had gotten used to living with Sam on the road and living in San Antone. She adjusted the pillows and sat up in bed. "What's up, Wildcat?"

"I got me a new car. Wanna go for a ride? Bought'er yesterday. Want to show her off. And I wanna show you somethin'."

She showered and dressed quickly and met him at the entrance.

He pulled up in a shiny new red Jeep Wagoneer.

"Hop in, Hat."

She tried to remind him her name was Lily but her words were lost in the wind as they rocketed out of the driveway, scattering unsuspecting tourists attempting to cross Las Vegas Boulevard in their path.

"Somebody needs to do something about the pedestrians," Lily commented.

"You mean, besides kill 'em?" Wildcat had fought every traffic ordinance tooth and nail. He believed in his "God-given right" to drive down the Strip as fast as his vehicle would permit. "Vegas ain't what it use to be," he said sadly, revving the engine in frustration as they stopped at their fourth light. The Strip was booming. The Sahara, the Thunderbird and the Dunes had completed major remodels. The Castaways and the Tally Ho both opened. And the Slipper was right in the middle of it all. She still thought of it as the Slipper. Wildcat called it the "Barefoot...No slipper, get it?"

"Damn it!" They were stopped at another light. He tapped on the steering wheel impatiently, looking up and down Flamingo for cross traffic. Unfortunately a taxi cruising through the intersection prevented him from running it.

"Love the Jeep," Lily tried to distract her friend.

"It's an off-road vehicle," Wildcat said. "Means we can go out in the desert."

"Is that what we're gonna do?"

"Yep. 'Cause that's where the something' is that I want you to see."

Wildcat turned east on Desert Inn Road. The pavement ended after four blocks. He kept going, ignoring the "Road End" barrier. He reached over and popped open the glove box, retrieving a flask. "Off road means no law's gonna stop us." He offered it to her. "Whiskey? Good stuff."

It was only nine-thirty. She would have refused anyone else. She unscrewed the cap and took a swig, coughing.

He laughed as the Jeep hit a small hill and moguled into the air. A bit of whiskey launched out of the flask, landing on the dash. She passed the flask to Wildcat. "So where are we going?"

"What do you see?"

"Desert."

"No, up ahead."

"The sun?"

"Nah. That's the Boulder Highway up there. See it?"

Lily stared straight ahead, swallowing hard to stop the lump creeping up her throat. The Boulder Highway, it was the road she first traveled with Sam and Junior to their new home. She remembered coming over Railroad Pass, rounding the bend and seeing the cottonwood trees, the small buildings. The beginning of her new life.

"Friend of mine tells me this here road, Desert Inn, is gonna be extended all the way to Boulder Highway. That intersection's gonna be a major commercial property."

"I see." So that was the reason for the trip. Wildcat never came out and said something direct. He had to sneak up on things. "So who owns the intersection?"

"Exactly! Answer is—a friend of mine owns a couple of lots. He's willin' to sell to me cheap and there's a lot of property up for grabs right next to it."

"So what would you do with the property, assuming we owned it?"

He looked at her like she was crazy. "Why build a casino on it of course!"

"A casino? Way out here?"

"Way out here's where folks are movin' to. Way out here's where you can have plenty of parking, shops, restaurants for the locals so they don't have to drive all the way downtown. A locals' casino complex. That's what I'd call it."

Lily looked into the early morning sun. They were bouncing

through the desert in the general direction of the Boulder Highway. She had retraced the full circle of her life, from the Dam, over the pass, down the highway to the city, out to the Strip and now back to here. Casinos had brought her to this city, they had been her life, her dream. She wasn't ready to start a new casino on the Strip. But out here? Far from the mob and the competition. A new concept, appealing to the locals. The local population continued to grow—more than sixty-five thousand in Las Vegas and more than double that in the unincorporated parts of the County that surrounded the city. Plenty of potential business. What would such a casino look like? Would it have a showroom, restaurants like the competition downtown, or would it be an entirely new invention?

She heard Wildcat laughing, bringing her back. "You love it. I knew it."

"I do love it, Wildcat. I'm just not sure I'm up to starting a new casino."

"Hell, Lily, you're not even half a century old. You're a spring chicken. And anyhow I'll help you. We'll be partners. I'll do all the dirty work, you just do the fun part. Meetin' with designers, doin' the publicity campaign, furnishing the place."

"And providing the money?" She laughed.

"Oh, yeah. That too. But it won't take near as much as buildin' on the Strip or downtown. And I'll put up fifty percent. Maybe my client and me. So you'll have plenty of that stash of cash for other things. So is it a deal?"

"Stop the car."

"What?"

"You heard me, Wildcat. Stop the car." Lily got out, her legs a bit wobbly. She walked around, looking behind her at the city in the distance. Ahead of her was Sunrise Mountain. She knelt down.

"You okay, girl?" Wildcat jumped out of the jeep and ran to her side.

"I'm fine." She looked up at him, then down to the ground. She picked up a handful of dirt. It was sand. As good as the sand on the Strip. She let it run through her fingers.

"What the hell you doin'?"

She dusted her hands and smiled up at her partner. "Just checking, Wildcat. I like it. I think we should do it. Let's try to lock up as many parcels as possible without letting people know we're involved."

"Yahoo!" Wildcat grabbed the flask and they toasted their new venture standing in the desert. Then he helped her back in the jeep.

He headed towards Sunrise Mountain, then turned suddenly towards their city, leaving a satisfying set of rooster tails in the desert.

"Yahoo!" he screamed again at the top of his lungs, waving the flask in the air, baptizing the sand with liquor.

"Yippee!" Lily's yell was as wild, as free, as joyful as her partner's. She grabbed the flask and anointed her patch of sand.